# The World Cup MURDER

# Pelé

## WITH HERBERT RESNICOW

# The World Cup MURDER

WYNWOOD™ Press
New York, New York

LIBRARY OF CONGRESS
Library of Congress Cataloging-in-Publication Data
Pelé.
  The World Cup Murder / Pelé with Herbert Resnicow.
    p.    cm.
  ISBN 0-8007-7204-0
  I. Resnicow, Herbert. II. Title.
  PS3566.E35W67 1988
  823—dc 19                                                    88-15505
                                                                    CIP

Copyright © 1988 by Herbert Resnicow
Published by WYNWOOD™ Press
New York, New York
Printed in the United States of America

## From Pelé

TO my revered grandmother, Vó Ambrosina, who never went to my games because she felt it was more important for her to be in church praying that I would not get hurt. Wherever she is, I know she is still praying for me.

From Herbert Resnicow
TO Kevin.
Welcome.

# The World Cup MURDER

# 1

## Meditations

by Marcus Aurelius Burr

FOR THOSE OF YOU who are surprised at today's Back Page headlines, who don't even know that a miracle has occurred under your ignorant noses, shut up and listen hard:

Never a soccer country, the U.S. was thought worthy of playing only Lower Slobbovia, or if we worked hard, possibly Monaco, so it was against all odds that the U.S. would host the quadrennial World Cup Games. Against all odds, yes, but we were chosen. That we would be eliminated in the first round was a certainty. But we weren't. Anyone from Brazil or Italy or Holland would have given a hundred to one that the U.S. Team would never make the quarter finals. But we did. As for playing for the World

Championship, only a damn fool would have bet a nickel on that. Well, when the U.S. beat Bulgaria this afternoon, the damn fools collected their bets and this Sunday, in Brooklyn's Koch Field, they will see the U.S. Team, led by some stubborn fools, playing East Germany for the World Cup.

There are three stubborn damn fools to whom this was not a surprise: Gregor Ragusic, Steve Vanderhook, and Luis (Grilho) Vargas. In the great American tradition, two of the leaders of the U.S. soccer revolution are immigrants. Ragusic, a Serb who had played on the Yugoslavian World Cup Team, made his fortune in Brooklyn importing foods from Eastern Europe. Looking for new worlds to conquer, he decided to bring soccer, professional soccer played with eleven men on a full-sized grass field, back to his adopted country. Ragusic teamed up with Steve Vanderhook, whose ancestors anted up the $24 that bought Manhattan, to organize the U.S. Soccer League, twelve franchises across the country in cities where there were successful NFL football teams, so that during the summer they would be able to give football fans their essential kicks. Ragusic, typically, kept the lucrative franchise for the Brooklyn Booters for himself, while Vanderhook, who had been preaching soccer ever since his football injury left him a paraplegic, became the first Commissioner of the USSL.

Ragusic hired Brazilian-born Luis (Grilho) Vargas as Head Coach of the Booters. Grilho (Portuguese for "grasshopper," because of his great jumping ability), the greatest soccer player of all time, even greater than the legendary Pelé, some say, molded the Booters into a world class team in only four years and forced the other teams to follow suit. With Grilho, Ragusic also hoped to get Cabot Hollingsworth Bonifacio (Boni) Vargas, Grilho's son, who even then showed promise of becoming the best forward in America. Boni is now a Booter and the USSL's leading scorer, so it should be no surprise that we have a good chance to win the World Cup four days from now.

Surprise, surprise: we don't. Soccer is a tough game, but the rules are designed to keep it from being violent. If a player commits a foul, the referee holds up a yellow card, a caution, which carries a free kick penalty. A caution can be called for actions which are perfectly normal in football or baseball, such as ungentlemanly conduct or dissenting from the referee's decision. For a second caution, the referee flashes a red card, which means the player is out of the game. No substitute takes his place; the fouling team plays shorthanded, which usually means a lost game. If the referee believes the fouling was deliberate, he can issue a red card for the first foul.

In today's semifinal, the Russian referee had his cards glued in his pocket. For the Bulgarians, at least. If an American looked cross-eyed at a Bulgarian, the yellow card came leaping out. But when a Bulgarian player assaulted an American, the referee didn't even wave a finger. In spite of this, the U.S. Team was ahead 2-0 in the last minute of play. There was no way the Bulgarians could tie, much less win, so they pulled out all stops and attacked the American forwards viciously. Was it pure coincidence, as the referee claimed, that three American forwards, including Boni, were so badly hurt that they can't play in the finals? Is it a coincidence that the referee for the big game is a Hungarian? Sure, if you believe in fairy tales. The iron curtain countries have turned the quotation about sports being the moral equivalent of war on its head. So don't bother betting where your heart is; the fix is in. East Germany will win the World Cup by a huge score and the East European government-controlled newspapers will print proud editorials about the superiority of socialist sport.

---

Julius Witter, Sports Editor of the *Daily Sentry*, placed the printout of Marc's column carefully on the near right corner of his desk, aligned it exactly with the edges of the desk, and leaned back in his swivel chair. He pushed his old-fashioned horn-rimmed reading glasses back on the gray hairs neatly combed over his bald spot and looked off through the glass enclosure of his office at the sea of hunched backs in front of the computers in the busy newsroom. For a moment Marc felt that these minor variations from Witter's ceremony of rejection meant the column might be accepted, but the hope died as soon as Witter spoke. "Too long."

"Come on, Mr. Witter," Marc said, "eighty words over the seven hundred? You can't fit that in?"

"Actually," Witter said, running his thumb over his graying military moustache—the kiss of death, Marc knew—"it would take the removal of three hundred words to make this column even marginally suitable for burying in the used-car ads. Have you lost your mind, Burr?"

"I'm good and mad, Julius. If you had been there, seen what I saw . . . if this had happened in Palermo or Glasgow or Buenos Aires, the fans would have burned down the stadium with the referee in it and then gone on to do some *really* bad things. And I would have helped them."

"Is that your goal? To turn American soccer fans into raving maniacs?" Witter shook his head sadly. "Did it ever occur to you that if Koch Field were burned down, our reporters would have to travel to Queens or even to New Jersey to report on major sporting events? Do you know how much that additional travel would cost in productivity? I might even have to put on another warm body to get the same incompetent coverage we have now. Have you any idea what our esteemed owner, Mr. Heisenberg, would say about the additional cost? Are you trying to make my life difficult, Burr? Because if you are, you know that my policy is to delegate headaches downward."

"I have to do what's right, Julius. I have to tell the truth as I see it."

"Really? And if you succeed in inflaming the populace to burn down a stadium or hang a referee, what next? Once they have tasted the joys of mob violence, what is to stop them from burning down the Sentry building if they don't like the way you criticized one of their heroes? I don't mind your going on welfare, but how am I to maintain my standard of living if Mr. Heisenberg stops signing checks? And even worse, you start by insulting our readers. Brilliant."

"I just told the truth."

"Exactly. In a newspaper. The novelty may have a certain shock value, but other than that, it is sure to lose us some readers. Which Mr. Heisenberg will notice. Unfavorably. It may come as a shock to you, Burr, but people, even our readers, do not like to be insulted. Nor, for that matter, do Russians, Bulgarians, Hungarians, and East Germans, particularly if it's the truth. Would you like to explain this column," he slapped his hand on the printout, "to the State Department? Or the FBI? The CIA? Would you like hordes of congressional investigators digging into everything we do here? Can you afford to take two years off without pay to prepare a case for your innocence, to prove you are not in the pay of some secret nihilist organization? Or even pay your attorney's initial retainer? Has Dahliah been promoted to President of the Oliver Wendell Holmes College of Criminology unbeknownst to me? Or won the lottery?"

"Dahliah isn't even up for tenure till next year. As a matter of fact, we are a little short right now and I could use—"

"Burr, you are unbelievable. Here am I, trying in my finest fatherly manner to avoid firing you, and you dare hint at a raise?"

"I just thought . . . it's a good column, Mr. Witter. Well written, accurate, and bound to promote discussion."

Julius Witter stared at Marc incredulously. "And knowing this, you still want me to approve it?" He reached into the pocket of his old gray cardigan, took out his dirty brown pipe, and began to load it with shaggy black-flecked tobacco. After all he had done to train Marc to be a *real* newspaperman, possibly even his successor, the lad still had his childish dreams. Fantasies. No understanding of the real world. Witter sighed. The coaxing, the stimulation, the careful bringing along, all wasted, down the drain. Well, all he could do was keep up the pressure. Marc, just the right age to be his son, had he ever . . . would just have to learn or crack under the strain. If you can't stand the heat, get out of the business.

"What about the game story I sent in? Will that be printed as it stands?"

"Of course, my boy. I liked it so much that I did the rewrite myself; just removed a few of the more offensive parts."

Marc stared at him. "You turned it into the usual crap?"

"To save you the trouble, Marc; I know how busy you are." Witter began lighting his pipe, talking through teeth clenched on the stem. "When you forced me to promote you to Assistant Editor and to allow you a column, I assumed that, after fifteen years under my paternal tutelage, you had learned that our basic function is to provide accurate numerical data, harmless information, and some mildly controversial opinions, the kind that could be argued by a team's partisans in a neighborhood bar. Occasionally, a savage attack on an out-of-favor personality, citing anonymous sources and unnamed informants, might be tolerated, provided the story was well hedged with alleged's, claimed's, and 'it is generally understood's.' Something like this," he nodded toward the manuscript, "is totally unacceptable." The pipe lit to his satisfaction, Witter took a deep pull and pointedly blew the smoke at Marc.

Marc moved his chair back. "Does this mean you aren't going to print my column as written either?"

Witter smiled, leaned forward, and puffed hard, trying to reach Marc with the smoke. "Don't play idiot with me, Burr; I was smart while you were peeing in your diapers. You knew very well that this jeremiad would never see print. Unless," he said hopefully, his eyes lighting up, "you wanted an excuse to resign? If so, I accept your resignation. Effective immediately. Good-bye." He unfolded his long, thin body, stood up and put out his hand. "Sorry to lose you, Burr, but I think you're doing the right thing. You were never really fit to be a newspaperman; why don't you try journalism for a change?"

Marc remained seated, ignoring the outstretched hand. "You know I can't afford to resign," he said bitterly. "And you don't really want me to go, do you? It would take you ten years to find another victim this perfect. If it weren't for Dahliah. . . ."

"Ah, yes, Dahliah." Witter sat down again. "Lovely girl. Too good for you, you know. Have you ever thought of emigrating? I hear Rupert Murdoch is looking for a stringer in Tasmania. Lovely climate, friendly people, ideal for your limited talents, and it would free Dahliah to marry someone worthy of her. Did it ever occur to your selfish little soul that you're dragging a wonderful woman down to your level?"

"Dahliah loves me," Marc muttered, "and I love her. As soon as I get enough money together. . . ."

"Yes, well, I'll do my best to see that that never happens. For Dahliah's sake, as well as Mr. Heisenberg's. Now," Witter turned businesslike, "since you are not a complete ninny, and you didn't intend to resign, and you knew that childish tantrum you wrote would not be acceptable, please give me the proper column."

Marc took a folded printout from his breast pocket and laid it on Witter's desk. "How did you know?"

"When I come home at night, overworked and weary, and my cat twists herself lovingly around my legs, I know she doesn't love me, she's just trying to persuade me to give her delicatessen chopped liver instead of canned cat food. If I can read her mind, why should I have any trouble with a lesser entity's?" He picked up Marc's printout and glanced at it. "I take it this is a simple song of joy describing how the U.S. Team beat the Bulgarian Team in the semifinals, with just enough of a hint of the violence that occurred to entice some of our more bloodthirsty sports enthusiasts to overcrowd Koch Field on Sunday and make Gregor Ragusic even richer than he is? And that it contains complimentary mentions of Steve Vanderhook, the U.S. Soccer League, and our great coach, Grilho Vargas?"

Marc nodded miserably. "Exactly the kind of junk you wanted."

"Excellent." Witter smiled wolfishly. "You may be slow, Marc, but you do understand the importance of eating regularly. And did you predict that the formidable U.S. Team was sure to win the World Cup against the effete East Germans? We want to make sure that the visiting out-of-towners leave enough money with our local bookies to support our statesmanlike politicians."

Marc nodded again. "Exactly seven hundred words."

Witter looked pleased. "I trust you, my boy, so I won't bother editing this." He tossed the printout to Marc, just short, so that it fell to the floor. "Go ahead, send it down. May I further remind you that it was at your request I promoted you from thrice-weekly columns to daily columns for the duration of the World Cup Games, so don't waste any more precious time writing unprintable self-therapy."

"It's impossible to do that much work during my regular hours, Mr. Witter."

"You have my sympathy, Marc," Witter smiled, falsely apologetic. "However, the words *overtime pay* are not in the vocabulary of assistant editors. And for the next few days, in addition to daily exclusive news items, I want personal interest stories, six hundred words each, on Grilho, Boni, Vanderhook, and Ragusic. On time. Also on the other Booters on the World Cup Team: Benjamin, Royal, and Velez."

"But everybody knows—"

"Everybody knows *Cinderella*, too, but they like to hear the story over and over again. So you will tell our readers what they already know, reinforcing their established opinions in your own inimitable style, plus any new dirt you can dig up. Why all the Booters hate Ragusic. And something about the feuds, too, please. Ragusic and the other owners against Vanderhook, Grilho against Ragusic, Boni against his father, Vanderhook against Grilho and Grilho against the Hollingsworths. Nothing bad about Vanderhook or the Hollingsworths, please; they're very rich."

"There aren't any real feuds; just disagreements."

"When you get through digging out the facts and writing the stories, they will be full-blown feuds. In the *Sentry*, at least. Nothing actionable, please; just intimations of blood flowing. Understood?"

Marc stood up, holding the printout of his column. "Will that be all, sir?"

"For the while, Burr. And it's all right with me if you spend the next five minutes thinking of revenge. Just don't take any foolish action; you're outclassed. Yes," he waved Marc's objection aside, "you did take advantage of some unusual circumstances in the past to squeeze some minor gains out of me, but ultimately, the odds are with the house. And don't slam the door."

Marc paused at the door. "Enough of those minor wins, Julius, and I'll be sitting in your chair. Be warned." He slammed the door. As usual. The glass shuddered but did not break. As usual.

## 2

$M$arc was hot and sweaty and in a foul mood when the slow-moving freight elevator let him off at the top floor of the loft building. He pulled down the big steel door and carefully snapped both locks; no way was he going to venture out again that night into the dark, deserted streets of the Chelsea manufacturing district in which he and Dahliah had to live. Dahliah, busy in the open kitchen area, greeted him with a wave and a smile. "I'm making a new dish," she called out. "Tofu saté. The recipe looked delicious."

"With meat?" He paused on his way to the front half of the loft, the gym, the reason they couldn't live in an apartment house. "On bamboo skewers? The tofu will fall off."

"Of course no meat; don't be disgusting. And I'm not using skewers; I'm marinating the tofu in the sauce and I'll stir-fry everything as soon as you relax."

"Why don't I smell garlic?"

"You'll find out later, darling. Or would you rather have garlic and no kissing?"

She looked so adorable in her old, worn T-shirt, with her long auburn hair pulled back and up, that Marc started back toward the kitchen area. "Supper can wait. Let's do the kissing now and eat the garlic later."

"You keep nagging at me," she pointed a warning spoon at him, "and you can have option three: no garlic and no kissing. So, relaxing first, eating second. I want you full of energy after supper."

"I'm full of energy now."

"Hating energy, not loving. Mr. Witter told me. And besides, you're all sweated up."

"Witter told you? *Julius?*"

"He called an hour ago. Said you had a hard day— writer's block and lots of rewrites—and suggested that I make a special meal and prepare a hot bath and give you a good shiatsu massage later. Very few bosses would bother to do that. The bath is ready and I've laid out your gym clothes."

"You don't understand, Dahliah. He hates me, wants to get rid of me. This is his way of rubbing it in—that's why he called you."

"He's trying to be a father to you, darling, so sometimes he may seem a little stern, but he really loves you, I can tell. As a woman and as a psychologist. And the reason he called was . . . did you ask him for the raise? So we can air-condition the loft?"

"He shot me down before I could even finish the sentence. I still think we shouldn't spend any more money on this place. We ought to save for a down payment on a building of our own."

"At our present rate, that'll take ten more years. Do you really want to sweat for ten more years? And I don't have tenure yet. Suppose they don't give me tenure?"

"They have to; you're their most beautiful professor."

"Assistant Professor; the lowest of the low."

"I'll overlook your low station and marry you anyway. Let me take you away from all this, Dahliah. We'll get an efficiency apartment in a nice neighborhood—"

"Which will cost more than this whole loft and you won't have room for your gym equipment and you'll get fat and blame it all on me and grow to hate me. Besides—"

"Never." He reached out for her.

"Later." She pulled back. "Besides, you know I'm not ready to get married yet. Maybe after I get tenure, we'll discuss it again. I also have more to tell you. The reason Mr. Witter called. He wants me to write an article for the Sunday Sports Section: 'Why They Play the Way They Do.' With a by-line: by Dr. Dahliah Norman. A cross-cultural analysis of the different psychological styles of soccer. Just in time for the World Cup. You have to help me. It pays three hundred dollars on publication. Maybe Mr. Witter can't give you a raise right now, but he's really trying to help us. And it gives me exposure; maybe I'll even write a paper on the theme."

Marc sighed. He loved Dahliah, and he respected her profession somewhat, but couldn't she see? He trudged back to the gym area. The walls were covered with big beautiful blowups of the photographs he had taken when he had competed in the '72 Olympics, when the Russians and the Japanese had swept the gymnastic competition and he had been the only American to place in the top twenty.

He dressed slowly and pulled a high stool over to the still rings. Usually he started on the horizontal bar, but today . . . Dahliah was right; he did have a lot of hate in him. Hate for the Bulgarian Team, hate for the Russian referee, for the system where what should have been a pleasurable competition between the greatest soccer players in the world became an instrument of state policy, hate for—no, not real hate—anger at Julius Witter, and of course, hatred for himself for allowing Witter's needling to affect him so. He climbed up on the stool, grasped the rings, and with one toe, threw the stool out from under him. He chinned up rather than kipping up—trying to use the most energy possible rather than the least—pressed up into a handstand, lowered his body into a planche, arms outstretched and body horizontal, then, still maintaining himself at arm's length, slowly dropped his body to vertical, holding himself in the crucifix position. He held the strained position for several seconds, until his pectorals started trembling, then flopped into a loose hang. *Like an angry idiot,* he thought, *to forget to stretch first; I'll feel this tomorrow.* He hung loosely, head back, for a full minute, feeling his body relax, get longer, longer, until peace flowed through him, from his fingertips down. He kipped up and dismounted with a simple front flip, almost perfectly.

Marc walked over to the horizontal bar, jumped up, caught the bar, and kipped up in the same motion. He went into a series of drop kips until he started tiring, then took two turns of a giant swing and dismounted with a sloppy double back flip. *Each year,* he thought, *I get tired more and more quickly. I was a has-been at twenty-two, and sixteen years later I couldn't even place in a high school competition.* He moved away from the cluster of equipment to the edge of the mats that covered the gym floor and went into a routine of floor exercises, rolls, twists, and flips, ending with a running double backflip and falling clumsily when he landed. *Enough,* he decided. *The state of mind I'm in now, I could easily break something, preferably my neck.* Time for the hot bath followed by—the way Dahliah was acting—a cold shower.

"I also baked a carrot cake," Dahliah said, "but it has a lot of honey in it, so only one small piece." She served Marc a slightly bigger piece than she took—Dahliah had the idea that a woman should not be *zaftig*, in spite of Marc's assurances that she was a raving beauty and he loved her exactly the way she was—a sign that he was forgiven. For what, he didn't know. Probably for proposing again after he had promised not to for six months. All that mattered, as far as he was concerned, was that they were at loving peace again. "Now tell me about the different styles of play."

"It's true," he said, "a soccer fan can tell which country the team is from by watching them play for five minutes. The Americans, for instance, run around like crazy, enthusiastically, giving it the old college try, each wanting to be the hero who scores the winning goal. The Brazilians move like a chorus line, rhythmically, passing to each other with short, fast kicks, moving the ball very fast toward the opposing goal, where their forwards can take a shot. The British like to take long, booming kicks, getting the ball into enemy territory at once and away from their own goal. This may be because of the British weather; when the field is muddy, short passes just drop dead. It may also be part of the national strategy: to fight the wars on enemy territory and never allow the tight little island to be invaded.

"The Argentineans play a rough physical game, like their gauchos, but technically perfect. The Dutch play a very flexible game. When they're attacking, you have ten forwards, any one of whom can score, but when they're defending, you have eleven defenders, four deep, guarding their own goal. And they change over in a second. The Germans are very well organized, with perfect strategy and tactics and excellent execution and, occasionally, surprises, as when a defense man will pull out of the backfield and lead a try at the goal. The Russians have probably the best-conditioned players of all. They play a deliberate, steady, obvious, methodical game, pounding away again and again toward the enemy until they drain his energy and force their way to their goal. The Italians play like a bunch of all-stars, but very defensively, keeping a sweeper behind the line of fullbacks who can go where he will to plug any gap that appears. But once in a while they break out into an attack and their forwards, who are great kickers, will slam in a goal. The Uruguayans—"

"Stop," Dahliah laughed. "I can't absorb so much at once. I have only a thousand words. Write it down for me and I'll work on it later."

"Tomorrow."

"How can I resist," she smiled irresistibly, "such a silver-tongued suitor?"

# 3

The yellow sun glared down from the brilliant blue sky, flaming the precisely mowed grass, the green-baize smoothness of Koch Field. The beautiful new stadium, the biggest and most modern in the New York metropolitan area—though only half the capacity of the two-hundred-thousand-seat Maracana Stadium in Rio de Janeiro—had been opposed by every automatic opposition group in the city, but economic necessity, the careful preparations of Gregor Ragusic and Steve Vanderhook, and the demands of 2 million New York soccer fans had pushed the construction through. No one outside of the soccer world had realized that in the melting pot that was the United States, the majority of the population was, at most, two generations removed from a culture where soccer was the only sport, where national pride was embodied in a country's soccer team, where fans would kill each other over which forward was a better dribbler, where referees and players often needed police protection after a game, and where the stadium was literally torn apart after a loss by the home team and its coach's home was burned to the ground.

Of course, now that the United States was host country to the World Cup Games, now that the final game for the World Championship was being played in Brooklyn, and the games had brought hundreds of millions into the economy and tens of millions in taxes; now that the U.S. Team had made the finals, with tickets for the big game with East Germany selling for a thousand dollars each, there were only muted grumblings from the professional gripers that the money the stadium cost should have been spent on improving living conditions for the poor, the homeless, the imprisoned, and the bureaucrats who would control the distribution of that money.

It had been estimated that the previous World Cup final game had been watched on TV by almost 2 billion people, and that in places as far as ten thousand miles away, there had been shootings and knifings over disagreements between partisans of one team and the other as to whether or not a foul should have been called on a charging tackle. The feelings were not quite that intense in the United States, not even in New York—though in the home of the Brooklyn Booters, with its Head Coach and four players on the U.S. starting team, one did not mention East Germany without spitting—still there were fans who had bet their life savings on the U.S. Team, in spite of the loss of its three top forwards and in spite of, or maybe because of, the odds of eight to five against the Americans.

The burning sun was slowly grilling the twenty-two players scrimmaging down below on the pool-table-flat field. Hot sweat drew irregular dark patches on the thin navy blue jerseys of the U.S. World Cup first team and on the bright red shirts of their opponents, who were dressed to simulate the East German Team. Marc Burr, sitting in the stands at midfield, though theoretically at work, had given in, relaxed, and was enjoying the game purely as a spectator. This was what he loved most about being a sports reporter: the friendly competition, the display of skills hard earned by years of practice, the flash of talent that unexpectedly broke through with astounding beauty, the pure game. For this was clearly a real game, played by the rules, nonstop, with the first-team players determined to prove they were the best and the reserves trying to show that they deserved to play.

Of all the team games, Marc loved watching soccer best. Football was a game played by huge supermen whom no ordinary citizen could hope to match and its emphasis on power and violence made it, for Marc, like reporting a war. Baseball, like Wagner's music, had moments of beauty separated by hours of boredom and, in spite of the extraordinary neuromuscular coordination required, was played by potbellied men who would faint if they had to run for five minutes straight. Basketball's action was fast and continuous but, except for the few magicians, consisted mainly of giants dropping balls *down* through hoops.

But soccer? Yes, soccer was *the* game; the fullest test of speed, stamina, skill, intelligence, reactions, team play, judgment, coordination, balance, determination—even of strength, though not of the weight lifting kind. To tackle a dribbler who was approaching your goal, driving the ball ahead of him with both feet alternately, meant judging his intended course accurately without getting faked out or caught off balance, getting the proper foot against the ball to wedge it against the dribbler's foot, and then, at precisely the right instant, to knock him off balance by the force of your shoulder against his chest without being called for roughness. Not easy, as many a sprawled defender could attest under his breath when he tackled a forward who was faster, stronger, and trickier than he was.

And another thing Marc loved about soccer: Height didn't count. Marc, at five-eight, had been almost too tall for world class gymnastic competition and was firmly convinced that, had he been three or four inches shorter, he would have won a medal. And worse, he had only that one shot at the gold. At twenty-two, he was already stretching the age limit; at twenty-six, it was foolish to even think of competing seriously. Soccer players could play professionally for twenty years and, in soccer, the greatest players were short: Pelé was five-eight, Grilho slightly shorter, and both weighed about 150, the same as Marc weighed now. Some fullbacks were a little taller, and some goalies hit six feet, but goalies didn't do much running. Jason Benjamin, at six-two, was the tallest man in soccer, but he was slim and light on his feet.

In a soccer game, a seven-foot basketball player would have looked helpless, nailed to the floor, and a three-hundred-pound football tackle would have collapsed just running from one end of the field to the other. And though soccer was not completely injury-free, it was almost as safe as *watching* football on TV. No wonder soccer was the world's most popular game and the fastest growing sport in America.

Marc loved watching, from above, the subtle shift of the team patterns as they went from attack to defense to attack again, sometimes within seconds. The moment a player was on the ball, had gained control of the ball, his team, no matter where or how positioned, was automatically on offense and, just as quickly, the opposing team went into defense. A forward, deep in enemy territory and trying to get loose to receive a pass, would suddenly, as his teammate lost possession, have to guard the man who had been marking him. The instantaneous change in gestalt reminded Marc of the time when, as a boy, he had been given a magnet and a box of iron filings. With the filings sprinkled on a piece of cardboard, Marc would move the magnet under the cardboard and observe how, without shifting position, the filings changed their pattern and orientation with each pass of the magnet. So, too, did the blue and red teams on the field shift as control of the white ball, with its evenly spaced pentagonal emblems, passed from one side to the other. The public address system was softly playing a fast, rhythmic, teasingly familiar South American song, and it seemed to Marc that everyone on the field, even the three referees in their zebra-striped shirts, was moving to that beat, dancing in a ballet conducted by the unpredictable flight of the mercurial white ball.

The blue team, the first team, was playing without their injured forwards, Fred Bremer, Herb Wendell, and Cabot Hollingsworth Bonifacio Vargas. The three, in full uniform, were jealously observing the game, sitting glumly on the long bench near the entrance to the locker room. Their places on the field of battle had been taken by Jamaican-born Cuffy Royal, a short, rugged, powerful black man with thighs like tree trunks; by slim, handsome José Velez, whose family had escaped from Cuba in an open boat when José was a baby, and by long-haired, fiery Teddy Pangos, whose father had once played professional soccer in Crete.

The red team was led by Grilho himself at the center of a five-forward attacking line. Though showing even more strain on their sweat-drenched faces than the first team, they kept pressing doggedly on toward the blue goal, driving intently, methodically, Russian style, to get the ball into goal-shot territory. The red shirts were playing a very physical game, using only standard tactics and depending on sheer strength to bull their way through the defense, breaking tackles with a force that would leave the blue halfbacks stretched out on the ground, forcing the whole red forward line toward the penalty area in front of the blue goal. In one ten-minute period Marc counted three shots on goal, one of which Jason Benjamin, the tall goalie, had to dive for and barely stopped.

Then Grilho took the ball at midfield and demonstrated the skill that had made him, at seventeen, the star center forward of Rios, Brazil's best team. He waved his flanking forwards out sideways, all the way to the touch lines, to spread the defenders, and began running at medium speed toward the blue half of the field, controlling the ball in front of him as he ran. Moving fluidly, with occasional reverses and bursts of high speed, a pinball on a fast machine studded with obstacles, he dribbled the ball from foot to foot without losing stride, seemingly effortlessly, past the defenders who tried to stop him, faking out one, catching another on the wrong foot and whirling past him, slipping their tackles smoothly, easily, as he approached the penalty line, only eighteen yards from the goal. By that time the three fullbacks had dashed over to get between him and the goal. Grilho faked a kick into the goal with his right foot and, in the same liquid movement, snapped a short pass with his left foot to Grosz on his right, who immediately arced a high kick to the left side of the goal, five yards out. Grilho sprinted to where the high pass would come down and jumped straight up, high. Three blue shirts rose simultaneously around him. Though shorter than any of the defenders, Grilho, the grasshopper, rose above the others, body facing to his right, to punch a header into the goal. Jason Benjamin, already moving toward the ball side of the goal, slammed on his brakes and shifted back to stop the expected header. At the last moment Grilho twisted his body in midair and headed the ball toward his left, his forehead slamming the ball toward the top corner of the goal. Benjamin dove at the ball and with the fingertips of his right hand barely deflected it so it hit the top crossbar and bounced away. A whistle sounded and everyone relaxed.

Already started toward the deflected ball, Grilho turned in one graceful, easy motion and started jogging to midfield. Just as quickly, a school of fish changing direction, the other players followed. The men of both teams formed themselves into four straight lines in midfield with Grilho facing them. Without pause, and working with them as well as counting the fast cadence, he led the soaking-wet players through a regimen of bending and stretching exercises that lasted a full fifteen minutes.

Marc marveled at the stamina of these young men, surely the best-conditioned athletes in the world, to be able to do calisthenics after a fierce, uninterrupted forty-five-minute session of play. A game of soccer has two forty-five-minute periods, with only a ten-minute halftime interval. During those ninety minutes the players are in constant motion on a field as much as 130 yards long and 100 yards wide, an area almost three times as large as a football field. They don't just jog when they move; they are usually running slowly, and they break into maximum-speed sprints at undetermined times every few minutes.

Theoretically, soccer is a low-contact sport, but when tackling a dribbler to get the ball away from him, it's not enough to trap the ball between his foot and yours; you have to overpower the dribbler to get control of the ball, otherwise he'll leave you on your butt as he shoots for the goal.

At midfield, Grilho checked his watch and ended the stretching session. He dismissed his team and led them, running at half speed, over to the tunnel leading to the locker room. At that point, he called out Jason Benjamin and the other goalie, the ones wearing the distinctive red-white-and-blue-striped jerseys, and started them running around the field.

Marc walked slowly down the steep concrete steps of the stadium to the barrier separating the seats from the field. He placed his hands on top of the fence as though it were a side horse, vaulted down to the ground easily, and walked slowly toward the locker room area. He enjoyed visiting a soccer team's locker room.

Football and basketball teams, and even baseball teams, left Marc feeling like a pygmy, and he was often over-looked in the crowd of reporters, most of whom were taller. Soccer players were all about his height and build, short, slim, hard men, with flat bellies—you begin to reconsider the pleasure of eating dessert when your livelihood depends on having to lug an extra five pounds around when you run for ninety hard minutes—and huge, powerfully muscled thighs and calves. That was the only difference between gymnasts and soccer players; gymnasts had big arms and slim legs. Of course, there was another difference: Gymnasts performed highly concen-trated maneuvers for a minute or two, trying for perfect form in the prescribed exercises. Soccer players worked like mules for ninety minutes with no thought of form; there was no time to think in a soccer game, just to *do*. So gymnasts had small, flat, muscular chests while soccer players had the deep, bony, rib cages that were needed to contain the big lungs and powerful hearts the sport required.

Even before he entered the locker room, Marc heard the song that had been playing outside. Though it was played very softly, he found himself walking in rhythm with its catchy beat. The room smelled worse than any locker room Marc had ever been in; the day was hot and soccer players have to sweat a lot to keep their blood from boiling. There was none of the towel-snapping foolery that characterizes a baseball locker room; the mood was rest and relaxation. Several of the naked men, already showered, were stretched out, with their eyes closed, on top of towels spread on the benches. There was plenty of room for all; soccer teams have fewer men than any other major sport because of the two-substitution limit. Some of the men were drinking water and eating salt tablets; a couple had their own little bottles of honey and water, laced with their favorite mixtures of vitamins and electrolytes. Not one of them looked fatigued and Marc felt that, given five more minutes of rest, they all would have gone out for another forty-five minutes of play without a murmur.

Piled near each locker were the wet uniforms, the jerseys and shorts and socks and jocks, ready to be washed. The piles were small; a whole soccer team can be outfitted for the cost of three professional football players' uniforms. The wiped-down shin guards stood against each locker, and the low leather shoes—each player had four pair, with his number on the inside—were laid on their sides, laces pulled wide open to permit drying, ready to be collected by the shoe boy to be cleaned and polished so they stayed supple.

Shoes are a soccer player's most important equipment, custom-made for his foot and built to give full support for running and jumping, for changing direction abruptly, and though very light, for kicking. The shoes are cut low around the ankle and padded there, with a raised padded support to protect the Achilles tendon. The molded plastic soles have either six big tapered plastic studs or sixteen small studs, depending on the preference of the player, screwed into plates embedded in the plastic.

Marc began making his way toward where Grilho was sitting in front of his locker at the far end of the room. Before he was halfway there, Grilho's fabled peripheral vision, which some attributed to his wide-set eyes and narrow face, came into play, and he turned to watch Marc approach.

Grilho had a broad, square, bony forehead, with outstanding bulges at the upper corners—like the horns of the devil, some said—with high Indian cheekbones hanging over the sharp axlike nose and the thin lips that bespoke Inca ancestors. The nostrils flared out from his sharp-bridged nose, intakes for the huge quantities of air that soccer players need, giving him an angry, dangerous look that was made even stronger by the tight lumps of muscle at his jaw. But the fierce, wild, animal look was softened by the broad, friendly smile, a wide expanse of perfect white teeth, and the soft, compassionate, hazel eyes that showed the true character of the great man, the greatest soccer player of all time. The Head Coach's skin was a clear light brown, the beautiful, typically Brazilian, café au lait color of the true *carioca*, the heritage of three continents. Grilho's hard-muscled body was shiny with sweat and he was breathing deeply and evenly, but other than that he showed no sign of tiredness. His naked body looked as good as any Marc had ever seen on an athlete half his age, the ripple of abdominal muscles attesting to the forty-two-year-old man's fitness.

With his right hand Grilho ran the blue towel up his face and back over his graying curly black hair to get the sweat out of his eyes, took three more slow, deep breaths, and said, "I am sorry, Marc, but I cannot spend much time with you now." His voice was soft and low, with a slight trace of an accent, more in the phrasing and rhythm of his speech than in the pronunciation. As he spoke, the fingers of his left hand were drumming the rhythm of the background music on the bench next to him. "Perhaps after the practice? You understand?" He looked truly regretful.

"Yes, of course, I can understand." But Marc couldn't understand. True, Grilho didn't look his age and was still as slim and muscular as he was at seventeen, when he was star center forward for Rios, but he had not played professionally for four years and couldn't possibly be in condition to. . . . "After the practice? More practice? I just got here and I don't know when you started. Didn't you just play for an hour and a half straight?"

"No, of course not. We had a very hard game yesterday so we just played forty-five minutes today." *Just* forty-five minutes? Marc was used to athletes bitching after ten minutes of calisthenics. "And we will have a thirty-minute rest." Thirty whole minutes? Practically a *vacation*. "I am not trying to overwork my players; we must be in good shape for the final game."

"But more practice? After this? Football players are exhausted for two full days after a game in which a man can have as little as ten minutes of actual playing time."

"That is true, but there is a great difference. In American football, there is an explosion of energy, people attack each other, fight with great violence. And many of them are very big, up to three hundred pounds. Size is not important in association football and the for-wards, who do the most running, they are not big. Even Boni, he is not very heavy. We have many times in a game when a player has just to run at low speed. Have no fear; after they rest, they will be ready for a good practice. Not difficult; just fundamentals. Always the fundamentals must be practiced; no one is so good he can skip that."

Marc stared at the short, slim man before him, the greatest of his sport, who was calmly telling him that, for a soccer player, a full-speed forty-five-minute practice game was a warmup for a "good" practice. Which, Marc understood very clearly, would be a hard practice. "Jason Benjamin and the other goalie—why did you punish them?"

"Punish?" Grilho looked puzzled.

"Make them run laps."

"That is not punishment. Goalkeeper is a very difficult position. True, there is little running, but he must be alert every second, ready to jump where it is needed, follow the play, see where the attack is coming from, throw himself at the ball, organize the offense when the attack is stopped. He must be in as good physical condition as everybody else and those two, they did not have as much exercise as was needed. Now, if you will please excuse?"

"One more question, Grilho? Why you?"

"Me? Why I work out, too? Oh, please, Marc, I must set the example. If I can, they must. I am always in condition, yes, because I work every day, but I was not in World Cup condition. When I was chosen for the team, I worked much harder so they would not be—I would not be— ashamed how I play, even in practice. So for three months I try to get in the best World Cup condition. It is unfortunate that I was chosen, but it was done. For the honor, you must understand, not because I am still good enough. I am not, and I know that very well. You noticed how I missed that goal?"

"I noticed that you dribbled through the whole U.S. first team and would have scored a goal if Jason Benjamin had been one inch shorter."

"Not the whole team; our three best forwards are not there." For a moment, Grilho's face twisted in concern for his son, Boni, the first to be injured that day. "Even so, ten years ago, five years ago, I would have scored. But the body . . . one gets old." He turned to Marc fully. "You see, this is what comes of permitting sentiment. They should have chosen a younger player but, you understand, I have never played in a World Cup Game. Injuries, sickness, accident . . . five times I would have, but each time it was impossible. Many times, some teams, they try to hurt me. I am careful, fast, but not always can I succeed. So this time, now, Mr. Vanderhook—he understands; he can never play a championship game, either—he insist that I be on the team. We have twenty men permitted for the World Cup Team. Only sixteen can suit up for a game, only eleven can play, and only two substitutions are allowed. Everybody thinks we will lose in the first game so, if we are very far behind, they will put me in for the last five minutes so I, too, can play in a World Cup Game. It was a big mistake. Now we—" he looked around and saw that none of the players was in earshot, but he lowered his voice "—now we may not have an easy job to win."

"Are you blaming yourself, Grilho?" Marc was truly sympathetic. "You had eight forwards on the roster and you play in a 4-2-4 formation. With only four forwards in the game and four more on the bench, who could possibly think, with only two substitutions per game, that you would run out of forwards?"

"I should have thought. But I was too wishful to play in the World Cup. Now I am in the position where if there is one more injury to a forward I must put in a halfback. And if there are two injuries, I must be ready to play myself. Against the best in the world. I can only hope that, if the East Germans play very—please put in your newspaper, Marc, that the whole world will be watching the referee, so that he must keep his eyes open and be fair, even if his country is friends with East Germany. Otherwise . . . I will pray that if there are two injuries, it is in the last few minutes." He shook his head regretfully and stood up, reaching for his towel.

"One more thing," Marc asked hurriedly. "About the stories that you're having trouble with Gregor Ragusic and Steve Vanderhook. Any comment?"

"Later, please, Marc." Grilho looked truly sorry. "Now I must go. Already I have lost some rest time. After I shower and suit up, I will not be enough rested for the practice. This afternoon after the discussion period, when we analyze the team play and the individual play, that might be a good time? Or, yes, I would like that better, tomorrow morning, before the eight o'clock practice starts?

For the remainder of this day I must concentrate on the team tactics and the game plan." He shook Marc's hand and trotted off to the shower room. *Trotted*. As an ex-athlete himself, Marc shook his head, too, in wonder. But as a reporter, he also noticed that Grilho had evaded the question.

# 4

For the World Cup Games, Gregor Ragusic had set up a temporary office for the Commissioner of the United States Soccer League: two rooms on the second floor of the stadium, near the elevator at the far end of the Brooklyn Booters' Koch Field offices. Vanderhook's secretary was away from her desk, so Marc tapped on the door of the inside office and, on Steve's loud welcome, went in. The Commissioner's temporary office was furnished just like his permanent offices in Radio City—at Vanderhook's personal expense, Marc was sure. Everything was subdued, old, authentic, and in good taste, from the carved mahogany desk to the worn leather easy chairs and the polished bronze lamps. The oak-paneled walls carried, at eye level, some small antique etchings of Cambridge University buildings.

Steve Vanderhook, at forty, was still movie-star handsome, with deep-blue eyes, a smooth, even tan, and thick, heavy, long blond hair that showed only traces of gray at the temples. Though he was over six feet tall, he looked chunky when sitting down because of the tremendous breadth of his shoulders, his huge chest, and the bulging upper arms that strained his navy blue blazer whenever he moved. His light-blue tie displayed the emblem of the U.S. Soccer League in gold. In his senior year at Princeton, Steve had been an almost certain Heisman Cup winner when he was stopped on a power plunge for touchdown by an even more powerful lineman, head to head. When the pileup was untangled, Steve lay on the ground, paralyzed from the hips down. He never played again, or walked again without crutches, never recovered the use of his legs or had any feeling in them, in spite of the dozens of doctors and therapists his family had retained. He sublimated his drive and his energy by upper body exercise—free weights, cables, pneumatic machines—building up his arms to where they were stronger than the average man's legs.

Once Steve had accepted that walking was not subject to his abilities or to his will, he made the best of what was left of his life. Fortunately, the Vanderhooks were old-money rich and Steve could devote himself fully to his crusade: to change the rules of football so as to decrease the chances of injury; to reduce the importance of football in American life; and to promote soccer as the perfect, safe team sport, both to play and to watch. He was unable to achieve his first two goals at all. The love of football and the need for its violence was too deeply embedded in the American psyche. At the end of ten years of blood, sweat, and tears, he had made only minor gains in his battle to make soccer a major sport in the United States.

It was then that Gregor Ragusic had approached him, suggesting that they join forces, combining Steve's name, contacts, and existing small organization with Ragusic's business acumen and drive. Each would provide half the start-up money required for the promotional campaign that would draw donations from the biggest companies in the country, particularly the insurance companies. Gregor also persuaded Steve not to waste his time fighting football or pushing soccer *generally*. He wanted Steve to concentrate on promoting a new professional soccer league that would, he claimed, develop interest in soccer automatically. The two men, the crippled blond giant and the fat, dark little trader, took to each other like magnets, alternately attracting and repelling each other, but woe to anyone who came between the two forces. So was born the United States Soccer League, with Steven Vanderhook as its first Commissioner.

Ragusic sold the first seven franchises—cannily keeping the choice Brooklyn franchise for himself—for sums that Vanderhook would not have dreamed of asking, and Vanderhook got concessions with a smile from governors and mayors who would never have spoken to Ragusic except to thank him, very shortly, for a big campaign donation. And now, after eight years of struggle, the World Cup Games were being played in the United States for the first time, a U.S. team had made the finals for the World Championship for the first time, and Ragusic and Vanderhook were tasting the sweet joys of their success and reaping the rewards of their labors.

"You're just in time, Marc," Steve boomed cheerily. "I want to show you something." He pushed a button on the arm of his wheelchair and steered himself jerkily out from behind his desk. "The controls are a little too sensitive," Steve said, "but we'll fix that in the next model."

"What was wrong with the old one?" Marc asked.

"Too unsteady and too limiting. I designed this one myself, with my engineers. Isn't it beautiful?"

"Looks more like a locomotive than a wheelchair. It must weigh a ton. Those big front wheels—how do you turn?"

"It's heavier than it's going to end up being, because I'm using lead-acid batteries—four of them, I'll explain why in a minute—so I need a steel pipe framework. It's painted black so we can see what it looks like when we get the lighter-weight batteries and can use an anodized aluminum frame. I'm able to use big wheels, front and back, because there are no axles. Each wheel has its own high-torque pancake motor built in, with its own battery for power. By eliminating the axles, I can lower the center of gravity and have a safer wheelchair. This model can't turn over or dump the occupant. Wheelchairs can be dangerous if you're not careful. Don't forget, legs are used for balance as well as walking."

"Okay, but how do you turn if the wheels are fixed to the frame?"

"Same way a tank or a tractor turns; by braking one side and speeding up the other. Or, in this case, I can reverse the left wheels, run the right side forward, and turn in place." He demonstrated by whirling around twice. "With all the power I have, I can use thick pneumatic tires with deep grooves, able to climb any normal curb."

"Stairs, too?"

"I have a prototype design for that, but it's much too expensive and very dangerous, too easy to tip over backward. But still, the freedom this new model gives me is unbelievable. On a flat straightaway I can hit over twenty miles an hour, faster than a sprinter, and maintain speed for two hours. Not for highways, but in New York, in any city, I can keep up with most traffic. And I can carry a lot. You know what that means for someone like me?" He indicated a pair of black leather saddlebags and, fixed to the base of the chair, a big leather quiver which held his hand crutches. Steve was not completely immobile. He could walk after a fashion, by locking the braces at his knees and, supported by the crutches, dragging one leg after the other.

Marc studied Steve's happy face. "You want this so you can play soccer yourself, don't you? A whole team of paraplegic soccer players. Two teams."

"Why not? Why shouldn't we be able to have fun like anybody else? It's not just for fun, either. It's the mental attitude. For twenty years I've . . . if you'd ever been laid up for just one month, you'd understand how debilitating, how discouraging, how *deadening* it is to see others doing so easily, so normally, so *often*, without thinking, what it would take a miracle for you to do just once. If some poor guy—or woman; it isn't just men who get hurt—sees me, and a hundred others like me, playing soccer on TV, seeing how fast, how easily we move, how much control we have, it would change his attitude toward himself and, just as important, change the attitude of others about us. We'll be human again."

"So that's what you meant when you said the stair design was too expensive? I wondered, with your money . . . so it's not just for yourself?"

"I have the corporation already set up. It won't be charity; we'll sell these at cost, and we'll try to keep the production costs down. Maybe even get approved for Medicare. It'll save the government money; no need for most of the special accommodations they now mandate. And—this is off the record; I don't want to raise people's expectations too high too soon—we're working on a design for quadriplegics."

"Breath control?"

"Chin, eye reflections, winks, whatever can activate a computer. They have some of these controls now, but the problem is backup. If the computer suddenly goes *blooey* while the chair is moving . . . but in time. . . ." He wheeled slowly over to the office door. "Come on,

I'll race you to the far end. Give you a ten-yard head start, because you're handicapped." He laughed triumphantly.

"Don't bother; gymnasts are built for grace, not for speed. I concede the race. You in a hurry to go someplace? Or could we stay here for a few minutes and talk?"

"Well, at least let me show you what the new chair can do. You have no idea. . . ." Steve opened the door and wheeled out slowly. Marc followed, hesitantly. As soon as Marc was outside, Steve positioned the big wheelchair so it was facing down the long corridor, toward the elevator bank. "Ready?" he asked.

"Sure," Marc answered. "For what?"

"This!" Steve shoved the joystick all the way forward, fast. For a moment, as the full power of the four heavy batteries poured into the motors, the wheels skidded on the slippery carpet, then grabbed, and the chair zoomed down the hall like a hopped-up drag racer. To Marc, it looked like the chair, and Steve with it, was going to blast out of the end of the building at sixty miles an hour, but just before he reached the end of the hall, Steve slammed on the brakes and the chair skidded a good twenty feet before it came to a stop only a few feet short of the end of the long hall. Steve immediately whipped it around in a standstill turn and came zooming back toward Marc again. Frightened, Marc dived back into the office. If that chair ever got away from Steve. . . . But this time Steve slowed down well before he reached the office door and moved back inside in a slow, graceful curve.

"Are you crazy?" Marc yelled. "You could have killed yourself. You must have been hitting—how fast were you going?"

"I don't have a speedometer," Steve said proudly, "but it was well over twenty miles an hour. Great, huh?"

"It looked like sixty to me. Now will you please come down from the clouds and talk to me?"

"About what?" Steve rolled back behind his desk. "Your column this morning was a real piece of nothing. I was hoping you would say what I couldn't."

"The Bulgarians? You're the Commissioner; why can't you protest officially? That was the rawest, most obvious fouling I've ever seen. We're lucky our boys weren't crippled for life." As soon as they were out, Marc regretted saying those words in front of a paraplegic, but Steve seemed to take no notice.

"I did file a formal protest, but I couldn't complain too loudly about the Bulgarians. This isn't just a U.S. affair, you know; there are international ramifications. The State Department doesn't want trouble with the Russians right now; there are some delicate negotiations going on."

"Is the Fédération Internationale de Football Associations going to do anything about it."

"Nothing that'll do us any good. They offered to make sure that referee would never work in an international competition again. Big deal; there's plenty of work in the Soviet Union for him for the rest of his life. I held out for his never refereeing any match again and they finally agreed. But that was all I could get. The Russians will probably give him a promotion to a higher-paying desk job in the Sports Commissariat, just to show what they think of our protests. I was hoping that all the papers, all the sports reporters at least, would blast them properly, so that the uproar would get the U.S.S.R. and Bulgaria barred from the next five World Cup Games. Not a chance."

"There are limits to what we can write, too," Marc apologized. "It's not outright censorship, but it's not far from it, either. Can we talk about other things? Like what are your predictions for the final game? On the record."

"On the record? I am confident that we'll win by a score of one-zero. The East Germans will have a lot of trouble getting past our fullbacks and if they do manage to do that once or twice, Benjamin will stop them. I sincerely believe he's the best goalkeeper in the business."

"Only one goal for us? We've hit two point three goals per game so far, the highest average in the whole match."

"That's my prediction, officially. Off the record, Marc, we're going to get clobbered and we're not going to score a single goal. We have only four forwards now, and not our best ones, either. John Geis is the only first-team striker we have left. He's good, but he's used to playing winger for Boni and Bremer. Cuffy Royal and José Velez are pretty good, too, but they're not of the same caliber as the men they're replacing. Thank God, at least they're both from the Booters and are used to working together. Theodore Pangos—well, he's very competitive, but he's not in the same class as Boni."

"You didn't mention Grilho. He's the greatest center forward of all time and he's eligible to play."

"He's even older than I am and he hasn't played in competition for four years. If we have to use him, it means the game is lost. Instead of Grilho, I'd rather see a halfback put in—Franczak or Barto. Grilho knows better than to put himself in, unless we're so far behind that there's no way we can win."

"You're assuming that only one of our forwards will be injured in the final game."

Vanderhook paled under his tan. "They wouldn't dare," he said in a shocked voice. "I'm assuming that *none* of our players will be injured. After what happened yesterday? The public outcry, the loss of respect, it would . . . no, that couldn't happen. The referee, even if he favors them, would never . . . two billion people will be watching."

"There are lots of times in a game where the referee has to make a judgment call, where the *intent* of the tackler, as the referee sees it, is what decides whether he was going after the ball legitimately or trying to injure the dribbler. Who's to say what the intent was on a close call? There have been other World Cup Games when the referee didn't show even a yellow caution card on some of the most obvious fouls ever committed."

Vanderhook clenched his jaw tightly, the veins standing out on his forehead. "I don't want to discuss such things, Burr; what you say just will not happen. The Bulgarian game was a desperate attempt by a losing team to eke out a tie. The situation here is different. You and I know that the East Germans will take a big early lead. They'll put away two goals in the first half and play very tight defensive ball for the rest of the game. Even if they're willing to risk international condemnation, there will be no need for them to descend to obvious fouling. After my protest yesterday, the referee won't be able to do any more than shade some minor decisions the wrong way.

"This whole talk is off the record, Marc," Vanderhook said grimly, "and I would appreciate it if you didn't broach the subject with anyone else. I truly do not believe anything like what you said will happen, but if it does, I'll handle it my own way." He angrily pushed the little lever that activated the wheelchair's motor all the way forward, and then jerked it back. The sudden braking almost sent him flying out of the chair.

"Hey!" Marc yelled. "Take it easy. You want to get out from behind the desk, I'll help you."

"I don't need any help," Vanderhook said irritably. "Just a little too sensitive. The controls, I mean, not me." He very carefully nudged the controls and moved out into the middle of the room. "I get tired of being stuck behind a desk all day," he explained. "Sometimes I just have to move around a little."

"It's not just the controls that are sensitive," Marc said.

"Yeah, I guess. But there's so much on my back, so many people I have to keep happy, so many pressures. . . ." He looked up at Marc and said, seriously, "I don't want any sensationalism in the media that will inflame the fans or the Congress; there's already been one war over a soccer game, between El Salvador and Honduras in '69, and I emphatically do not want to start another."

Marc wanted to change the subject; Vanderhook looked worn out, even this early in the morning. "I read the other day that an American doctor in Mexico succeeded in regenerating some nerves leading to the spinal cord by bridging the gap with fetal cells."

"I know all about it; knew about it a year ago. He's had signficant success with cut nerves in rats. But it's not yet ready for human beings or for the spinal cord. Be three more years, at least, to complete the experimentation and testing. I've asked my neurosurgeon to look into it, head a team to start duplicating the experiments here. Told him I'd provide as much money as needed."

"You know about that guy who's using computerized impulses that bypass the gap in the spinal cord to activate the leg muscles directly?"

"Dammit, Marc, don't you think I know about everybody who's doing anything in the field that has the slightest possibility of—"

"Hey, relax, Steve; I'm only trying to help."

"Yeah, everybody wants to help me. Nobody asks me what I want. Like my father keeps reminding me I'm the last of the line. Once a week. Discreetly."

This was the first time Vanderhook had mentioned anything personal to Marc. Though they were only three years apart in age and each had had the experience of being top athletes in their early twenties, though they often talked as equals and Marc really liked and admired Steve, the Commissioner had always shied away from personal matters. Nor had he asked Marc about his own life outside sports reporting. Marc sensed a story and automatically seized the opportunity. "It was very insensitive of your father to—I mean, in your condition, to rub it in. No disrespect intended."

"My condition? You mean . . . you think I can't . . .? No, no, that's not it at all. It's my legs, the voluntary muscles, that I can't control. Otherwise I'm a perfectly normal—not *perfectly*, that is, I am handicapped—but the problem is . . . you won't believe this, Marc, but it's money."

"Money? I thought you were very—that is, if anything went wrong, you still have a good salary as Commissioner."

Steve smiled. "It's too much money, not too little. There was a woman I liked, was considering marriage. If I were poor and she wanted to marry me, be willing to be tied down to a husband in a wheelchair, I'd have had several children already, made my mother happy. But with my money . . . I asked her to sign a prenuptial agreement. She refused. She wanted my money, not me. I would have burned the agreement right after the ceremony if she had truly loved me as I am."

"No other candidates?"

"Lots of candidates; all imperfect in some way. Like me," he added bitterly. He changed the subject. "Look, I'm sorry to inflict my problems on you. It's just what you said before, about the game, that they'll foul out all our forwards—that really upset me."

Marc decided to overlook the implicit criticism. "I was just passing on information, that's all. You want to talk about something else for a change? I still have to get an interview," he said apologetically, "and you said everything you told me before is off the record." Vanderhook nodded, resignedly. "Okay, what about the rumors I hear about you and Grilho? That you've had a major argument?"

"A minor disagreement," he said wearily. "Really. About technical matters. Nothing that affects either the final game or our relationship. I really respect him, you know; it's just that he's so stubborn."

"Okay, tell me about the minor disagreement. I've got to come back with something or Mr. Witter will put one of his hatchet men on the story and it'll blow up into a chain-saw massacre."

Vanderhook thought for a moment, then said, "It's about the future of our American teams in international play. Grilho has worked wonders with the Booters and especially with the World Cup Team—but he's not an American."

Marc stared at him, amazed. "Come on, Steve; I never thought I'd hear anything like that from you. Hell, he's been a citizen by marriage more than twenty years; he's as American as you are. Because he's part black? Part Indian?"

Vanderhook flushed. "No, no, of course not. You know me better than that."

"I thought I did, but . . . all right, I shouldn't have said that. But you know, Steve, not being an American is considered a plus in soccer. All the greatest players have been not American: Pelé, Cruyff, Beckenbauer, Chinaglia. . . ."

"Yes, exactly. Soccer isn't really an American game. We learn to throw, not to kick. And, as a nation, we're bigger, stronger, healthier, better fed than any other group in history. Grilho doesn't take that into consideration."

"He's done very well for the U.S. in spite of those terrible handicaps."

"Don't go sarcastic on me, Marc; I know what I'm

talking about." He paused to organize his thoughts. "What I meant was, Grilho was brought up on Brazilian-style soccer. Short passes, perfect control of the ball, moving rapidly toward the goal area, coordinated team play, and attack, attack, attack, all the time."

"That's bad? He's also combined that with the Dutch style where, on attack, even the defenders take part, come all the way forward. And on defense, even the forwards move back to overwhelm the offense. To me, that looks like a perfect combination. His 4-2-4 formation gives you four forwards and four fullbacks, with the halfbacks moving where they're needed. And it's worked. Look how far we've gotten with—let's face it—inferior players. Except for maybe Boni and Benjamin, none of our first team can match the stars of even small countries like Uruguay and Denmark."

"Exactly my point. There's no reason the U.S. can't have the greatest soccer teams in the world. All we need is to inculcate the love of soccer and to develop an American style of play, one that utilizes our physical characteristics and our cultural characteristics. One that fits the American psyche."

"And Grilho hasn't done that? Won't do that?"

"He can't. His style is modified Brazilian. He thinks Brazilian, he plays Brazilian, and he teaches Brazilian. Even his son, Boni, the greatest American soccer player we've ever had, is not an American soccer player, he's an American who plays soccer like a Brazilian. Brilliantly, but like a Brazilian. Watch our team play with this in mind, then watch a Brazilian team. They move like the Rockettes, all in perfect coordination with one another, all dancing to the same tune. Have you ever been to Rio during *Carnaval?* Tens of thousands of people, hundreds of thousands, all dancing, moving, singing, to the same beat, all over the city, perfectly—*unconsciously*—coordinated with one another. Beautiful. But not for Americans.

We don't have that samba beat in our blood. Or any beat. We're individualists, marching to the beat of a million different drummers; anarchists, two hundred fifty million strong."

"He's been very successful, Steve."

"That makes it even worse. We've done wonderfully well under Grilho, better than anyone had a right to expect, and because of that, we're going to follow his system for a generation. His way will feel uncomfortable for Americans, not consciously, but they won't do—won't be able to do—as well under it as they could under a system that fits the American culture and the American body and the American mind. And that will set soccer back in the United States for two generations, maybe forever."

"Are you hoping we *don't* win the final game?"

"No, no, of course not. All I'm saying is that next year, the South Americans and the Europeans will have solved the way we use our present system, and we'll never do as well again as we did this year. Just as each culture has developed its own style in everything—cooking and clothes and music and dancing and literature—we have to develop the American style of playing soccer. One that fits us easily, comfortably, naturally."

"And Grilho refuses?"

"Worse," Steve said. "He can't. And he doesn't know he can't."

"Well, what do you want him to do? I don't see—you want him to resign? You're crazy, Steve. He'll never . . . the greatest player of all time, the one who led us to the World Cup finals? With a shot at the World Cup itself? How did you get the nerve to even *mention* this to him?"

"I didn't. I just began hinting and he misunderstood. He thought I was criticizing him, his play, his team."

"You were. Did he slug you?"

"Grilho? No, he's too civilized for that, too controlled.

You know him. Even as a player, when they were trying to cripple him, he used to smile and help the attacker up from the ground where he had dumped him. He's the one man in this world who never got a red card. With him the team comes first."

"What did he do?"

Vanderhook smiled ruefully. "Slowly and carefully explained to me, as to a backward child, that now was not the time to make changes, no matter how badly he was performing as Head Coach. It ended up with my assuring him that I loved him and admired him and respected him and swearing that I wouldn't think of changing one tiny thing he had done. And he has a very good memory, too."

"You don't want me to print one word of this, do you, Commissioner?"

"That's why I told you everything, Marc. In case you get part of this story from anyone else, you are now obligated not to say a word. I understand how you think better than you do."

"You're a crooked politician, Commissioner, the worst kind: an *educated*, intelligent, crooked politician. I should have known better than to put myself in this position. But if this comes out from someone else's digging, I'm going to print what I know, too."

"Fair enough, Marc. But exactly the way I told it to you. Grilho doesn't deserve to be hurt. Or criticized."

"Yeah, I love him, too. But you've got to give me something. I can't go back to Mr. Witter with only good news. What about your problems with Gregor Ragusic? I heard—"

"It's not true." Struck gold, Marc thought.

"What isn't true?"

"I'm busy, Marc; piles of work on my desk and too many people to see. Thanks for the information about the new neurological techniques." He rolled back behind the desk, very jerkily this time, and pulled a stack of papers in front of him. "Would you mind letting yourself out, please?"

*These* Mayflower *types,* Marc thought, *or, rather,* Half Moon *types; all politeness and tight lips; tightest when they are most angry.* Well, now that he knew something was wrong, Ragusic would tell him all about it; Serbians did not conceal their emotions. On the other hand, they were known to lie. And who didn't, especially to reporters. Marc left quickly and quietly. No sense riling Steve up again.

# 5

Gregor Ragusic was marching back and forth in front of his gigantic white desk, yelling at Marc. "What the hell is the matter with you, Marcus?" he shouted. "You are afraid to tell the truth?" It was hard for Marc to imagine that twenty-four years ago, this bald, fat little man with the thin moustache, who would have been perfectly typecast as a twenties gigolo, had played flanker for the Yugoslavian World Cup Team and had actually, though they had lost to Peru, scored a goal. Nor did Ragusic look like the captain of industry he now was: Chairman and CEO of a conglomerate of companies that imported and distributed Eastern European products, and owner of the most profitable franchise in the USSL. True, his silk tie cost more than Marc made in a day and his soft, gray cashmere suit more than Marc took home in a week; true his hair was trimmed weekly, his nails groomed semiweekly, and his plump body massaged daily, but none of this altered Marc's vision of Gregor Ragusic: a brilliant Machiavellian mind, goaded by the glands of an enraged Donald Duck, trapped in the body of a Casbah guide. Ragusic bent down and thrust his face right in front of Marc's. Marc pulled back as far as the chair would let him. People were always pushing Marc, Witter with his smoke and Ragusic with his face. And with his breath, which smelled of garlic even this early in the morning. "You think Derzhavna Sigurnost will not try anything because you are American journalist?" Ragusic sneered. "Ha!"

"I'm not afraid of him," Marc said. Ragusic's office was not much larger than the Oval Office. His restraint, Ragusic had once explained, was due to his great respect for whoever could get elected as President. This year's decor was pure white, from the deep-piled angora rug to the enameled high ceiling with its bright recessed lights glaring down on the albino-cowhide overstuffed chairs. Lightning flashes of brilliant red abstractions on the walls highlighted the barren ice-floe effect. "I don't even know who Dersh—whatever his name—is. Mr. Witter's the only one I'm afraid of."

"Good. Better you shouldn't know. And tell me, please," he stopped screaming and taunted Marc, "how can it be that a journalist does not know from the Bulgarian secret police?"

"I'm a sportswriter. I have enough trouble knowing who slugged whom in last night's hockey game. Do you know how many vitally important sports events are going on every day that we don't even mention—that one of the *Sentry*'s loyal readers will call up about and ask why the hell we didn't print a full-page story of how his son drove in the winning run that put his high school team back in second place in the standings?"

"In my country, every little kindergarten schoolgirl, so

big, she knows who is political important. Why you think I go away, hah? You think I *like* for political tell me what to do?" He pushed his face into Marc's again.

"You've been an American citizen for fifteen years now, Mr. Ragusic; *we're* your country."

Ragusic stood erect again and shrugged impatiently. "My *old* country, natch. But why you change the subject? Why you don't tell about those bastards? How they cripple up my team? If they break Boni's leg, how I win League Championship next year? You know what this will do to attendance? Cut in half, absolute guarantee. Maybe more. You know how much that cost in money?"

"I thought you were worried about the World Cup finals."

"Oh, sure; that, too. But tickets for that game already sold. All gone. I tell mayor, for New York, especially for Brooklyn, you must make biggest stadium in world. Two hundred ten thousand. Minimum. You think he listen? Never. Now he is sorry, sure, but what good that do me? Or him? You know how much more money we make if . . .? Stupid peoples. I hate stupid peoples. I, Ragusic, happy to tell them what is right, smart. All of them. For free. No charge. Do they listen? No! Why? You tell me why, Marcus; I don't understand it."

"Uh—maybe they think that what you tell them is to make more money for you?"

"Of course it is to make more money for me. That is wrong? I am smarter, faster, I deserve. I *think*, not just to watch TV; why I shouldn't make more money? But they make more money, too, no? So why not? If I make hundred million—I don't say I *make* hundred million; just for example—city get ten million tax, minimum. Actual more. What you think I do with hundred million? Keep? Buy chocolate chip cookies? Okay, maybe some, but most I got to give for salary, rent, lawyer, accountant, expense. What you think happen with money I give? *They* buy cookies? Okay, some, but they *spend* my money. So there is more tax. And so on. By time I am finish, all government—county, city, state, Washington—have *most* of money. So why they not listen to Ragusic?"

"Okay, Mr. Ragusic, why?"

"Why? You asking *me* question? You suppose to be interview me and you ask me? Don't change subject again, Marcus. I ask you, you going to let bastards get away with ruining me?"

"Well, I agree that it was a terrible thing, Mr. Ragusic, but I don't quite see it as ruining you. Your franchise cost you practically nothing, and right now you could probably sell it for forty million. The World Cup Games will multiply the interest in soccer ten times what it was before, even if we don't win. So—"

"Exactly!" Ragusic was triumphant. *"Only* ten time. And for why? Because we don't win. And for why we don't win? Because those bastard, they cripple up my team. If we win World Cup, then interest for soccer multiply one *hundred* time. That's how much I lose. Now you understand? See, talk with Ragusic, you get smart. For free."

"Do you really think the U.S. Team could have won the World Cup? Against East Germany?"

"Sure. Why not? You know why? Because they are not smart. *Could* be smart, but government does not allow. Always do one way. Like one million tanks. Line up straight. Smash." He stiffened up in an imitation of Frankenstein's monster and walked forward clumpily, the effect ruined by the soft rug. "Like so. Okay for fighting another million tanks, but what good for fight fox? They think everything must be one way, you do another way, they go crazy. I tell Grilho, don't do everything like same old way, do a different *new* way. You think he listens? No. Why he don't listen, Marc?"

"Maybe he feels there is insufficient time to change

what they've been practicing for six months; to become familiar with a new system. Maybe he doesn't know a new system that's better than what he knows now."

"You see? You do it same way, too." Marc noticed that the more excited Ragusic got, the stronger his accent became. "I don't say make a new system. You think I don't know in three day it is impossible? What I say is . . . look. Go right now to Meadowland, where enemy trains. What do you see? You see one hundred blue uniforms for playing against German Team. First team. You see strong black forward—even looks like Cuffy Royal—and skinny little Cuban—he looks just like José Velez—and a big keeper, Jewish, exactly like Jason Benjamin. And they play exactly like who they look. And they all play *only* Brazil-Dutch system from Grilho, so first team learns how to beat Grilho system. Those Germans, they are from Communist country; everybody must be the same. Think the same. Do the same. It is for control by the government, you see? Of people. Cannot make any change. So what you must do? *You* must change. Yourself. Right?"

"Well, that sounds reasonable," Marc admitted, "but what system do you change to, *can* you change to, in three days?"

"Do I say system, Marc? No! I don't say system. You are not listening again. I say *change*. So if you cannot do new system, how do you change? Easy. *No* system. For Americans, it's easy. Normal. Americans don't like to be told how; just tell him what you want. This I learn first day in America. In some ways is bad, yes, but in some ways is good. Very good. So now, when I want something, I don't tell him how, I just tell him what. See?"

"How can you play soccer without an underlying system, without set plays?"

"You sure you are American, Marc? You look American but you don't think American. Look, in soccer, you cannot have set plays, I don't care what anybody say. Soccer is like mercury. You know mercury? You try to pick it up, you *touch* it, it goes around you, breaks up, *through* you. You cannot stop it, you can only let it go where *it* want to go. Sure, if you see your forward has the ball on your flank, you run to the penalty line by the goal for him to kick a pass to you. Yes, that is smart, not a play. But in soccer, you must see, must *know*, where everybody is, the pattern of everything, all around, even in back, and do what is best that second. Not hesitate, not *think*, just do what is smart. The American way. So if we stick to the system the Germans expect, they will kill us, score two, three goals in the first half, then make a solid wall in front of the goal, and play the Italian defense in the second half, and no more scoring. We lose. You understand? But if the style is not what they expect, they'll go crazy. If *their* system fails, they won't know what to do. So we win."

"You know, Mr. Ragusic, just an hour ago, Steve Vanderhook told me very much the same thing."

"Sure, of course. I been telling him this for two years. Now he begin to understand. Trouble is, Steve is very nice boy, but not smart."

"Not smart?" Marc was astounded. "Steve is considered one of the most intelligent . . . some of the articles he wrote when the two of you were promoting—"

"Oh, sure, Steve is *college* smart, but not *real* smart. How Steve can be smart? He inherit money from great-grandfather. The great-grandfather was *real* smart; Steve can not be so much."

"Does that mean your great-grandchildren can't be smart?" Marc needled. "Or your children?"

"Yes, too bad." Ragusic faked regret. "First I work hard; in office six o'clock every day, my children still sleeping. Then, can never be exact another me, beautiful sweet nice genius. But also they cannot be all stupid ugly bad either. Can only be mixture. Is science. Same for Steve Vanderhook. Nice, beautiful, but he only inherit money, so he cannot be genius, just smart. So I must tell him what he must do. Only, he is American. Does not listen."

"About how to play the East German team?"

"No." Ragusic shook his head wearily at Marc's inability to keep up with his mercurial mind. "The game I fight with Grilho about. He is *South American* American; almost bad like North. Very stubborn. No, we will lose that game. Too bad, but no use to crying. Must look to future. What Steve does not listen to is . . . look, when iron is hot, you can make it how you like. When iron is cold, you can only break your teeth. So, now there is big interest in soccer, big headline in paper. If America win, that is very good. But if lose, it is not terrible bad. Everybody will say, just wait for next year, we show those bastard who cripple up all our great player. So now, right *now*, is perfect time to get more stadium, make another league, twelve more team, play Soccer World Series in America *every* year."

"That's not the World Cup."

"Do I say World Cup? You are not listen to me, Marc. The World Cup is every four years. Too long; American don't like wait. No, I say World Series. The *American* World Series. Maybe every *two* year we make *All*-American World Series, too. South America, Central America, Mexico, Canada. Plenty big crowd. Very big. Make soccer *big* major sport."

"And make you richer?"

"So? Why not? I don't deserve? For five year I lose money on soccer, now I am not allow to make?"

"You'll sell the franchises?"

"Sure as hell not *give* away free. But we all get share fair, all the owner."

"Equally?"

"Please do not be so stupid, Marc. Fair, not equal. Fair mean in proportion to attendance, no? Is in bylaws—I put in when we start league, just in case—so there must be no arguing."

"Steve and the others didn't notice?"

"Sure they notice; just do not see how plant can grow from seed. I told you, college smart."

"And Steve opposed you on the expansion?"

"Did not oppose; Steve just always want to go slow. But no matter, all the other owner want money, big money, so we must expand."

"You've discussed this with them? It's all arranged?"

"I do not discuss; I *explain.* They all *business* smart, so they understand money very fast. And now time is right. I tell them everything right after final game."

"Is Steve going to try to stop you?"

"Steve cannot stop anything; only owner can vote."

"Doesn't Steve's opinion carry a lot of weight with some of the owners? And the public? If you and he quarrel, won't that hurt the whole process?"

"Oh, sure. But I never fight with Steve; I *explain.*"

"I got the impression from Steve that you and he had serious differences."

"Serious? No. Only Steve does not understand how American think so good."

"Vanderhook? He's an eighth-generation American. From the New Amsterdam days."

"Sure. Is why. Steve is inside America; does not see. I *study* American; I see. American do not like normal: like *big.* Soccer score: one-zero, two-one, even zero-zero. One and one half hour of play and no score? Hah! That is big disappointment for American. Next week maybe not come to game. American like to see goal. Two, four, *eight* goals, maybe. More. More goals is *better.* American like big hero to score big goal. So for new league rule, I must to make two little tiny change: First, offside line must be thirty-five yard from goal, not midfield. Two, to not be call offside foul, only one man must be between the goal line and offense man who does not have control of ball, not two men. Very small little tiny change, no? Make big improve."

"No." Marc stared at Ragusic in amazement. "That would change the whole character of the game."

"Yes! Very big improve. Those tiny little nothing change must to produce more goal. High score. Like football."

"No wonder Steve fought with you."

"What fight? We do not fight; just discuss. But cannot make no difference. When all new owner come in, I have enough vote to make new rule. Steve can do nothing."

"He'll resign."

"Of course. Sure. What else? Steve is man of great honor. So we get new Commissioner. Big politician. Old senator; maybe even old president. Strong man who has lot of influence in Washington. Make it easy to build new stadium. All owner make lot of big money. Everybody is happy. Beautiful, no?"

"I . . . why are you telling me all this?"

"I like you, Marc, that is why. You learn good, some day get smart, be big help. I'll give you big good scoop, you give me big good publicity in column. Make mind, heart, *soul*, of American soccer fan happy. Tell them now is time for soccer must have twelve more city and World Series every year. Do not mention about big score. Not time yet. You understand?" Ragusic beamed at Marc.

"And Steve agreed to all this?"

"Not have time to tell Steve *everything* for first time; is too complicate for Steve. But I explain to him again, later, tell him more, then he must to understand. No problem. Steve not real smart, but when I finish explain *everything*, he will understand. For sure." Ragusic smiled sweetly. Beautifully. Geniusly. "You come see me every day for next month, okay? I give you big scoops. Everything. Very interest. Little bit at time, so you understand. Then you write what I tell you. Not from my mouth, but like you find out yourself. But come in morning, before my secretary come in, or at night, late. Is not good to make other reporters jealous if they see you come here too much. You understand?"

Marc understood. He understood all too well that Ragusic hadn't told him everything the first time either, that in Gregor Ragusic's eyes he, too, was not *real* smart and had to have things explained to him slowly and only at the right time. What else was in Ragusic's mind, Marc did not know, nor would he know until Ragusic chose to use him again. An undeclared war had been declared and Marc, if he cooperated, would be the only combat zone correspondent, getting exclusive after exclusive and headline after headline. Maybe even a raise. If he cooperated. But he would be a correspondent who couldn't tell the truth, not now, at least, not until the World Cup final was over. By which time, knowing Ragusic's speed of mind and action—for all he knew, the whole deal was already set—it would probably be too late to change anything.

So Marc would have to write exactly what Ragusic wanted, favoring the new league expansion, which was really a good idea, and pushing for it to be done now, since this was truly the proper time. Even if he exposed what little he knew of Ragusic's hidden agenda, he couldn't stop the wily little fox; Ragusic would still have the votes to change the rules. At best, Marc's early opposition would be like throwing gasoline on the fire that could destroy professional soccer in the United States.

Marc smiled back at Ragusic, with his lips only, knowing that, to Ragusic, he looked stupid ugly bad. And there was nothing he could do about that, either.

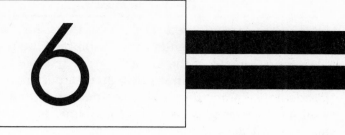

# 6

Marc got back from lunch just in time to meet Cabot Hollingsworth Bonifacio Vargas, now dressed in casual street clothes and hobbling slowly on crutches, coming out of the stadium. "All alone, Boni?" Marc asked, looking around. The twenty-two-year-old star forward of the American team was a full six feet tall, with his mother's light blond hair hanging over his pale blue eyes. Though his face was tanned from the long hours of playing under the sun, there were still touches of pink showing, baby-like, on his ears and under his light brows. He had the Hollingsworths' pointed nose and thin broad smile, with the long horselike teeth that made people think he was some unrecognized member of the British Royal Family. Boni's big hands and feet came with his early fast growth, but even hobbling on crutches, he had the grace of the natural athlete, the skittish energy of a nervous thoroughbred. Broad-shouldered and very thin, he was truly "bony," giving his friends two reasons for the nickname. "Where's the rest of the gang?"

"Still going over minor individual imperfections." The handsome young man looked pained and Marc had the feeling it wasn't just because of his taped left ankle. "My father can't accept that a soccer player, a member of a World Cup Team, should do anything that is not quite up to his own towering standards. He explains what they should do and shows them how to do it, over and over, patiently, and still they don't get it exactly right."

"He's not entirely wrong, you know," Marc said. "These are the world's best we'll be facing, and one little mistake can lead to a goal."

"Yeah, sure," Boni said bitterly, "but there's no point in my listening; I won't be playing. And the reason it takes so long is that he just won't believe no one else in the world can do what he used to do so easily, if they would only try a little harder."

"You want to talk to me about it? I could use an interview."

"Some other time. I'm going home now to brood."

"The Vargas East Side house or your West Side apartment? We can talk in the taxi."

"Grandpa and Grandma Vargas, and the whole contingent from Brazil, are staying at my father's house. I haven't seen them since Christmas, so normally I'd be staying there, too. But Grandpa and Grandma Hollingsworth had already arranged for me to have dinner with them tonight, so that's where I'm headed."

"Another session in the pressure cooker? Boy, I wish somebody would force me to become Secretary of State. Or even Ambassador to Monaco."

"All very sweet and polite, understated, but in their own way, as stubborn as my father. And my mother. I told them I'd go back to school soon—I don't want to only play soccer for the rest of my life—but they think I'm wasting my time. They want me to be a diplomat, the Vargases want me to be a soccer star, and my father wants me to be better than he was. Or any other miracle. If you think it's fun to have people always pressing you to be what *they* want you to be, try it sometime. Especially people who love you and think it's for your own good. There's no way to tell them what I . . . at least, if they'd all agree on *something* . . . ah, the hell with it."

"Okay, Boni, relax. You know I won't push you to be anything. All I need is one lousy little story you'll let me print. You want a lift to the shuttle? That'll give us plenty of time to talk."

"My folks came up from Washington to see us play, so I'm on my way to the Greenwich house."

"Okay, I'll give you a lift to Grand Central Station; I really need an interview."

"I'm driving, Marc. You want to go for a ride?"

Marc eyed him suspiciously. "With that ankle? In a Lamborghini?"

"My grandfather's old Silver Shadow. A truck horse, fully automatic. Yes or no?"

"If you'll give me a good story. And drop me off on the Upper West Side so I can get a bus home. You want me to drive?"

"If my grandfather found out I let anyone touch that car, especially someone who doesn't even *own* a car, he'd horsewhip both of us. I have enough trouble with him as it is."

"So take up polo; that'll make him happy."

"Yeah, polo for my grandfather, the Foreign Service for my grandmother, soccer for my father, and the Hollingsworth Foundation for my mother. And what can I do for you, Marc, to make you happy?"

"Think positive thoughts and drive within the speed limit while my fair white body is in your tender care."

They entered the parking garage. "Give me the ticket, I'll get your car. And really talk to me; some inside dirt that I can print, for a change."

---

The interior of the Rolls was not quite as silent as the ads claimed, but it was a lot better than a winning team's champagne-drenched locker room or some of the other impossible places in which Marc had interviewed athletes. He sank back on the fine leather seats, relaxing as the big car took them smoothly through the Brooklyn-Battery Tunnel up the FDR Drive. "I'll cut through Central Park," Boni said, "and drop you off at One Hundred Tenth Street and Seventh. Okay?"

"Fine," Marc agreed. "But how did you get away so early? I thought Grilho insisted on everyone being at every practice full time in full uniform, unless he got a note from his intensive care unit."

"I told him I wanted to get an early start so I wouldn't have to fight rush-hour traffic with a sprained ankle and maybe be late for dinner with my grandparents. Father is very big on family, even the Hollingsworth side."

"The ankle isn't bothering you, is it?" Marc glanced at the speedometer. The smoothness of the ride had lulled him into forgetting to worry about Boni's passion for high speed. "We're going awfully fast for city traffic."

"Relax. You know what a terrific driver I am; great peripheral vision and superfast reactions. Inherited. My father's side."

"I also remember the last time I drove with you and, frankly, I'd rather have a worse driver with better judgment. Inherited from your mother's side." Making a big show of it, Boni slowed down to sixty. *I keep forgetting,* Marc thought, *this is a twenty-two-year-old boy who is used to having his own way in everything.* A golden lad, who inherited his father's skills, his mother's beauty, and the

Hollingsworths' money. And the Vargas money, too, someday. Smart, too, even if it was only—in Ragusic's contemptuous words—college smart. Not deliberately, Marc was sure, Boni unconsciously let the powerful car gradually speed up again, steering with his left hand and tapping out a fast rhythm on the wheel with his right. The road was sufficiently open for Boni to weave in and out of the blocking traffic pattern at maximum speed—just as he did on the soccer field—and, if a cop stopped them, the Hollingsworth political power would ensure that Boni would never lose his license.

Marc decided to ignore the light poles flashing by like the pickets of a tall brown fence and tried to get Boni's mind off his troubles by changing the subject. "What's that song they're always playing during practice?"

"That one? *Tico Tico.*' Father's favorite. One of the best sambas ever. Must be fifty years old. Sort of a nonsense song, about a little blackbird in the cornmeal, but a beautiful melody and a very fast rhythm. During *Carnaval,* one song becomes the favorite, *the* song. Everyone plays it, sings it, dances to it. Beats out the rhythm all the time, in every way."

"Like you're doing?"

Boni glanced down, surprised. "Yeah, I guess so. Didn't notice, but it sort of grabs you. It's called *batucada*—'the beating out of the cadence' might be a way to put it. People tap the rhythm on tables, desks, cars, you name it. The kids do it on garbage cans, drums, books, all the time."

"Don't you get tired of hearing only one song all the time?"

"Sometimes, but you don't notice after a while. It becomes . . . people forget I'm half-Brazilian, got a great sense of rhythm, and that's not a joke. Ever been in Rio? An experience not to be missed. Everyone moves all the time, beautifully. Brazilians *dance* when they walk down the street; we're probably the most graceful people in the world. My mother is a good dancer, but when she dances with my father she looks as stiff as a board. He's *good.* Hell, my grandmother Vargas can make me look muscle-bound."

"Is that what makes you so good at breaking tackles?"

"Might be an important factor, my genetic inheritance. But I was also trained by the best; I had a soccer ball in front of me from the day I learned to walk."

Beautifully done, Marc congratulated himself, getting Boni's mind off speeding—the car had slowed down to fifty-five; a major victory—and into the interview. "How did you feel," Marc asked, "when that Bulgarian fullback tackled you?"

Boni took his eyes off the road for a moment and glared at Marc. "I used to think," he said bitterly, "you were one of the more intelligent reporters, but as long as you ask the same stupid questions, you're going to get the same stupid answers." Marc started to object, explain, but Boni took his hand off the wheel and stopped him with an open palm. "I felt just wonderful, marvelous. I'd been looking for a chance to get out of that stupid final World Cup Game, the one I had been training for, dreaming about, the last four years, so I could continue my serious drink-ing. Therefore, I feel no animosity toward the poor fellow who accidentally hurt me and I'm terribly pleased he sustained no injury from my clumsy fall." Boni snapped his mouth shut tightly and stared straight ahead through the windshield. The Rolls started speeding up.

"Reporters have to ask those questions," Marc said mildly, though he grabbed the door handle harder, "in the hope that the injured athlete will blow his top and say something controversial enough to get a big headline on the back page. You know, 'Boni Blasts Bulgar Bully', something like that." He paused for a moment, then asked, "You wouldn't feel like telling me the truth on the record, would you?"

Boni smiled grimly. "On the record? Truthfully? On the record, I wouldn't tell you the right time. I'm not going to play professional soccer forever, you know, in spite of what my father thinks. When I go into the Diplomatic Corps I had better be skilled at not telling the truth and at never speaking for the record unless it's as a highly placed anonymous source. And it still won't be the whole truth. But off the record? You saw the game. That sonofabitch came to me from the left, didn't have his eye on anything but my left ankle, plowed into it just when it was carrying all my weight. With the heel of his shoe, can you imagine? The *heel?* From the side. Bypassed my shin guard. I still have the cleat marks, sharp and clear. At that moment, the ball was on the outside of my right foot. From where he was, there was no way he could have made a clean tackle to get the ball; he was just plain out to cripple me. I'm lucky it was only a sprain. An inch in either direction and he would have broken at least two bones. And that bastard referee? He was right on top of it. No way he could claim he didn't see the whole thing. A red card? Forget it. A yellow card, a caution? Hell, we didn't even get an indirect free kick out of it. Nothing."

"You think the same thing will happen in the big game?"

"Three injuries in three minutes? All forwards? They wouldn't be that stupid. But I wouldn't put it past them to get John Geis early on. John's the last of the starting forwards and that would cripple our attack completely. Who are we going to put in as a substitute? A halfback? My father? That's how they'd make sure we couldn't score a single goal."

"Grilho's the greatest."

"For Pete's sake, Marc, he's old enough to be—" Bonie stopped and smiled sheepishly. "Well, he *is* old enough to be my father and, sure, he's very good—for about five minutes. After that, he can act as the general leading the troops, but that's all."

"He did very well today after forty-five minutes of play."

"Against a crippled team, sure, and even then he missed the goal, but Sunday we'll be facing the East Germans." Boni drove in silence for a while, then said, "Can we get off the game, please? And my father? I left the stadium so I could relax my mind and you're bringing everything back again."

"Okay, tell me how you get along with Steven Vanderhook. As Commissioner, I mean."

"Commissioner Vanderhook," Boni said in his formal voice, "is a fine, upstanding gentleman of the old school; a perfect—" Boni smiled, then recited:

"In all his life, unto no manner wight.
He was a very parfit gentle knight."

"Showing off your education again, kid?"

"Come on, Marc. Everybody knows *The Canterbury Tales*."

"Everybody who went to Princeton, maybe, though I doubt that. Not my readers; that's for sure." He sighed. "Okay, Boni, I can see you're in *that* mood. From now on—for this trip only, I mean—no attribution for anything. Though I reserve the right to use it as background or if someone else gets hold of it."

"Vanderhook is a wimp," Boni said flatly. "A miserable wimp who's going to ruin the whole league."

"Steve? Wimp? Are you crazy? After what happened to him and how he made a new life out of nothing? Most men would have—"

"I don't mean his personal life, Marc; I'm talking about the way he lets Gregor Ragusic pull his strings."

"I spoke to Steve today and I got the impression that he's fighting with Ragusic about something, not just giving in."

"I don't mean giving in; Ragusic is just too shrewd for him. Take the team expansion. . . ." Boni glanced at Marc. "You know anything about it?" He casually pulled off the highway toward Fifty-ninth Street.

Marc smiled. "Are you trying to pump me now? Is this for attribution?"

"Hey, don't you ask me lots of questions?" He turned serious. "Look, Marc, I've always leveled with you. All I have is some snatches of conversation I overheard. I look like a Yankee, so no one believes I'm half-Brazilian and speak Portuguese. Also Spanish, French, and Italian. So I find out a little here, a little there. Ragusic's been sending out feelers to some of the stars from the other teams. Nothing firm, just feelers, but to too many of the players. More than he could possibly use on the Booters. And I'm probably the only one who knows this. I need to make sure before I do anything. Tell me what you know."

"It shouldn't affect your . . . oh, you're concerned about your father."

"You think I'm worried about myself? I love soccer and I really wanted to play in the final game but let's face it, I'll have to pack it in anyway, a couple of years from now, leave soccer—and I don't know how I'm going to tell that to my father—and finish up at the Woodrow Wilson School. Then I'll go into the Foreign Service, make Grandmother Beverly happy and Grandfather Grinell proud of me. Soccer is the greatest, I love the game, but I'll be damned if I'm going to devote my life to making that sonofabitch richer than he already is."

"You don't like Ragusic?"

"Don't like him? He's the slimiest . . . everybody who's ever had anything to do with him, hates him."

"Everybody? The players, the coaches, the office help?"

"Even his kids. He treats us all like dirt. Lets you know how much better he is than you are, smarter, all the time, in every way. You can see him laughing at you, figuring out how to screw you as soon as he's finished using you."

"They say his word is good."

"Oh, sure, he never lies. But you have to listen carefully to everything he says, word for word, especially when he puts on that phony accent."

"The players hate him, too?" Marc sensed a story. "Benjamin, Royal, Velez, the ones on the World Cup Team? Why? He's made them rich, hasn't he?"

"Money isn't everything."

"What did he do to them?"

Boni tightened up. "You'd better ask them."

It was clearly not the time to probe that tooth deeper. Another day, when Boni was in a better mood. . . . "If it's that bad, why do you—especially you—stay with the Booters? You have so many options open to you."

"One of the reasons I'm with the Booters is that Ragusic hired my father. He knew that when he got Father, I'd have to play for the Booters eventually; no choice. It would have killed my father to see me with another team."

"You could always leave. Right now."

"Leave? Now? Leave my sweet, innocent father at the mercies of that conniving little bastard?"

"Your sweet, innocent father is the richest athlete of all time and runs a dozen businesses while he's coaching the Booters as a hobby. He can take care of himself."

"He has *investments* in some businesses, he doesn't run them; goes into his office maybe once a week. He hasn't even *thought* about business in the past three months. Soccer is not a hobby for him; it's his life. If Ragusic—you don't know what a bastard he can be, in his own subtle way—tries to mess up my father's life, I've got to stop him. And you have to tell me what you know."

Marc thought for a moment, organizing his thoughts, then said, "Ragusic is going to start another league, twelve more teams."

"So that's why—but there aren't enough American players of professional caliber to make twelve more teams. He'll need two or three hundred European and South American players and . . . he's going to offer them so much money that he'll strip the world of all the best players. Doesn't he know the ramifications? Soccer is the most important thing in the lives of sixty percent of the world's population. People *kill* over soccer. The diplomatic uproar . . . it would be the biggest foreign affairs disaster you could imagine: the rich imperialist Yankees buying the national treasures of some poor colonial country. Of the whole world. We wouldn't have a friend left, no allies. The Soviets would have a field day. Stupid, stupid, stupid." Boni was trembling.

"Watch the road! Do you want to kill us both?"

"If I had that bastard in the car with me. . . ." Boni slowed down a bit. "Tell me I'm wrong, Marc. Please. Tell me he's going to do this slowly, build up a team a year, just one team, with mostly American players. I just flew off the handle, right? Jumped to the wrong conclusion?"

"That may be what Vanderhook is fighting Ragusic about. Steve isn't a wimp, really. You've misunderstood him. But the facts are that the owners can start a new league if they want to; there's nothing in the bylaws to stop them. The only hope is that the ones who are friendly toward Steve, who respect him, will vote to do it slowly."

"But you have to make them understand, Marc. Write about it. A new league? Twelve more teams? New teams? The existing teams will have to sell some of their players to the new franchisees. Ragusic will make a fortune. They'll all make a fortune."

"That's why I doubt if anything I can write will help."

"You must, Marc. What this will do . . . Brazil is not a

rich country. If they offer the best Brazilians the kind of money that American athletes get, it will kill Brazil's chances for a World Cup for a generation. The soccer drain. Brazil will look like the breeding corral for the United States. And Father will be blamed. They don't understand how little power he has with Ragusic. It'll kill him."

"I can explain that in my column."

"It won't matter. You think they read the *Sentry* in Santos? And Ragusic can sell me to San Diego or Tacoma; I have two years to go on my contract. Maybe even Nome, with that crazy bastard. And coaches. They'll need head coaches. He can sell Father to . . . the family will be separated."

"Grilho doesn't have to go. He can afford to break his contract. He can always leave professional soccer, too."

"Father doesn't break agreements, and he can't leave soccer; it would kill him. There's something else you can write about, Marc, that nobody seems to have thought of. It's not just Brazil; England, Italy, West Germany, France, Holland . . . the Russians will dominate the sport, gain a tremendous diplomatic victory. In the eyes of much of the world, the best soccer team means the best country."

"You're overreacting. If we have the best players in the world, we'll have the best World Cup Team."

"And you're forgetting that anyone who played on a World Cup Team for one country can't ever play for another country." Boni drew a deep breath. "Does anyone else know about this? Besides us and Vanderhook?"

"I don't think even Steve . . . I got the impression that Ragusic has been feeding Steve a little at a time, preparing him slowly for the idea. He wants me to prepare the American public for the expansion slowly, too, a little at a time."

The lump of tight muscle on the side of Boni's jaw stood out, hard. "Ragusic has to be stopped. I'm going to talk with my grandfather; he still has lots of influence in Washington." He glanced sideways at Marc. "Are you sure my father doesn't know?"

"I don't think so. As a matter of fact, I wouldn't bother your father about it right now." Might as well get it all over with at once. "Ragusic is giving your father a hard time about Sunday's game. Wants him to drop his Brazilian-Dutch system."

"Is he crazy? The way we play has the best elements of both systems. How does he think we got to the finals, anyway? How the hell are we going to find a new system, practice a new—" Boni took a deep breath. "Ragusic is really crazy. Don't worry, Marc; my father will never do it. People think he's soft. They forget he grew up in a *favela*, one of the toughest slums in the world, raised himself out of it all by himself. He's not soft; he's *polite*. There's a hell of a difference. I know. What I don't like is that Ragusic's bugging him right now, before the big game. Father needs a clear mind and this isn't going to help."

"Uh, it's not just a new system for the game, Boni; it's a whole new ball game." They had just pulled into Central Park and Boni was speeding past the slow-moving horse-drawn carriages. Marc waited until they got to the north end of the park and Boni pulled off onto Central Park West. "Put the car out of gear and shut off the engine." No way was he going to tell Boni anything else with the car in gear, ready to pile into some immovable object. Boni looked at him, curious, and turned the key. "Ragusic wants to speed up the game, make it more aggressive."

"Good. I wouldn't mind smashing a few East German ankles myself, if I could play. It should be the guy who got me, but since I can't get at him . . . they all work together anyway. But Father will never do it. To him, soccer is holy; a matching of mind against mind and body against body, precisely within the rules. Regardless of what Ragusic wants, we'll play the final game the way Father wants to."

"It's not just the final game. Ragusic wants to change the rules for the USSL."

"Change the rules? How can he—"

"He can. He's going to—that is, there will be a vote after the second league is formed that—" Marc couldn't help it; it just came out. "The offside line will be thirty-five yards from the goal and only one man has to be between an attacker who doesn't have the ball and the goal line." He quietly opened the door latch and cautiously eased the door out an inch.

"He's crazy. What will happen . . . the whole team will go on attack, congregate around the goal, scramble for the ball. Like rugby or water polo. It won't be just more aggressive; it'll be a slaughter. Players will get hurt every game. Scores will go through the ceiling: ten goals, twenty goals a game. The old records—Father's and Pelé's—will be worthless. It'll kill the game." Boni's face grew dark and grim and, in that light, somehow he stopped looking like a magazine model of an All-American boy. The hard lines and flat planes of Grilho's face showed darkly through the light tan, revealing a rigid inner Boni, exposing the son of the stubborn, ambitious boy who, at thirteen, had lifted himself by his bootstraps from Brazil's toughest slurn. "Ragusic's got to be stopped," Boni said softly. "I'm going to stop him, Marc. And you're going to help me."

# 7

It was half-past seven when the freight elevator door opened and Dahliah came home. "Where the hell have you been?" Marc yelled. "Thursday's your early day; I almost went crazy!"

She came into his arms at once. "Oh, darling, you shouldn't worry. I'm a big girl and I've studied karate."

"That's not the point." He held her tightly. "It's not the best neighborhood and there's no one in the streets after business hours."

"You come home late lots of times. You don't care if I worry."

"I'm not a beautiful girl. They want my wallet, they can have it." He stroked her hair. "Please, if you ever again—if you can't avoid it—leave a message on the machine."

"I know; I should have. But I was so busy today . . .

wonderful news. Mr. Witter loved my article; he's going to put it in the Sunday Sports Section. With my by-line."

"But just last night . . . when did you write it?"

"After my last class, I decided to go to the library and research the story. Not real scholarly research; just checking a few things. I started with what you told me yesterday about how each team played—not all the teams; just a selected few—and what ideas Americans have about the people of that country. There was a pretty good correlation, so I made notes and called Mr. Witter and he said I could come in and use his computer. I wrote the story in one hour and he liked it and said he would edit it himself. Isn't it wonderful? I made three hundred dollars in three hours."

"That still doesn't work out to coming home so late."

"Oh, after I was finished, we talked for a while. About you. He really likes you, you know."

Marc looked at her, astounded. "And you believed him? Don't you see? He was just trying to find out more about me so he could find my weak spots, give me a still harder time. He hates me. What did you tell him?"

"Nothing much, really. And he doesn't hate you; he looks on you like a son. I'm a psychologist, remember? I can tell. He really wants to help us. He offered me another assignment, too, for much more money. It pays a thousand dollars, but I have to finish it fast. He even gave me a temporary press pass."

"A thousand dollars? Witter? It's a trick. I hope you turned it down."

"Turn down a thousand dollars? In our condition? For one little article? You know how much I get for a scholarly article that takes a month to write? Nothing. Not one penny. And newspaper writing is so easy."

"Easy? That's it. He's trying to destroy my confidence—your confidence in me—by paying you a lot of money for a simple job so you'll despise me when I tell you how hard I work for how little I make."

"Please, Marc, it's not like that at all. I really admire you. Do you think I could love a man I didn't respect? And we could use the money. Put it in the bank and make believe we don't have it."

He looked at her suspiciously. "What's this thousand-dollar assignment?"

"It's for the Women's Page. 'The Sporting Woman.' "

"For Nelda Shaver? That moron?"

"She happens to be a remarkable woman. You're just jealous because she's achieved so much. She was very nice that time you were in the hospital."

"Sure because I worked it so that her interests and mine coincided. You should see her when something doesn't go her way. She's a snake. She got her job in the first place because her family is friends with Mr. Heisenberg and there's rumors that she and he . . . on top of that, Nelda— she must be sixty, though she only admits to 'over twenty-one'—is the most sex-crazy person I've ever seen. Or heard of. No one in her department is safe from her. Or in the whole paper."

"You, too?"

"Me? Of course not. Even if I didn't love you, she'd be the last . . . I hate her. And she's incompetent, too. Can't write, can't edit, doesn't know a thing about sports. Her whole page is nothing but gossip."

"You're exaggerating, just like all men when they meet a competent woman, but it doesn't matter. I won't have anything to do with her directly; the article goes on her page in this Saturday's edition."

"*This* Saturday? A thousand-dollar article? Do you know when it has to be in? By eight o'clock Friday. Tomorrow. Witter's kidding you. When are you going to do the research? The interviews?"

"It's only twelve hundred words and my first class

tomorrow is eleven o'clock, so that's no problem. Mr. Witter said you'd give me the background and help me."

"Me? Do you know what I have to do tomorrow? I have to do a column every day from now till Sunday. And my regular column Monday. Plus whatever fantastic exclusives I can pick up tomorrow and two personality stories." Marc decided not to mention the interview he was going to get from Gregor Ragusic early tomorrow morning or the story Boni wanted him to write that would stop the evil league expansion in its tracks.

"Well, if you're *that* busy," Dahliah sounded miffed. "I helped you lots of times when you were overworked. And the thousand dollars was for *us*, you know, not just for me. So if that's how you want to be. . . ."

"No, no, it's all right. I'll help you. What's the assignment?"

Dahliah brightened. "Give me a second to change and I'll make supper while you talk." She walked quickly into their sleeping area at the back of the loft, changed out of her conservative suit into a brightly flowered dress, and went directly into the kitchen area. "Set the table. We'll just have some raw vegetables with a spicy yogurt dressing. I want to start working on my article and not wash the dishes. Unless you'll wash while I work?"

"No," Marc sighed. "Raw vegetables with yogurt is fine. What do you want to know?"

"Luis 'Grilho' Vargas. You know all about him? What does 'Grilho' stand for?"

"Not all, but a lot. Grilho—which means 'grasshopper' because he jumps so high; don't you ever read my column?—is pronounced 'Grill-yo.' The Portuguese way. He's Brazilian. Was Brazilian. Married an American girl, Kimberly Hollingsworth."

"Yes," Dahliah said from the sink where she was washing tomatoes. "That's the story. Mr. Witter said it was very romantic. A modern Romeo and Juliet."

"Well, yes, in a sense. But everybody knows the story, what there is to know."

"Mr. Witter said you'd say that, and to tell you that you're wrong, as usual, whatever that means. He wants me to write the story again, from a woman's point of view, and with my own psychological insights."

"Yeah," Marc sighed. "And did he tell you everyone knows the story of Cinderella, too? Forget it. I'm sure the way you write it, it'll sound new and interesting and besides, a lot of people are now reading about soccer who never knew the game existed before." He finished setting the table: two plates, two glasses, two knives, two forks, one spoon for the dressing, a holder of paper napkins, a loaf of whole grain bread, a shaker of sea salt, and a bottle of organic apple juice. Marc sat down, facing Dahliah's back, and began speaking. "Grilho was a very poor boy whose family lived in one of the *favelas*, the shantytown slums on the side of the mountains alongside Rio de Janeiro. He shined shoes and did odds and ends of work to help support his family, while going to school. Like all Brazilian boys, he loved to play soccer. He couldn't afford a regulation ball, but he played with a sack stuffed with rags and whatever else he could find."

"He was a juvenile delinquent? Got into trouble?"

"No, no, the *favelas* are not like some of our big city slums. I don't mean there's no crime there, but most of the people in a *favela* are just poor, not evil. I don't doubt that, when times were especially hard, Grilho might have snitched a piece of fruit from the market, but certainly nothing worse. However, after five years, he gave up school."

"Is he really illiterate?"

"Grilho? You're kidding. Five years of Brazilian school is more than equivalent to eight years in ours. You automatically take Latin and French and English, as well as the standard subjects. There are very few illiterates in

Brazil, especially in the big cities. And Grilho . . . anyway, his income was needed, so he worked in a factory. And played soccer on the factory team. He was a natural player—as he puts it, 'I have a gift from God'—and had as a coach an ex-forward from the Santos Team, one of the best in Brazil. By the time he was thirteen, he was playing regularly on the intermediate team for Rios, and was making a good living, by *favela* standards. Because he was so much younger than any of his teammates, and couldn't easily socialize with them, he took to reading and educated himself.

"How far did he go?"

"After he got married, he earned a university degree in business administration, but that's another story. Anyway, by the time he was fifteen, he had become star center forward for Rios, and Rios was accepted as the best team in Brazil. At that time, this meant that Grilho was the star scorer—his average was one point forty-four goals per game; equivalent to Babe Ruth hitting two hundred fifty homers a year—for one of the best teams in the world. At fifteen. He was world famous, becoming very rich, mobbed wherever he went, and still yelled at by his mother."

"I can see a no-man-is-a-hero-to-his-valet complex developing."

"Nothing like that, but his mother, like all mothers of favored sons, proud as she was of him, did want him to give up this foolishness and become a doctor."

"Did she pressure him? Make him feel as though he had not lived up to his goals? Did she put down his father for not earning more than his son?" Dahliah put the bowl of vegetables on the table and mixed curry and slivers of jalapeno peppers into the yogurt.

"No, nothing like that. They're a close, loving family. But she pushed Grilho to study specialized subjects, premed subjects, in case he was injured and couldn't play anymore. He didn't, just kept reading for pleasure and to satisfy his curiosity. Anyway, by the time he was eighteen, he had been selected for the Brazilian World Cup Team, but on a bad foul had his ankle sprained, and couldn't go to Tokyo." No wonder, Marc realized, Grilho was so upset by the foul that put Boni out of action. He was reliving those days when he thought his own career was ended forever. "While he was recuperating, he was invited to a party at the American Embassy, and there he met Kimberly Hollingsworth, the only child of Grinell Hollingsworth, the American Ambassador."

"Cinderella? Was that what Mr. Witter meant?"

"Exactly. But in reverse. The dark-skinned boy from the *favelas*—"

"He's black? You never told me that."

"If you would read my column once in a while. . . ."

"Oh, Marc, you know I'm not really interested in sports. Just karate. For protection, not as a sport. And gymnastics, of course. I think gymnasts are the most beautiful—"

"Yeah, well, I also write good stories. And columns. Try one someday; it won't kill you. Anyway, nobody in Brazil is black, practically, or white or Indian or anything. Brazil is probably the most mixed, racially, of any country. There are no blacks, whites, browns, reds—just mixtures. Oh, some people are darker skinned than others, have more visible Indian features or whatever, but no one really cares. There is no racial prejudice; the only segregation is economic. Anyway, there was this dark-skinned, Indian-featured, eighteen-year-old, unsophisticated, self-taught boy from the slums who had become the world's most famous athlete and the beautiful, blonde, seventeen-year-old, well-bred, Swiss-finishing- school-trained daughter of wealth and power, meeting at the embassy ball. Like Cinderella. In reverse. And they fell instantly in love. Deeply. Totally. Unexpectedly. Beautifully."

"Oh, Marc, what a lovely story. I can write that."

"There's more. You think it was that simple? You think that Grinell Hollingsworth was going to let his only child . . .? Kim's parents hit the roof when they found out she had been seeing Grilho secretly. Not that anything had gone any further than some kissing. Grilho was a deep, believing Catholic, and Brazil is a Catholic country where a woman's virtue is her proudest possession and a loss of virginity can mean a blood feud. He truly loved Kim and would have died rather than hurt her in any way, or damage her relations with her family.

"When Grinell Hollingsworth ordered Grilho to come to his office to be ordered never to darken his doorstep again, the eighteen-year-old boy, with manly dignity and the greatest respect, proudly announced his love for Kim and politely asked her father for her hand in honorable marriage. When she turned eighteen, of course. Though the Hollingsworths believed they were not racially prejudiced, they were shocked and hurt by their daughter's love for an uneducated, black-skinned, foreign athlete. It took a full year for Kim to persuade her parents that Grilho was worthy of marrying their only child and for them to get to know the sweet, intelligent, gentle young man. At the end of the year, they gave their consent."

"I would have written that story for nothing, Marc. Maybe it'll do some good, get people to look at one another as people rather than as stereotypes. Thanks. I wish you had told it to me sooner."

"There's a little more, Dahliah. Kim and Grilho were married on her eighteenth birthday, the wedding was attended by all the highest officials in Brazil, and half the world of soccer. A year later, their son, Cabot Hollingsworth Bonifacio Vargas, was born. Cabot was, much to his grandmother Hollingsworth's delight, blond and fair skinned. As the only child of their only child, the Hollingsworths enrolled Cabot, at the age of three months, at

Exeter, Princeton, and the Woodrow Wilson School of Foreign Affairs. Grilho had other ideas, and he spent much of his time teaching his son, Boni, how to play soccer the Grilho way. To please his in-laws, Grilho maintained a home in New York, a large brownstone on the East Side, as well as in Santos, intending to spend half a year in each country. But after Boni entered Exeter, the Vargas family went to Brazil only during the school vacations. Grilho became an American citizen after he married Kim, but by now he was an American at heart. Though he never forgot Brazil, he began playing for the Brooklyn Booters of the new United States Soccer League. Owner: Gregor Ragusic." Marc stopped and drew a breath. "Okay? Now we can eat?"

"Of course, darling." Dahliah spooned the dressing over a bowl of vegetables for him. "That was beautifully done. I wish I had taped it."

"I can do it again. The trouble is, this is the story everyone knows. Nothing new in it. The Hollingsworths and the Vargas family keep things pretty private."

"That's all right. When I interview them, I'll find out everything I need to know. I'm a psychologist; very good at interviewing people, bringing out hidden information."

"Interviewing?" Marc put his spoon down. "Nobody interviews Grilho's family. That's completely private."

"Give me his number. I'll explain that I'm not going to dig into private things; I just want a personal interview in depth. How Kim and Grilho feel about things."

"I don't have his private number. Nobody has."

"Well, I've got to talk to them. Mr. Witter said it was very important. Without personal contact, he might not accept the article."

"Grilho keeps his family life completely separate from his professional life. Completely."

"You talk to him, don't you?"

"Sure, almost every day. His son, too. But that's about soccer."

"Fine, I'll talk to him about soccer, too. And after I get to know him, after he sees that I'm on his side, I'll ask him if I can write a sensitive story about him and his wife."

"Forget it; it's been tried before. He's not stupid, you know."

"Has it ever been tried by a woman? One who has a doctorate in psychology? Or are you afraid I'll succeed in your own field?"

"Oh, why do women always . . .? Don't answer. I'll do it."

"Women don't always *anything;* it's men who . . . I'll need your little autofocus camera, to take some pictures of her and their home."

"All in one day? Grilho and Kim Vargas? Brooklyn and Manhattan? And get your story in before five o'clock tomorrow so Shaver and Witter have time to make you rewrite it twice before 'The Sporting Woman' page closes? And you have a class at eleven? Yeah, sure, I know. Being a reporter is easy; you can do it in your spare time. Okay, take the autofocus; I'll drag around the good one, probably get mugged for it. I have to be at Koch Field very early tomorrow, to see someone—" no sense confusing the issue by mentioning Ragusic—"as soon after six as possible. Grilho is going to give me an interview before eight o'clock practice, and with you interviewing him in detail about his family and how they met and their first kiss and all that, we'd better get up at five."

"Make that six, Marc. The story you told me made me feel very romantic tonight and I need my eight hours sleep."

"Then we'd better go to bed right after supper."

"Eat quickly, darling," Dahliah said.

# 8

It was past seven and the sun was already high and bright when Dahliah and Mark came onto the field. Grilho was sitting next to the locker-room entrance, suited up and ready to start practice, impatiently tapping his fingers on the wooden bench, unable to understand why the whole team wasn't waiting eagerly to start playing soccer; to get in an extra hour of fun. Marc knew the players had all come early—no one dared be late for a Grilho practice—but were resting in the locker room until one minute to eight; a Grilho practice was enough work in itself. Grilho stood up gallantly when Marc introduced Dahliah as a new reporter and his fiancée. The minor social deceit earned Marc an indignant sideways look from Dahliah's usually loving green eyes and, after a quick glance at Dahliah's bare left ring finger, an additional disapproving look from Grilho's sharp eyes.

Dahliah asked Grilho if she might take some casual snapshots and then get his opinion about the national characteristics of World Cup teams, the only soccer subject she knew anything about. Grilho posed obligingly, then joined Dahliah on the bench. Marc would have loved to watch Dahliah get a polite, formal, absolute turndown when she broached the subject of the Vargas family. It was time she learned that reporting was an art not easily mastered. But he had to talk to Gregor Ragusic privately, the way Ragusic wanted, secretly, well before anyone else went up to the second-floor office area. He excused himself, without being specific about where he was going, or why, and slipped into the locker-room tunnel, bypassing the locker room and turning right down the main corridor to the elevator bank nearest Ragusic's office.

The outer office was empty, so Marc went directly to Ragusic's office and knocked on the door. There was no answer to his second, louder knock either, so he turned the knob, opened the door a crack, and said as he peeked in, "Mr. Ragusic?" Mr. Ragusic did not answer. Mr. Ragusic was slumped on the floor in front of his desk, the right side of his head down, the left side bashed in, covered with blood, the wet red pool on the white carpet making an abstract expressionist splotch that matched, perfectly, the paintings on the wall. Marc pulled the door closed fast. Loudly. He jumped at the noise, and looked around. There was no one to see or hear.

He opened the door again, a tiny crack this time—the killer could still be inside; the blood had looked very wet—but there was no one in the bare office. Looking around guiltily again, he slipped into the office and silently closed the door behind him. If he had killed Ragusic with a club, or whatever, the killer probably didn't have a gun or a knife, so Marc tiptoed over to the closet door, even though the pile of the white carpet was deep enough to quiet an army, and from the side, flung open the door. Only coats and hats. He closed the closet door quietly, tiptoed over to the bathroom door on the left side of the room, and flung that open suddenly. The bathroom, too, was empty. Slowly he walked across the room, staying as far as possible from the body, to the left side of the desk—the right side, actually, from the entrance—and gently touched Ragusic's neck. Just in case, he told himself, though he knew the man was dead. No pulse.

Thinking fast, he quickly unsnapped the camera's case, set the shutter on flash, and focused on the body. If he played his cards right, he could squeeze at least one twenty-five-dollar raise out of Julius Witter for the exclusive and another for the pictures. Maybe more. Then he lowered the camera. He could also, he remembered, thinking hard, simultaneously put his life into the greedy, grasping, merciless hands of Lieutenant Harvey Danzig, the shame of Brooklyn Homicide, who would have no compunction about using Marc as a staked goat to trap the murderer. He would make Marc *happy* to tie himself helplessly to an immovable stake so as to avoid—by dying—the *really* bad things Danzig could do to him.

Danzig's favorite tactic—maybe his only tactic, but it was a good one; it had worked on Marc twice before—was to get something on his victim, no matter what it was, that would let the fat little detective arrest Marc and threaten to put him in the holding pen with the worst criminals in Brooklyn, murderers who had nothing to lose by cutting one more throat, diseased drug addicts who would kill Marc for his shoes, psychopaths who liked to kill short young reporters. Of course, if Marc were to cooperate by finding the murderer in the next twenty minutes, Danzig might consider dropping the charges. And if Marc didn't move fast enough to suit Danzig's timetable for maintaining his position as the detective with the most arrests in Brooklyn, Danzig could hurry things up by letting it be known that Marc was the only one who knew who the murderer was and that the only way to shut him up was for the murderer to kill Marc fast. Whereupon Harvey Danzig would spring from the shadows and arrest the killer while he was still twisting the knife in Marc's heart.

Was this worth a possible fifty dollars a week? Plus Witter's enmity for forcing an additional fifty a week out of the paper? *Additional* enmity? Fifty dollars a week times the possible week—if he was real lucky—the *maximum* week he had to live after Danzig got his hooks into him, came to an even fifty dollars. Total. *Maximum.* For that much—little—it was not the height of intelligence to take pictures or to hang around any longer or even to phone the story in to Witter from a phone inside the stadium. He had been trapped that way, once. Or even a phone *near* the stadium. He had been trapped that way once, too. Maybe he was slow, but eventually he got the picture. Which meant *no* pictures and get out fast.

Marc rapidly closed the camera case and looked around. His fingerprints were on the doors: closet, bathroom, and entrance. He'd get them on the way out. Touched anything else? No, thank God. Footprints? From the front door to the closet to the bathroom and around the body. And back to the door again, on the way out. The pile of the carpet had evidently been vacuumed during the night, because he saw the marks where the murderer had smoothed out his own trail, but the murderer's smoothing traces would be obliterated by Marc's own. That was too damn bad. Better a million murderers go free than one innocent young reporter get hung by Harvey Danzig. Marc picked up two heavy manila legal folders from the desk, slid the contents out onto the desk, bent over, and started backing away, dragging the folders along the carpet as he went. He stopped at each door and carefully wiped off the knob with his handkerchief. Once he was out of the inner office, he repeated the pile-straightening procedure in the outer office, and folded the manila folders to fit his breast pocket, so he could throw them away later. He peeked into the corridor—no one there—and ran down the fire stairs to the main corridor; no way was he going to chance the elevator.

Casually, he walked out the front entrance and away from the stadium. The security guard had taken only one quick look at his press pass. Let somebody else find the body. And get the story. His story. No, not his. No way would he be identified with *that* story. Still, the *Sentry*'s. Let the *Times* have the story? *His* story? The one he had risked his life for? Bravely (stupidly?) opening the closet and bathroom doors? The story Mr. Ragusic himself would have wanted Marc to have? To hell with the *Times*. They didn't deserve to reap the benefits of his labor. Neither did Julius Witter, but there was no one else he could talk to. Feeling tremendously loyal, he made the decision. Call from where he could not be traced, from where a million calls a day were made to the *Sentry*.

"Borough Hall," he told the cabdriver. There were lots of phones there and he had every excuse for making a call from the center of Brooklyn's government.

---

"I have a terrific exclusive, Julius," Marc said.

"Where are you?" Witter asked.

"What difference does that make? Are you taping this? I'm in a place where no one will be able to trace my call."

"Good. Now tell me where you are."

"Has the *Sentry* suddenly gone out of business?" This did not sound like the Julius Witter Marc knew. "What's going on there?" Witter didn't answer. Finally Marc said, "I'm at Borough Hall; what the hell difference does that make? I'm reporting—an anonymous caller is reporting—that Gregor Ragusic has just been murdered. In his office. Take this down while it's still hot."

"You don't want a raise for this fantastic front page,

stop-the-presses story? Or for the pictures you took? Why, Marc," Witter's voice was mocking, "that's very generous of you. Unlike the other times when you blackmailed me. I'd be happy to give you a raise for this, too; just ask."

"I didn't take any pictures and I don't want a raise; I'm doing this only out of a sense of duty. To you. It's my job, after all. Just doing my job, what I'm paid to do."

"I'm proud of you, my boy. All my efforts, all the time I've put in training you . . . it makes this old heart leap with joy. Now here's what I want you to do."

"Do? No, no, you don't understand. I don't have the time to get involved with this story. That's why I'm calling from here. I happen to be very busy completing the research on a very important—you can have all the credit; nothing for me. Just send down one of the guys to Koch Stadium with a photographer. I have to go to the Meadowlands, interview some of the East Germans. I've been neglecting them lately."

"I think you should go back to the stadium yourself, Marc. It wouldn't be right to deprive you of this tremendous scoop, especially since you're doing it as part of your normal job, without extra compensation. Only you'll have to share the by-line."

"I don't mind. In fact, you can give the other guy all the credit. Spread the wealth. Fair is fair. Now start writing; I'll give you the whole picture."

"Don't bother, Marc; I already have the whole picture."

"You already have—but how? It was only twenty minutes ago that I—"

"You're not the only great investigative reporter we have, Marc. Fortunately."

"It's not possible. The only one who could have . . . oh, my God."

"Well put, Marc; your command of the language is an unfailing source of inspiration to us all."

"Dahliah? DAHLIAH?"

"A reporter in the old *Front Page* tradition; a natural. When she couldn't get the cooperation she needed for her assignment from Grilho, she went looking for you. Not in the locker room, of course, but one of the players told her that they hadn't seen you. She checked the first floor and, when she didn't find you, she went to the second floor."

"But she's not a reporter. You shouldn't—"

"She's an excellent reporter. Kept her head, took a whole roll of pictures—the messenger should be there right now to pick up the film—locked the office door behind her, and called me. Directly. As any good reporter would have done. Should have done. A reporter who is loyal to his editor first, his paper second, and to the protection of his own miserable cowardly skin last. She doesn't know it yet, but I will reward her for this. Yes, the thousand dollars I had intended to give her for the feature story."

"No, Julius. Don't. You can't. That will give Danzig proof that she withheld information from the police."

"Too late; the check has already been made out. In her name. With the reason for this payment to a nonemployee. And the time I ordered the check made out. You know how efficient our comptroller is. I've included an additional ten dollars for the rental of *your* camera, the one you gave her to take pictures with."

"Danzig will arrest her. He'll—"

"Yes, now that you mention it, I do believe he will." Witter's voice dripped false sympathy. "You know how hungry he is for arrests. And convictions. However, I am even now checking to see if our attorneys can properly represent her. After all, she is not a union member. If they can, I am prepared to battle Mr. Heisenberg to provide for Dahliah's defense. You know that Julius Witter never forgets a loyal employee, even if she's on a temporary assignment."

"You did this purposely, Julius," Marc raged. "You set

it up so you could print an editorial about how a brave *Sentry* reporter defied the police to get the story to our readers."

"Hmmm, that is an interesting thought. Thank you, my boy, I wish I had thought of it myself. Yes, I will write a blistering editorial as soon as Danzig charges her formally. I was sure, if you watched me long enough, you'd absorb some of the more elementary aspects of being an editor."

"But she'll go to jail. Danzig will . . . oh, no."

"Only for a short time, Marc; have no fear. There are dozens of attorneys in her school, brilliant ones, who will gladly take her case, to the Supreme Court, if necessary."

"Julius, you bastard, I'll get you for this."

"Really? That should be interesting. How big a handicap do you want?" He waited, but Marc could not answer. "Now, as to your going to the Meadowlands . . . I think that's an interesting idea. We really have been neglecting the East German point of view on this earthshaking contest; fair is fair. I'll send one of the warm bodies I have hanging about, unwarrantedly drawing salary for breathing, to the Koch Stadium to cover the story of Dahliah's arrest and to interview Lieutenant Danzig. Wise of you to go to New Jersey; I have a feeling Danzig doesn't like you very much."

"Save it, Julius. I'll go. You knew I would the moment I called."

"How brave of you, Marc. I'm sure Dahliah will appreciate the unexpected gallantry."

Marc hung up hard. The phone did not break. Nothing was working right on this day.

"Go away," Lieutenant Harvey Danzig greeted Marc, the piggish little blue eyes in his fat round face glaring through the gold-rimmed glasses. "I'm busy." He was standing in the main corridor, in the middle of the second-floor office area, blocking Marc from getting any closer to Ragusic's office at the far end of the complex. "You're interfering with official police business."

"But I'm here to cooperate with you," Marc pleaded. "Remember how much I helped you on the Bean Ball case? And the Super Bowl?"

"I remember," Danzig said grimly, "what a pain in the ass you were." He took off his hat and carefully wiped his head so as not to muss up the strands of blond hair he had combed across his bald spot. He put his hat back precisely on top of his head. "Always bitching, never doing what I told you, screwing up the whole case, messing up the evidence like a damn amateur. Even though I was trying to get you off the hook on a bunch of charges."

"But you were the one who filed those charges."

"What'd you expect, Burr? You perpetrated the crimes, didn't you? I got to keep my arrest record up, don't I? And I didn't file them charges; just sat on them. Risked my whole career just to protect you. And my pension. So what did you do? Got yourself sent to the hospital just to make me look bad. You call that gratitude for all I done?"

"I got myself sent? You sent me to the hospital. You!"

"While I was saving your life, right? Because you wasn't following my orders exactly like I said, right?"

Marc was sure he could feel his brain curling at the edges; Danzig always had that effect on him. No matter what he did, in Danzig's mind it was only to help Marc. Pure altruism, and if in the course of his trying to make an arrest Danzig happened to put a couple of holes in Marc's hide, that was Marc's fault for being so clumsy and uncooperative. The fat little detective had only one interest in life: to make arrests. It didn't matter whether or not the arrestee was guilty, whether or not Danzig's handcuffed prisoner could have committed the crime, or whether or not there was any evidence at all against him. By the time Danzig got through with a suspect, he would be begging for a chance to confess to another officer, any other officer but Harvey Danzig. This Lieutenant Harvey Danzig would allow only after the broken perpetrator had confessed to the crime Danzig had arrested him for, as well as several of Danzig's past unsolved cases, plus the assassination of President Abraham Lincoln, and the sinking of the *Maine*. All on tape, of course, starting with an oath that under no conditions did the confessed murderer want an attorney present. In Marc's heart, he knew there was no sense going on like this; he would never change the detective's image of himself as the symbol of chivalry bravely protecting an unappreciative populace against the onslaught of the barbarians. What Marc had come back to the stadium for was to save Dahliah. That was what he had to concentrate on. "I was the one who discovered the body," Marc confessed. "Ragusic. Me."

Danzig looked at him in disgust. "What stupid trick you trying to pull now, Burr? I got the one who. She already confessed. Soon as I finish up here, I'm taking her downtown to book her."

"Book Dahliah? For what? It's no crime to—"

"She didn't just find the body; she called your buddy first. Julius Witter. Gave the perpetrator enough time to be halfway to Canarsie by now. Obstructing justice. Interfering with the police. It ain't as good as murder first, but it's still an arrest."

"No, you don't understand. You've got to listen." Marc grabbed Danzig's lapels. Danzig just looked at him. Marc let go, fast. "Look, when did she say she found the body?" Danzig took his time smoothing his lapels. "Okay, okay, you don't have to tell me, but it had to be after seven-thirty, am I right?"

"Where'd you get that idea?" Danzig asked so casually that Marc knew he was deeply interested.

"I *know*. Believe me, I know. If I tell you how I know, will you let Dahliah go?"

"She your girl friend or something? Not just a reporter?"

"Yes, of course." It would have to come out anyway. "We live together."

"So that's where she learned to call the designated authorities last, right? You told her to do it, right?"

"No, I never—yes, yes, it's all my fault. Let her go and I'll tell you everything I know."

"I don't do deals with perpetrators, Burr; you know that. You talk straight, and maybe I'll consider."

"All right. I found the body at seven-twenty. The blood was still wet."

"And you didn't call me? Knowing how much I like a

murder one arrest, you didn't call me right away? After all I done for you?"

"Yes, well, all I could think of was to get out of there. My head still hurts from the last time."

"I told you, Burr; that was to save your life. What else did you screw up?"

"Well, I happened to—accidentally—rub up against the doorknob."

"The door to Ragusic's office?"

"Uh—yes. And the front office door, too, maybe. Also possibly the closet door and the bathroom door, now that I think of it."

"You wiped the murderer's fingerprints off all the doors at the scene of the crime?" Danzig's usually pale face grew red. "You destroyed the evidence? You stupid bastard amateur, you're getting worse each time I see you. And you want to make a deal with me? After ruining my case?" Danzig drew a deep breath, another, then spoke in an overly sweet voice. "What else did you screw up, Burr? Don't lie—I know you. You don't screw up just one thing. Not you."

"I—uh—well, I didn't want you to think I had anything to do with the uh—crime, so I wiped out my footprints. On the carpet. With some folders. I walked backward."

"Folders. You're the guy who spilled the papers on the desk."

"I didn't touch them. Really. I left them in the same order, in case they were important."

"In case they were important," Danzig repeated. "In case . . . the perpetrator's fingerprints and footprints you wipe out but the damn bills you take good care of. Smart. Real smart. Okay, you went to the closet and the bathroom? That was you, not the killer?"

"Uh—yes. That is, I didn't *go* to the bathroom; just opened the door. In case the murderer was still there. Then I went behind Ragusic's desk and I touched his neck to see . . . then I went back around and wiped the knobs and went out."

"In case the murderer was still there. Brains." Danzig tapped the side of his head. "You idiot! You think you was being brave? Hell, if I was the killer, I would've protected you like gold, knowing how good you screw up the evidence." Danzig's hands were trembling, half-closed, making little aborted movements toward Marc, struggling to keep from strangling him. "Where was the perpetrator's footprints that you wiped out?"

"I didn't wipe out his footprints; he did that himself." As Danzig started to get red again, Marc hastily added, "From the door to the side of the desk. The right side."

"Behind the desk?"

"Yes. Next to Ragusic."

"And after you kill the case, you want to make a deal with me?"

"No, no, not for myself. For Dahliah. Let her go and I'll tell you everything."

"First of all, Burr, I don't need you to tell me anything. With what I got on you, I could put you away for—" Danzig poked his finger into Marc's chest. Hard. "Even before that, I'm gonna put you in the holding tank with the animals, and I'll make a deal with three of them—the worst three—that if they take care of you good, they can walk. This time. Then, right after you get out of the hospital—"

"Murder one!" Marc said urgently. "Wouldn't you rather have a murder one arrest? I'll get it for you—I did it last time, the last two times, remember? You'll get all the credit."

Danzig stopped boiling and looked at Marc suspiciously. "You know who done it?"

"No, of course not. Not *yet*, that is. But I know who was fighting with Ragusic; it had to be one of them."

"One of who? Who was fighting with the victim?"

"Well, the Commissioner, for one."

"The Commissioner? What are you, crazy or something? You trying to make me lose my pension?"

"Not the Police Commissioner; the head of the United States Soccer League. Steven Vanderhook."

"Ain't he rich or something? He's no good. I need . . . what other suspects you got?"

"There's all the guys on the team that worked for Ragusic. From the Booters. Grilho—he's the Head Coach—Boni, Cuffy Royal, José Velez, Jason Benjamin."

"Yeah, that sounds okay. All foreigners, right?"

"They're all American citizens."

"Yeah, sure. But Velez—he's PR, right?"

"Cuban descent, but—"

"Same thing. And Royal? Cuffy? With a name like that, he gotta be sort of darkish, right?"

"Black. But so is Grilho, too, sort of. And he's even richer than Vanderhook."

"Okay, that double leaves him out. Benjamin—he Jewish?" Marc nodded. "So he probably got a brother-in-law that's a lawyer; that leaves him out, too. I hate lawyers. Always making trouble; can't even sweat a perpetrator *easy* with a lawyer. So you're gonna concentrate on the rest, right? Make sure one of them did it, got me?"

"Boni is Grilho's son and he inherits the Hollingsworth money as well as Grilho's money."

Danzig started yelling again. "This is a hell of a case you got me into, Burr. All them suspects—they all rich?"

"Well, the other three players—Royal, Velez, and Benjamin—are stars, but soccer doesn't pay like baseball and their contracts were signed several years ago. Ragusic is not famous for giving away money. I'd say they make a good living, but they're not rich."

"Okay. They're the killers. Concentrate on them; the

two I said before. Don't waste time on the innocent suspects."

Marc felt as though he had volunteered to escape from a straitjacket under water and then found himself glued in. "I have to talk to them all to establish a motive," he said desperately, "before I can tell you who the murderer is."

"*Tell* ain't enough." Danzig sounded as though he might be softening a little. "I gotta have evidence in this town. Enough to make the collar."

"Yes, sure, of course. Evidence. With enough evidence to make the arrest. Yes, that's exactly what I'll do."

"Me alone, right? You don't talk to any of the other detectives? I got plenty of other guys in the house very jealous of my record, and I don't want none of them to have a smell of this."

"No, no. Nobody else."

"And you'll report to me every day? Everything?"

"Oh, yes. I'll phone your office at nine every morning."

"Not the office. We'll meet, breakfast, eight o'clock. The usual place."

"The diner? *That* diner?"

"Where else? It's the best diner in Brooklyn, ain't it?"

"Oh, sure, terrific." Marc would have promised eternal slavery to get Dahliah off. He was not looking foward to tonight's pillow talk. Or even to this morning's conversation—monologue. If Danzig let Dahliah go now, it would give her time enough before her eleven o'clock class to discuss with him how he had gotten her into this fix. At length. Through his male stupidity. Or even deliberately, out of jealousy for her newfound Witter-encouraged reportorial skills. On the other hand, the longer Dahliah stayed in durance vile, the more time she would have to plan what to say to Marc when she was finally freed. "I'll do everything you want," Marc promised, "exactly the way you want it, Lieutenant."

Danzig thought this over. "Maybe I'll consider it. *Maybe.* Meanwhile, here's what you do. Come downtown with me when I'm finished here and dictate everything to a stenographer and . . . no, too many ears in the house. Go upstairs to the press box and type out the whole story, everything you done wrong, complete. Don't forget you're doing this, confessing, of your own free will, like a good citizen. Including I asked you if you wanted an attorney and you refused. Got that? Then go to a notary public and get it notarized and bring it to me personal. If I like what you say, maybe I'll do what you want with your girl friend."

"Let her go?"

"You nuts or something? Why should I let her go when I already got her irregardless of what you do? No, what I'm gonna do is sit on her case while you—*until* you—find me the killer. *If* you find me the killer. Otherwise . . . what I mean is, until you bring me the evidence that'll let me figure out who the perpetrator is."

Marc sighed. "Okay. Agreed."

"By *when?*"

"When?"

Danzig couldn't believe how little understanding Marc had about how the police department functioned. "You think this is my only case? I got plenty of other cases to take care of, you know; can't spend all my time on one murder. Not in Brooklyn, I can't. So, by when?"

"But it's only an hour after the murder. I don't have anything concrete to go on yet, so how can I tell you—"

"Okay." Danzig smiled evilly. "You can't do it? Tough. I'll just arrest you and the dame and take care of it myself." He sighed. "That's the way it always is: Danzig got to do everything himself."

"No, wait. I didn't say I couldn't. I'll find the killer for you. The evidence, I mean."

"You sure?" Danzig stared at him doubtfully. Marc nodded wildly, reassuringly, "Positive?" Marc put his right hand up, swearing to heaven. "Well, okay," Danzig said grudgingly. "You talked me into it. By when?"

"I can't tell you that right now." Marc had to stall for time. "I need to talk to the suspects first. With Dahliah." The sooner she got out of Danzig's clutches, Marc computed, the lower the decibel level of the discussion would be. "She doesn't have anything useful to tell you anyway."

"You want me to let her loose *now*? We only went around with her a couple of times, so far."

"She's a professor at the Oliver Wendell Holmes College of Criminology, Lieutenant. They have lots of lawyers on the faculty. Close friends. Big shots."

"Yeah, I came up against some of them bastards already. You know what they teach them there? Criminology, that's what. Not how to get the animals put away fast; how to *rehabilitate* them, would you believe it? Okay, I'll let her take off now, but that's another one you owe me, and I'm holding you responsible for her. So if she helps you— and she's gonna do it my way, right, not like in college— when do I get the answer?"

"I need some information from you first. What did the medical examiner say? What kind of blunt instrument? The time of death?"

"What the hell's the matter with you, Burr? You know I can't tell you nothing. I could lose my pension for that."

"I can't function unless I know the basic facts of the crime. You might as well arrest me right now." Marc put his hands out for the cuffs.

Danzig took a deep breath. "If I wasn't so damn busy . . . all right, but just remember how much I'm sticking my neck out for you. You better be worth it." He looked around stealthily; except for the uniformed policeman stationed in front of the elevator bank, no one was within sight in the corridor. Danzig took Marc thirty feet farther away and lowered his voice. "The medical examiner said between seven and seven-thirty, but with what you said, it's gotta be between seven and a quarter after. And you better not tell that to anybody. Ragusic was killed by a compression of the left temporal area—that's a kick to the temple—by a soccer shoe. The kind with the two big round studs in the heel."

Marc thought for a moment. "Some soccer shoes have four studs in the heel, slightly smaller studs. Maybe it was just the two rear studs that—"

"Nah, forget that. It was the whole heel. The imprint showed. Smashed in the whole skull, practically. These soccer players—they got powerful legs, right? Any one of them could've done it?"

"Oh, yes, very powerful. Easily. Did you find the shoe? For top players, the shoes are very individual, practically custom-made, broken in to each player's feet. Numbers written inside."

"We didn't find the shoe yet, but we will. The department is good at that, especially if a big-shot rich guy like Ragusic gets it. The way I figure, it'll turn up in some garbage container not far from here; he can't afford to keep it." Danzig was silent for a moment, then said, "Which one of those guys was a rightie? The ones you told me about?"

"It was done with the right foot?"

"While Ragusic was sitting down at his desk. With the heel to the back and the toe pointing frontward. So he had to be standing on the left foot and kicking with the right foot. Like karate. Now which ones?"

"Cuffy, José, Benjamin, and Grilho are right-handed; Boni is a leftie. But that doesn't matter. Every soccer player uses both feet equally well."

"I told you before, it wasn't the rich kid, right? Especially since he's a leftie. And especially since he got a bad left foot; can't stand on it. Vanderhook—he's a wheelchair cripple. And it can't be the coach; aside from him being rich, the killer was wearing soccer shoes, like I told you. Which leaves out the rich kid double."

"Actually, Lieutenant, Boni wears soccer shoes when he's here; the coach insists that everyone suit up for practice. And he can stand on his left foot easily, with a cane. And soccer players can jump up, even off one leg, and kick while they're in the air. As for Grilho, he plays in practices, so he wears soccer shoes, too."

"I don't want to hear that kind of crap, Burr. You think arrests is everything? Well, you're wrong. Convictions is even better. And you know how hard it is to convict a rich guy? With all the lawyers and the psychiatrists and all? Hell, the guy who shot the President in front of the TV—he's still around and pushing for parole. So concentrate on the other three. Two. Leave Benjamin alone till I check him out; see if he's got a lawyer in the family."

"I still have to talk to all of them; they're the ones with grudges against Ragusic. What I learn from one may be applicable to—"

"Yeah, yeah, okay, talk, but work over the two real suspects good. Okay? Wait downstairs by the security booth at the players' entrance. I'll send your girl friend down in ten minutes."

"Time. I have to know . . . there's only one entrance open outside of game time. Check with Security who was here at seven. Before seven."

"You teaching me my business, Burr? First thing we checked. Everybody was here, the ones you said. The Commissioner, the coaches, all the players, the trainer, the boy. Everybody. Now you tell me: When you gonna have the answer for me? The evidence?"

"By tomorrow I may be better able to project more accurately when I can—"

"Project? What the hell're you talking about? All these suspects—they're part of the big game, right?"

"The World Cup Final. Yes."

"And that's Sunday?"

"This Sunday, yes."

"After that, they all take off? Go back where they came from?"

"Well, there are the celebrations and parties and everything, but yes, essentially." Marc could see where this was going. "All the suspects live in the New York area."

"No difference. Right now, we got them all in one place and nobody's gonna take off. After the game, they're all gone."

"But today's Friday already, Danzig. Have a heart."

"Sunday morning, that's it."

"I can't. No. That's too tight; I need every minute I can get. The game is in the afternoon. You've got to give me until Sunday night. At least. Please."

Danzig clenched his jaw, then relaxed. "Okay, but just because I like you. Sunday six o'clock."

# 10

"Can I talk now?" Dahliah asked in exasperation. There was no way for Marc to stall any longer. He pushed the button on his portable terminal's modem that sent the more detailed follow-up on the murder of Gregor Ragusic to the *Sentry*'s central computer, the story prominently featuring that intrepid nemesis of Brooklyn crime, Lieutenant Harvey Danzig, swiveled his chair toward Dahliah, and nodded resignedly. "You went away without even telling me," she complained. "Just ran off. What was I supposed to do?"

"What I thought you would do," he said wearily, half his mind working on the logistics of becoming a beachcomber in Tahiti by Sunday, the other half on how to murder Danzig in absolute safety by Sunday, and the third half on how the fickle finger of fate transforms a perfectly sensible impulse to avoid disaster into the agency which brings on an even greater disaster. "You should have continued the interview."

"But I couldn't. Grilho told me flatly that he never discusses personal family matters and neither does his wife or his in-laws. So I went looking for you and when I opened the door I found. . . ." She shuddered. "You know. And that detective. He's *horrible.*"

"I know, I know." *And little do you know, my sweet, innocent, beautiful Dahliah, how horrible he really is. You'll never find out from me and, if I can help it, you'll never find out from him either because I'll save you from. . . .* "Look, people are always telling reporters they don't want to discuss something. It's your job to get them to tell you what you want to know in spite of that."

"But he said—"

"They all say that. A *professional* reporter—" she deserved the dig, for her swelled head in getting a thousand dollars for a story "—would have asked him how he feels about having two members of his family, father and son, playing on a World Cup Team, something that has never happened before."

"But I don't know that's never happened before. Has it?"

"A good reporter does his research before he goes out on an interview, but even so, you could have asked the question. If you were wrong, Grilho would have corrected you. Then, regardless of his answer, you could have asked if Mrs. Kimberly Vargas is just as proud. Of both of them. Especially her son. He can't say she isn't, and he wouldn't refuse to answer a question like that. Then you tell him his wife must be very proud of him, too. What can he do? Say no? That she hates the idea that her forty-two-year-old husband has been chosen as a player as well as Head Coach of America's World Cup Team? That she's ashamed her husband of twenty-three years is in perfect physical condition while her friends' husbands puff after nine holes of golf?"

"But that isn't what I wanted to write about. I was supposed to do the story of their fairy-tale romance."

"You'll never get that story. I knew that and Witter knew it when he gave you the assignment. He just gave it to you to raise your hopes so that, when you failed, you'd feel even worse. Lose confidence in yourself. Then he'd have you under his thumb. As a way of getting back at me. But if you were more experienced, you'd know that if you can't get exactly the story you want, you take the story you can get. You could have led Grilho into how the Hollingsworths are also proud and happy about how well he and Boni—Cabot, they call him—are doing and how the honor of playing on the World Cup Team and getting to know all the foreign dignitaries will be helpful when he goes into the Foreign Service. Although the Hollingsworths would have been much happier if Cabot had stayed in school, Grilho would never tell you that. Actually, I don't think he really knows why Boni left school; I'm sure he thinks it was because his son loves soccer as much as he does. I don't know this for a fact, but I'm sure Boni joined the Booters to make certain his father would have a winning team and to win Grilho's approval. I have no doubt that, in a year or two, Boni will go back to school to please his mother's side of the family. The poor kid is always going to be torn between—but that's another story.

"Anyway, after that, you ask about how the Vargas family—Boni's Brazilian grandparents—feel about having their son and grandson on the World Cup Team—which has never happened before and will probably never happen again—and Grilho would answer that question too. By the time you were done, you'd have had a solid thousand-word story, one that would also have built up good will between you and Grilho and that Witter would probably have bought from you. And by that time, I would have been back and taken you away and you wouldn't have been involved with the murder in any way."

"I don't care about the story; you're just trying to make it look like it's all my fault. It isn't; it's all your fault. If you had just had the decency to tell me you were going . . . leaving me alone in a strange place with strangers—I didn't know *anybody*—where there was a murdered body. All you had to do was stick your head out of the entrance and tell me you had to go someplace and you'd meet me somewhere, anywhere, so I wouldn't have to wonder where . . . or worry . . . or go looking for you."

"I couldn't. I was trying not to be noticed, not to be involved with the murder."

"So you involved me instead. That's really rotten, Marc. I thought you loved me and you—" She burst into tears. Marc held her close, not saying a word, resting her head on his shoulder, until the tears slowed. "He acted like I was the murderer," she sobbed, "even though I was the one who called the police."

"I do love you, Dahliah. He was going to arrest you and I prevented that."

"Me? Arrest me? Why? I didn't *do* anything."

"Well, you did call Witter first."

"I'm a reporter. I have obligations. The people have a right to know. It's in the Constitution."

"Yes, sure, of course. But after the police. And you used the phone on Ragusic's desk?"

"*His* phone? Certainly not. I didn't want to go near his . . . him. I used the phone on his secretary's desk. I *forced* myself, even though I wanted to get as far away as possible. To tell the police *faster*."

"And to tell Witter faster. Big scoop," he said bitterly, "just like in the movies. And you wiped it off afterward?"

"Well, I didn't want the police to think I had anything to do with it."

"And you wiped off the doorknob and locked the door?"

"To protect the evidence. I found out about that at Holmes."

He held her away a bit so he could look into her lovely green eyes. "Darling—Dahliah—between us, we've destroyed all the evidence for a murder. What you did—we did—is against the law."

"But I only . . . I'm a psychologist, not a criminologist."

"It's all right, darling. Don't worry; I fixed it. Danzig won't make any trouble for you." At least not until one minute—one *second*—after 6:00 P.M. Sunday. He'd have a talk with Julius Witter, persuade him that Dahliah deserved the protection of the *Sentry's* attorneys. Even then, there would be no way to stop Danzig from arresting her and holding her for several hours. Unless Marc came up with the killer in three days.

"You can relax, darling; I'll see to it that Danzig doesn't bother you." *If I die for it, that's one promise I'm going to keep.* "He doesn't really *want* to arrest us; he'd much rather arrest the murderer."

"Then let's find the murderer." She brightened. "You're good at that."

"I was lucky before. It doesn't necessarily . . . don't you have a class soon? Shouldn't you be leaving now?"

"Not till eleven. And stop looking so worried. I'll help you."

"That's wonderful!" Marc said enthusiastically. What else could he say?

# 11

The blue and red teams were hard at their game when Marc and Dahliah reached the field. Grilho would not call off a practice if the sun exploded, but the spirit Marc had seen at Thursday's practice was not there. Though Gregor Ragusic was not the most popular man in the world of soccer, still the death of someone you know is a shock, a reminder of your own mortality, and a murder in your midst is of worse magnitude. Not only is there the anxiety about death but there is also the apprehension as to where the killer will strike next and who the killer is; sidelong glances at the man next to you and fear of the man behind you.

In spite of Grilho's exhortations, the men were moving in a spiritless manner, in direct contrast to the previous day's sharp, rhythmic, coordinated patterns. *"Tico Tico"* was still being played on the PA system but right now, such a short time after the murder of Gregor Ragusic, it sounded cheap and garish rather than cheerful and bouncy. Marc could see how exasperated Grilho was as, in midfield, he took the ball away from Cuffy Royal, dumping the bigger man on his butt with a perfectly executed tackle, and dribbled through the entire blue team to score an easy goal past Jason Benjamin, who moved as if he were wearing lead boots. As soon as the ball went into the goal, Grilho blew his whistle and motioned the whole team to come to him. They gathered around the Head Coach in a semicircle and Grilho began talking to them. Although he clearly was not shouting, from his posture Marc knew exactly what he was saying, and it certainly wasn't congratulations on a job well done.

Marc escorted Dahliah over to the bench near the locker room entrance and introduced her to the three crippled forwards: Herb Wendell, Fred Bremer, and Boni Vargas who, in spite of their inability to play, were fully suited up. Grilho's discipline again. This time, when Marc called Dahliah his fiancée, she did not merely give him a dirty look. She explained to the three soccer players, with a little more emphasis than was necessary, "We're not formally engaged; it all depends." On what it depended she did not say, but Marc clearly got the idea that he had better get her *dis*engaged from the Ragusic murder fast. And that Sunday, 6:00 P.M., was not *her* deadline. Within the next five minutes, if he read her rightly, would not be a moment too soon, as far as Dahliah was concerned.

Marc motioned Dahliah to sit on the bench and then sat down between her and Boni, who shifted his cane to the other side to make room. "Nothing stops your father," Marc said. "Neither rain nor snow nor gloom of night. . . ."

"Nor murder?" Boni added dryly. "Why should it? There's still the big game on Sunday and in the record book no one's going to write that we lost to the East

Germans six-zero because we stopped practicing out of respect to Gregor Ragusic. Hell, one week from now, all they'll know is that we got skunked. Besides, he—" Boni turned to the men next to him and said, "Hey, fellows, do me a favor. I have to talk privately to Marc. Do you mind?" The two got up slowly and limped to the other side of the entrance, fully out of hearing. "Ragusic wasn't the most popular guy in the world, you know. In fact, I'm not going to cry at his funeral and I don't know anyone who is. He made a lot of problems for a lot of people."

"Still," Marc said, "don't you think murder is going a little too far? I mean, there are lots of unpleasant people in the world, but that doesn't give anyone the right to kill them. There are better ways of solving problems than committing murder."

"Yeah, sure, I didn't mean that it should become the accepted procedure. After all, I'm going to go into diplomacy, where we talk out our problems, do our best to avoid conflict. Work things out peacefully."

"Is that what you meant when you mentioned stopping Ragusic?" At this, Boni shot a worried glance at Dahliah. "It's okay," Marc said. "She's reliable."

"No, that's not what I meant," Boni said hotly, "and you know it. When I said you'd have to help me stop him, I didn't mean help me kill somebody. If you think I did, then maybe you should turn yourself in, too." He waited, but Marc didn't respond. "Okay, as long as we understand each other. I already made my statement to the police and I told them I didn't know anything about anything. I'm just a soccer player, period. I don't want that bastard detective quoting back to me anything I told you in confidence, is that clear?"

"Oh, sure, but right now . . . what I'd like to do is get to the bottom of this fast. There's a hell of a lot of pressure on all of us now, especially your father, and the last thing we need is to have a police investigation on top of that. So if there's anything we can do to close—to help the police close—the case, we should do it fast."

"To hell with that. Whoever did it deserves a medal. Don't forget, when he killed Ragusic, he took a hell of a lot of pressure off us, all of us. Remember what we were discussing yesterday? A little questioning by the police will be like a vacation by comparison."

*You don't know Harvey Danzig like I do,* Marc thought, *and if you keep talking that way. . . . Poor innocent kid; I keep forgetting he's only twenty-two. Was I ever that naive?* "What exactly did you have in mind as to how to stop Ragusic?" Marc hated to do this to Boni, but he had to have something to tell Danzig tomorrow morning.

Boni stared at him suspiciously. *"We* were going to start a campaign to stop him from ruining American soccer. You would expose his whole scheme in your column and I would get my grandfather to use his influence in Washington to have a congressional committee set up to investigate monopoly practices in professional soccer. I'd also have Father use his influence with the other owners and with FIFA to prevent Ragusic from even getting started with the rules change and the league expansion. Mr. Vanderhook would back us, too. And the Players Association. And that's just a start."

"Boy, you play hardball."

"I learned that from my grandfather. You want to stop someone, hit him first and *hard.* Kill him before he has a chance to get started. And I don't mean kill *that* way. You know what I mean."

"Yeah, sure, I know exactly what your grandfather meant." The Hollingsworth wealth might have been inherited for the past three generations, but originally it had been put together in the violent railroad wars by some very tough Hollingsworths beating out some other very formidable opponents; Hollingsworths who *did* mean kill *that* way.

To Marc, Boni did not sound like the effete, thin-blooded descendants of the powerful founders of dynasties Ragusic had described, but rather like the future sire of a new line of more mighty, even more ruthless, in their soft-spoken way, indomitable warriors. Probably the influence of his father's genes, brought to full flower in the environment of the *favelas,* mixed with the stubbornness of a mother who, when she was seventeen, had defied Grinnell Hollingsworth to marry out of her class, color, caste, and country. With that combination, Cabot Hollingsworth Bonifacio Vargas might very well have intended to try the modern methods, the legal methods, of stopping Gregor Ragusic, first. But if that failed, Marc had no doubt that Boni would have done what had to be done when it had to be done. Without thinking. "Yes," Marc agreed, "and I'm sure I know what you meant, too."

"Okay, then," Boni seemed to have cooled down a bit. "What else is on your mind?"

"I'd still like to close this case, and I'm sure your father and Steve Vanderhook and everybody concerned would like that, too. Just to clear the air. And I'd like to show that it wasn't one of my friends who did it. Among other things, I'm under suspicion, too—for reasons we don't have to go into right now—and I want to clear my name. Whatever Lieutenant Danzig annoyed you with, I got ten times worse. So if you let me interview you about the case, I'll present it in the best possible light in the paper."

Boni thought for a moment, then said, "All you have to do is tell the truth. There's no need to try to make me look extraordinarily innocent; that would only make the police suspicious." He drew a deep breath, and began. "I got here about a quarter to seven and went to put on my uniform. With my left ankle the way it is, it was a slow process. There was only one pair of shoes in my locker, so I went to the equipment room to remind the shoe boy to make sure I had another pair in my locker for the afternoon practice—the dew makes the shoes wet and I always put on new shoes when I change. He wasn't there, so I left a note for him. I went to the bathroom, then got a chopped egg sandwich and a coffee from the machine, and then I just sat in the locker room until all the commotion started."

"Did anyone see you during this time?"

"In the locker room, everybody. At the vending machines, I don't think so."

"So you were not in anyone's sight from about seven o'clock on?"

"Approximately. Was that when Ragusic was killed?"

"Approximately. I think."

"There must be twenty other people with a similar lack of alibi."

"Oh, sure. I'd be very suspicious of anyone who had a perfect alibi other than by accident."

"Is that all?" Boni asked. Marc nodded. "I'd like to get up and move around a little. Father doesn't like to see me sitting around very long even when I'm not playing." He stretched his legs out and picked up his cane.

"You're wearing six-studded shoes," Marc noticed.

"Yeah, I used to wear them because Father always wore them and they gave me a better grip on soft ground, then I got so used to them that now I wear them even when the ground is firm." Boni got up, leaning on his cane.

"Any of the other Booters wear them?"

"Only in wet weather; they all like the multistudded shoe for regular play. A couple of the fullbacks from other teams wear them. Why?"

"Might be an article in it, one of these days." Marc got up, too, and motioned Dahliah to come with him. Ragusic had been killed by a kick from a six-studded shoe. The right foot. No other Brooklyn Booter wore six-studded shoes in good weather and there was nothing wrong with Boni's right ankle that would prevent him from kicking Ragusic's head in. Boni's left ankle, taped as it was, would certainly hold his weight long enough to get one kick off. Even if it couldn't, there was always a variation of the bicycle kick, in which you took off from the right foot and kicked with the right foot; not overhead, but straight ahead. Into Ragusic's head. Maybe there were some other things Boni had learned from his grandfather, the diplomat. Such as looking truthful while lying.

# 12

"Why were you in such a hurry to get us out of there?" Dahliah asked as soon as they reached the main corridor inside the stadium.

Marc continued walking toward the players' entrance. "I wanted to make sure you wouldn't be late for your class." Danzig still had to be prowling around the stadium, and the sooner Marc got Dahliah out of there, the better. There was no need to remind the detective about Dahliah's involvement; Danzig might have deluded himself into truly believing he was a man of his word, but experience had proven only that he could find a rationalization for any dirty trick he decided to pull on Marc. "Traffic is heavy at this time of day."

"My class is at eleven," Dahliah said, "and it's only nine-thirty." She grabbed his arm and pulled him back. "Whom are we going to interrogate next?"

121

"Well, actually, there's no one. They're all at practice and Grilho would kill me if I interrupted him."

"And that's another thing. You impeded my—you sat between Boni and me, so I couldn't ask him any questions. If we're going to work together, I want to ask the questions, too."

"Well, actually, what I wanted—need from you—is your psychological insights." What he really wanted—needed—was to get Dahliah away from the stadium before Danzig figured out more ways to use her against him. "The character, the personality of the suspects; things like that."

"Then I have to ask them questions, too, not just look at them. What if I think of something you didn't think of? Are you going to *gag* me?"

"Gag? Certainly not. Anytime you want to—but do you really want to get more involved in this? You have a full-time job."

"So do you, and if you can do it, I certainly can. Besides, I want to get even with that stinking detective for giving me such a hard time when I was trying to help the police; I'm going to show everybody how stupid he is. And the sooner we solve this case, the sooner I can think about more important things." She turned around and started back toward the locker room.

"Wait!" Marc panicked. "Where are you going?"

"The Commissioner's office. He isn't practicing."

"Of course not, but why? He must be very busy right now, making arrangements for . . . and a public statement about the murder. And checking who the new owners of the Booters will be and a million other things. Besides, why would you want to see him?"

"Boni said that Mr. Vanderhook would help him fight Mr. Ragusic, so if there's some conflict there, friction between Ragusic and Vanderhook, he's a logical suspect."

"But he's crippled; he couldn't—"

"Granted, but I'm sure he knows more about possible motives for everybody than anyone else does. He must have had more contact with Ragusic and was more closely connected with Ragusic's plans than anybody else around here."

"Yes, but—how about tomorrow, when you don't have any classes? I'll hang around here, pick up what I can, and tell you all about it tonight."

She looked at him distrustfully. "I have the feeling you're trying to get me out of here. Why? So you can solve the case all by yourself? Be a big hero? Male dominance again? Because if that's the case, forget it. I'm staying with you until I have to go to class, and then I'm coming back right after class. Or if you really want to get rid of me, okay, I can take a hint. You go your way and I'll solve the case without you."

"But you can't. . . ."

"I can't? Only men can? You and Danzig? Hah! Between the two of you. . . ."

"It's not that I think Danzig can do any better. It's just that he can be very—unpredictable. You remember I told you about the hard times he gave me during the Super Bowl case? And the World Series murder? All I'm trying to do is keep him from making trouble for you."

*"You're* going to protect *me*? Don't I beat you every time we practice karate? And I was in the Israeli Army for two years, remember? Army Intelligence, and I know a lot more than you give me credit for. I've solved cases, psychological problems, hidden problems that my colleagues, my *male* colleagues, couldn't even get started on. So you decide. Do we work together or do you eat TV *meat* dinners for the rest of your life?"

"No, no, we'll work together. I *want* us to work together." How else could he protect her from Danzig? "And it has nothing to do with eating. I love you, that's why."

123

"And respect? Have confidence in? Openness?"

"Oh, yes, certainly. Definitely respect. Confidence and openness. Yes."

"Then you can start by telling me what all that phony talk was about the six-studded shoes. You think I didn't notice? I can read you like a book. Even from behind. Boni might have bought that bullshit about your doing an article on soccer shoes someday, but I knew you were lying."

"Well, actually. . . ."

"Marc?" she warned. "Don't even think about it."

"Think? About what?"

"Lying," she said firmly. "Talk. Straight. And also tell me why you look so worried. I'm a big girl now and I can share that, too."

There was no way out; at her own insistence, Dahliah was going to be fully involved in the case. A hostage to fortune. To *Danzig*. About the best he could do was to keep Danzig's threat quiet; not to worry Dahliah unnecessarily. "Gregor Ragusic had his head smashed in," he said. "The marks fitted a six-studded soccer shoe perfectly. These shoes are used when the ground is soft, although a few players use them all the time. The studs are sort of conical, with the points chopped off; they're bigger and a little longer than the studs on multistudded shoes, which have lots of smaller studs. The six-stud shoes have two studs on the heel and four on the sole, with the heel studs placed transverse to the long axis of the sole. And the reason I look worried is—" he couldn't tell her about Danzig "—is that Boni's my friend, sort of; I really like him. And I just found out that he's the only Booter who wears six-stud shoes."

"Like a karate kick?" Dahliah closed her eyes for a moment, visualizing the action. "The studs, the holes from the studs, were vertical? With respect to the normal position of the head?"

"Yes, exactly. So the police will think it had to be Boni. And I don't want it to be Boni."

"He said his father also wears six-studded shoes."

"I don't want it to be Grilho, either."

"You don't want it to be anyone, do you?" She looked at him compassionately. "But it has to be someone. Probably someone you know. Maybe even someone you like. So live with that. *We'll* live with that." Well, at least it was *we* again. "Now, Boni is much taller than his father. Can't they tell from the size of the shoes, the spacing of the studs, whose shoes they were?"

"Maybe they can, but I don't have that information."

"Have they found the shoe? It has to have blood on it. And other—uh—evidence."

"If they have, I don't know. Danzig doesn't tell me everything. In fact, he tells me as little as possible."

"So we'll find out for ourselves. Where's the equipment room? Isn't there a place where they store equipment, repair things?"

"Yeah, sure, good idea. There's a boy who's responsible for drying and polishing the shoes. It's very close to— right before the elevators."

"Good." She started walking. "We'll interrogate Mr. Vanderhook right after we see the shoe boy."

---

Francisco Guzman kept the polished shoes neatly in numbered cubbyholes on the left side of the big equipment room. Next to the shelves was a set of four electric rotary brushes and buffers and, below that, a low, raised-edge shelf that held bottles of oils and polish. To the left of the polishing equipment, a shoe-drying rack was fixed to the wall, completely filled with soccer shoes airing out, waiting to be treated. Near the front of the room, a few feet from the steel-mesh door that separated the equipment room from the main corridor, was a pile of shoes that had not yet been sorted and for which there was no room on the drying rack. On the right side of the room were racks of jerseys and shorts, neatly hung on numbered hangers. A commercial-size washer and dryer stood in the back, next to a mangle and a big table. In the middle of the room were two heavy-duty sewing machines.

Marc leaned on the door's waist-level shelf, his right elbow sticking through the low horizontal slot through which equipment was passed. "Hi, Frankie. How're you doing?"

"Okay, I guess," said the slim young man who was working at the polishing wheels. "You heard?"

"Yeah, too bad. You know anything I don't know?"

"You kidding? I thought maybe you could tell me. You the reporter, not me."

"Yeah, but you hear things I could never find out."

"Nothing important. Loose talk. Bitching."

"About what, Frankie?"

"Hey, you got a job for me on your paper? I got a good job here, make a living."

"Okay, Frankie, just testing. How is it that things are so calm around here? Nobody's running around screaming, crying, even worrying."

"Hey, it's a big company. The man goes, be another man here tomorrow. Don't even know I'm alive. Sign my paycheck; that's all I worry about." He put down the shoe he was polishing and looked directly at Marc. "What's on your mind? You never talk direct to me before."

"Yes, well . . . for a story. Could you pick out a six-stud shoe, show it to my fiancée here?" Marc did not look around at Dahliah's face.

"Don't have too many of them on this team," Frankie said, reaching down into the pile and placing a pair of shoes, tied together by the laces, on the door's shelf. "Just Mr. Grilho and Boni. This one is Mr. Grilho's."

"Without checking the number?"

"Hey, twice as small, see?" Marc moved over to let Dahliah examine the shoe.

"You have all the shoes here?" Marc asked casually. "Any missing?"

Frankie looked at Marc suspiciously. "Why? You on to something?"

"I think I am. The police will be here any second to ask you the same thing, so why not tell me?"

"The police been here already, first thing. I told them one pair of Boni's is missing. Now you tell me what's going."

"Off the record? Completely? I mean it, Frankie; I could get into a lot of trouble." Frankie nodded. "Mr. Ragusic was killed by a kick to the head. With a six-stud shoe."

Frankie nodded again. "What I figure. That's why they took away Boni's other pair. To match."

Marc thought for a moment, then asked, "How long have you been here? Did you see anything?"

"I come in six-thirty. Mr. Grilho, he likes a full uniform in each locker before seven and another before one. For eight o'clock practice and two o'clock. Clean and press. Crazy. Don't take an hour to put on a uniform."

"You have a key to each locker?"

"Pass key. You want me to carry a whole bunch?"

"You open up in the morning?"

"And close at night."

"Who else has a key to the equipment room?"

"Mr. Mantanero. He's the boss of equipment, so he comes when he feels like. That's okay with me; plenty of overtime."

"Who else has a key to the equipment room?"

"Security. That's it." He hesitated for a moment. "The police think Boni did it?"

"It looks like they do."

Frankie shook his head. "Not him. Rich guys don't have to do *anything;* they got guys do it for them."

"Who else could have?"

"Nobody liked the man; he was real mean. And he smile too much. Don't trust nobody who smile *all* the time. Man like that—could be anybody do it."

"Somebody on the team?"

"Nobody from the street, that's for sure. And nobody from the new guys. Got to be a Booter." Frankie looked worried. "You think Boni did it? Maybe blew his top?"

"I hope not," Marc said. "I sincerely hope not."

"Boni—he's half Hispanico, right?"

"Portuguese."

"Same thing. You write that story so Boni looks good, you hear?"

"I'll do my best." Marc turned away and began walking toward the players' exit.

"Where are you going?" Dahliah asked.

"To the street. Find a taxi for you." He felt sick, knowing Danzig was preparing a case against Boni.

"Come back," Dahliah said, stopping at the elevators. "We still have time to see Mr. Vanderhook."

# 13

"Thank you for seeing us, Mr. Vanderhook." Dahliah was at her most charming. "I know how busy you must be with this unexpected unfortunate incident on top of your normal World Cup Games duties." Sickening to Marc. She never spoke to him this way.

"I needed the break." Steve Vanderhook matched her in charm and, yes, in beauty, too, Marc had to admit, as long as he stayed behind his desk. Dahliah's smile (was it more than polite?) had made Marc suddenly conscious of the fact that Vanderhook was only three years older than Marc, much handsomer, much richer, and had a much better job: Commissioner as against Assistant Editor. He was also taller, stronger, better dressed, better educated, had better connections, and was a better catch in every way than Marc. In every way except one. "I've just finished a session with Lieutenant

Danzig," Vanderhook went on, "a most disagreeable session, and I'm not in the mood to go right back to thinking about the ramifications of Gregor's death. There will be big problems."

"I'm sure he left a will," Marc said. "His wife will be the new owner."

"Oh, sure, but until the will is probated I'll probably be dealing with an executor or an administrator, an attorney who knows nothing about soccer and who'll be afraid to make the necessary decisions. The Booters will be badly hurt. The league, too."

"Can't you recommend that full management responsibility be given to Grilho? He can handle the job. Grilho not only knows soccer, he has a business degree, I understand, and lots of business experience."

"Oh, yes, he'd be ideal, but there are several hitches. It wouldn't look right for me to recommend anyone in the league; I could be accused of not being disinterested, of having an ulterior motive. Then, too, it wouldn't be fair to Grilho: Head Coach is enough of a headache for any man, and to add management to it would be a killing job. It would also hurt his reputation. There's no way the success of this past year could be repeated, and Grilho would be slaughtered in the media and by the fans— especially by the Brooklyn fans—every time the Booters lost a game. Then there's the matter of having his own son on the team. It must make his heart swell with pride, but what does he do if he has to negotiate a contract with Boni? Whatever he does, the new owners, or their stockholders, will accuse him of favoritism, of selling out their interests."

"I have a possible solution," Dahliah spoke up. "Let Grilho buy the team. He's rich enough and, once he's owner, he could hire a business manager and remain Head Coach which, I believe, is what he really loves."

Marc felt a stab of jealousy as Steve stared at Dahliah

with new eyes. Not only was she the most beautiful green-eyed, auburn-haired professor at Holmes Criminology, she also had business brains. Fast, practical, business brains. "Yes," Vanderhook said. "Yes. Definitely yes." Like the end of *Ulysses*. Too damn much like the end of. . . . "A perfect solution, Miss Norman. Perfect." Well, at least he'd gotten off the yeses. "But I'd rather the suggestion came indirectly. Perhaps you could make it to Grilho, next time you see him. Or you, Marc—and this would be even better, I think—you could suggest it in your next column. Build up a ground swell of favorable public opinion, giving credit to Miss Norman, of course." He smiled warmly at Dahliah.

"Yes, sure," Marc agreed reluctantly, "give credit. Of course." Dahliah was smiling back at Vanderhook. "Now can I—we—ask you some questions that have to do with the murder?"

Without taking his eyes off Dahliah, Vanderhook murmured, "Of course."

"I understand you and Mr. Ragusic had some differences. Serious differences. What were they about?" There was no way Vanderhook could have known that Ragusic had told Marc about his plans and, if Steve lied, Marc would have him. Not exactly *have* him, but it would be a strong indication of something. Of course, there were good reasons the Commissioner of the USSL would not want to discuss the problems, even the fights, he must have had with the strongest owner in the league, but still, if he lied . . . Marc found himself *hoping* he would lie.

"Gregor wanted to make rule changes that would permit much higher scoring and would tend to increase the violence. I opposed him strongly on that, on the basis that it would change what is essentially a perfect game and would kill our chances of ever playing for the World Cup again. And you know how I feel about violence in sports. In addition to that, he wanted to increase the number of teams and form another league, so as to make soccer a major sport in the United States and, not incidentally, to make a good deal of money for all the owners. I supported that, but I wanted to do this slowly, gradually, with a minimum of disruption, both in the U.S. and in the rest of the soccer world. Gregor wanted to do this all at once, precipitously."

"Would he have succeeded, the way the league is set up now?"

"Doubtful. The majority, a small majority, of the owners think as I do; they support me. But if the new league were formed, it's probable that the majority would swing the other way. Gregor was a very forceful personality, very persuasive, and a good deal of money was involved. And I would have nothing to say about who the new owners would be, other than that they would have to have good reputations. Or, rather, would not have bad reputations."

"So Ragusic's death comes as a relief to you?"

"I will not respond to that, Marc, and you must not even hint publicly that you asked me that question. If you wish to speculate on the matter, I can't stop you, but it would be in poor taste, very poor taste. As a matter of fact, I will give you some information, if you promise to support me on what I want to do. How do you feel about the two matters you brought up?"

"The second soccer league and the new rules? I'm in favor of a slow, careful buildup and I don't want the rules of soccer changed one bit."

"Good. I am about to start a campaign among the owners to allow the formation of another league by adding teams to the USSL. Two teams annually, until there are enough so we can break up into two parts, then add more teams slowly until we have twelve teams in each league. And at the same time, I will push for a change in the bylaws which ensures that we can never change the rules and must abide by the FIFA regulations."

"I can support that. Let me know when I can go with it. Now, I'd like to ask you some questions about the murder."

"In front of Miss Norman? For the record? The police have already satisfied themselves, if such was needed in my case, that I did not—could not—have had anything to do with it."

"Yes, for the record. I'm still a reporter, you know, and I have had some success in other investigations. I'm sure you want this matter cleared up as quickly as possible. Okay?" Vanderhook nodded resignedly. "Okay, when did you get here?"

"About six-thirty. This week has been especially busy for me and I have a good deal of work to do. Unfortunately, the post of Commissioner is also a ceremonial position, and I have appointments all day with visiting dignitaries, some of them very highly politically connected. Soccer is very important in most of the other countries. National pride is deeply involved, and I have to keep things quiet, operating smoothly. The only chance I have to do my regular work is early in the morning. At night, I have to attend diplomatic functions."

"Yeah, my heart bleeds for you, Steve, but at least there's no heavy lifting."

"There is much worse. I had a hard struggle with the FIFA officials and the Russians late yesterday, not to mention the Bulgarians. I'm sure as soon as Gregor's death is announced, there will be a hundred people, important people, who will insist on seeing me, trying to force me to make decisions that should not be made. And I have an appointment to talk with the Head Referee and the East Germans and the Hungarians this afternoon. If you think that's a piece of cake, or that you can do better, you're welcome to try."

"No offense intended, Steve; you know I'm on your side. But I have to ask. What did you do after you got here?"

"Came up the elevator and directly to my office."

"Anyone see you?"

"Not that I know of. I was one of the first ones in, according to the Chief of Security. When he reported the killing, he told me that only Gregor, Boni, and the equipment boy came in before me. And Grilho. Well, yes, of course, the Security people saw me, if that's what you mean."

"Anyone on the second floor see you?"

"Not that I know of. Gregor must have already been in his office. He keeps very long hours. Kept."

"I meant, anyone who might have sneaked in."

"That would be very difficult. Only one entrance is open at that time."

"Someone could have stayed here overnight."

"Possible, but very difficult. All gates close after six except the players' gate. Security checks who goes out as well as who comes in."

"So you think the murder was committed by one of the team members? Or staff?"

"You didn't ask that question, either, Marc. Be reasonable, will you? In my position, I can't answer, can't even respond 'no comment' to certain questions."

"Yeah, I guess not." He turned to Dahliah. "You want to ask anything?"

"Just one question," she said. "Who came in after you? Immediately after?"

"Many of the players came within the next few minutes. Grilho likes them to be here very early, so he can be sure who's available and who isn't. I think that, with him, it's more a matter of showing the right spirit than preparing for a change in lineup. I had Security give a copy of their logs to the police. Anything else?"

"No," Dahliah said sweetly. "Not right now, at least."

"Anytime at all, Miss Norman," Steve Vanderhook said. "Come around anytime at all." It sounded very innocent to Marc. Too innocent.

# 14

"You didn't say a word when he called you *Miss* Norman," Marc accused. "Not one word." They had just come down the elevator and were walking toward the players' entrance.

"He's old-fashioned," Dahliah said. "That's all. Meant nothing by it."

"You never accepted that as an excuse before."

"As soon as I explain it to him . . . he just doesn't understand that it's demeaning to differentiate between married and unmarried women when you don't do the same for men."

"Explain? We'll never see him again. He didn't . . . Ragusic was killed by a *kick.*"

"I'm sure there's a good story there for me, how he didn't give up when he was injured, how the power of his mind . . . he's a very inspiring figure. How a man can be so attractive even though . . . it'll be a great story; Mr. Witter will have to assign it to me. I'll tell it from a woman's point of view."

"I'm sure you will," Marc said through gritted teeth. "Why not take Nelda Shaver with you? A perfect combination."

"I think I can handle this better alone. Don't you have confidence in me? My ability as a writer?"

"As a writer? Sure. But you were there to psychoanalyze him as a psychologist. Analyze him as a possible suspect. Murderer. What did you come up with?"

"Not psychoanalyze, Marc; you should know the difference by now. And it's very hard to get to know a person well in such a short, specialized interview, practically a first impression. I'll have to talk to him at length, freely, about a lot of things. Just the two of us, in a less structured environment."

"Yeah, I was sure of that. Okay, give me your impressions." First impression? Marc would do his damndest to make sure it was her last.

"Well, he's a very powerful man, sure of himself, confident of getting his way. He overcame his handicap and stayed in the world of sports, of action, the world he loved. Although I'm sure he's capable of killing, if necessary, he's a very civilized man, and strong enough to use civilized methods to get his way. In everything."

Get his way? "You mean he could be the killer?"

"Obviously not. You weren't listening. I was just describing his psyche. Psychologically, yes, I suppose he could be, but only as a last resort."

"And between him and Boni? Which?"

"If they were the only possibilities? Boni, of course. Steve is too mature." She glanced at her watch. "I've really got to run, Marc, otherwise I'll be late for my class."

"Okay, I'll see you tonight and report on my other interviews."

"Other interviews? Without me?"

"What else can I do? I don't have enough time before Sunday—it must be as soon as possible, I mean; while the trail is hot. I have to talk with Benjamin, Royal, and Velez. And Grilho. Grilho keeps them practicing till eleven and then they have to shower and rest and eat, and he starts them again at two. Until five. So I have a very short time to talk to as many of them as I can. Then there are some stories to get in; I don't want Julius wondering what he pays me for. And I have to talk to him, too, today, face-to-face. Straighten out some things." Such as involving Dahliah in a murder case with Harvey Danzig. And giving her the idea that she can be a reporter and do women's-angle stories on inappropriate subjects. Such as Steve Vanderhook. "When the hell else can I—"

"Go write your stories now and I'll be back by twelve-thirty. Meet you in the press room upstairs. Don't start without me." She gave him a warm kiss and ran off. A very warm kiss. Nice, if it was meant for him.

---

Marc sent in two routine stories. The first was about how the police were progressing on the Ragusic murder, which was mainly about Harvey Danzig and what a great job he had done on other sports murders—anything to put Danzig in a better mood—with Danzig claiming it was too early to comment, though he had some interesting leads. The second story was a think piece on how the murder of Gregor Ragusic would affect the league next year. Maybe later Marc would throw in one on how the Sunday game would be affected, although he didn't think it would make a hell of a lot of difference. By now, Julius would have reporters getting reactions from Mrs. Ragusic and the rest of the family and, if possible, one of them might sneak in a few questions about what changes could be expected in the management of the Booters. Julius, after all, ran the Sports Section, not the news pages.

There was something bothering Marc; he couldn't quite grasp what it was. Color? Something about color? He glanced out the big inward-sloped windows of the press box at the flat green field below. The blue uniforms, and the red ones, too, were gone, off to shower and rest and eat. He hoped that at least some of the players he wanted to interview about the murder would still be around when Dahliah came back. Grilho would be there, of course. He hated to leave the stadium. Just in case somebody started a pickup game of soccer, Marc thought wryly. After the thousands of games he had played in his lifetime, from boyhood to professional, how he could still look forward to yet another game was beyond Marc. *I love gymnastics,* he thought, *but at my age a few minutes a day is enough for me. And I'm five years younger than Grilho.*

Marc would rather have talked to one of the three players from the Booters; he hadn't spoken to any of them, other than Boni, in the past few days. Preferably Jason Benjamin. He was the most intelligent of the lot and the most likely to know something important. Marc had already interviewed Grilho once. Not about the murder, true, but the three players were . . . the three players in the blue uniforms. That was it. No, not the blue; the red. There wasn't any. *That's it,* Marc exulted.

There wasn't any red on the white carpet. Somebody— the murderer—had just kicked Gregor Ragusic's head in. There was a pool of blood on Ragusic's head, deep enough to hide the cleat marks. So there had to be blood on the murderer's right foot—shoe. And he walked on the white carpet and didn't leave any red? Unbelievable. The smoothing out of the carpet was presumably by using folders the way Marc did—there were enough loose papers on the desk to fill ten folders—and walking backward, but there was no way to not leave any trace of blood. No way.

Marc sat back and let his mind work. It was racing. How could the murderer . . . He didn't fly. He didn't levitate. He—hopped. It was only three steps—hops—from Ragusic's desk to the bathroom door, maybe four steps, tops. The killer hopped to the bathroom—any soccer player could do it in his sleep—took off the shoe, washed it, dried it, and . . . he'd have to tell Danzig to check the towels, see if any of them had traces of blood on them, and that would prove . . . what? That the killer had washed and dried his . . . worse, if a towel was missing, all it meant was that the killer didn't waste time washing and drying . . . all he had to do was wrap the towel around . . . not even that. He could have just taken off the shoe and wrapped it in the towel and walked out. . . . It might look funny, if someone saw him, but still. . . .

Even worse, if the murder was premeditated, the killer could have brought a plastic bag with him; it was that simple. Put the bloody shoe in that. But then he'd be walking around with only one shoe on; somebody might notice. Idiot! If he brought a plastic bag with him, couldn't he have brought another pair of shoes along, too? Quietly, calmly, taken off the murder shoes and put on the other pair? An opaque plastic bag, of course. Unlikely someone would see him, but you never know.

But why carry around a plastic bag? Someone could remember that X, the murderer, was carrying a plastic bag around. Which he had to bring to the stadium with him; couldn't take a chance on finding an opaque plastic bag the right size at that time of the morning. That was the whole point. If it was premeditated, why kick Ragusic's head in? And if it wasn't premeditated, the killer didn't have a bag. So it's back to hopping over—or even taking off the shoe at Ragusic's desk—and *walking* over to the bathroom, washing off the shoe—the bottom only—drying it, and wrapping the shoe in a towel. Then, when he got outside the offices, put on the shoe as he stepped out into the corridor—in fact, just before he stepped out—with the right foot, of course—onto the hard tiles of the corridor, and walk away safely. Then go out onto the field, where the grass and earth would remove all traces of blood and all traces of the crime, and be absolutely safe.

No, he couldn't be sure of removing *all* traces—the police with their chemicals, remember? He had to get rid of the shoes. Easy. Drop them in a garbage dumpster. But if he went outside, the Security people would note that down. So? So drop them in an inside garbage can. Which means the police have them already. All this terrific thinking for nothing. Danzig could have told me, the bastard. On the other hand, if the crime wasn't premeditated, would Boni be so stupid? Boni? Well, who else? Even if his father could wear shoes six sizes too big for him, would he implicate his own son? Never. Not Grilho. And would Boni, who was very bright, drop his own shoes into a garbage can where they would easily be found by the police? Never. On the other hand, he could always claim someone was trying to frame him. How could anyone prove otherwise? But if someone else was trying to frame Boni, it would have to be premeditated, and then the killer would have brought the plastic bag with him and saved himself a lot of trouble.

Okay. Could one of the others have put on Boni's shoes by mistake? Ridiculous. A soccer player's shoes were like his own skin. Nobody—even if he wore the same size—could *not* know he was wearing another player's shoes. And again, why would anyone, on the spur of the moment, go up to Ragusic's office, have a fight with him, and kill him? And wear somebody else's shoes to go up there in the first place? Impossible. Another dead end. What was needed was more information. Much more. But he couldn't talk to any of the players without Dahliah. And she would be here any minute. Stuck.

No. Not really. Marc went to the elevator, then decided to take the stairs. Much quicker. He dashed down and ran to the equipment room. Frankie was ironing. Mangling. Same thing.

"Frankie, a couple more questions."

"You trying to make out like I know something? Or like I give a damn?"

"No, no, just some technical . . . no one has keys to the equipment room but you and Mr. Mantanero? And the Security people, right?"

"That's what I told you before."

"When you give out the uniforms and shoes in the morning, do you leave the equipment room open? Closed? Locked?"

"Who said I give them out in the morning? The subway messes up and I get fired and it ain't my fault? I got a system. I make sure every player got two sets everything in his locker the night before. That way, no matter what, I'm covered."

"Yes, fine." It wasn't really; one good idea shot to hell. "Do you lock the door?"

"How I do it is—you see the wagon?" He pointed to a small cart, about twice the size of a supermarket cart, with two bars across the top, on which were hanging some jerseys and pants on numbered hangers, like a cloakroom setup. "I fill up the wagon with what I need, and after everybody goes home, I go around and put what I have to in the lockers. That way, I got no problems in the morning, no pressure. And I always lock the door. Anytime I leave the room I lock the door. I'm responsible." He waved his hand around the equipment room. "For everything."

"You lock each locker, too?"

"And I check it. Something missing, it ain't gonna be

142

my fault. But I tell you something—a kid could open one of them lockers with his nails. Why? Something missing? I didn't do it."

"No, no, thanks. Nothing missing." Damn right, something was missing. A motive. A method. A solution. He walked over to the elevators and pressed the "up" button, then decided to run upstairs. For speed. Too late. Dahliah was there already, impatiently tapping her foot.

"I thought you were in a hurry to interview some more suspects," she said. "Where were you?"

"I was just—uh—in the men's room." He drew in a deep, relaxing breath. It didn't work. "Let's go downstairs. Interview somebody. Whoever we can find." That *whoever*, whoever he was, was going to get a real good grilling. About time somebody else sweated for a change.

# 15

$M$arc and Dahliah found Cuffy Royal in a small Szechuan Chinese restaurant a block from the stadium. "Only place around here for proper *hot* food. Fresh cooked, not defrost," Cuffy explained. "Can't stand the stuff in most places; can't even *taste* it." Though he tried, there was no room behind the fixed table in the booth for him to stand up, but his hard black face had a friendly smile.

"Are you a vegetarian?" Dahliah asked, seeing what was on his plate.

"Not just, ma'am. But after a Grilho workout, I am *hungry*. If I eat regular food, I gain twenty pounds just *looking*, so if I eat just vegetables—no meat, no sweet—I don't get fat. With plenty spices. Need that when you sweat."

"Mind if we join you?" Marc asked.

Cuffy waved at the seats opposite him. "You want an interview, your paper pick up the check."

"Of course," Marc said. "Be my pleasure. But I'm going to ask you about the murder, too, not just the game."

Cuffy stopped eating. "Oh, the police, they give me a hard time about that already. I tell them same as I tell you. Three monkey: I don't know, I don't see, I don't give a damn."

"It doesn't bother you that Mr. Ragusic, the owner of your team, was murdered?"

"One boss, 'nother boss, no matter." He turned to Dahliah. "Excuse me, Miss, but Marc, he got too much on his mind. I be Cuffy Royal." He held out his hand. "Very pleased to meet you."

Dahliah shook his hand; it was hot, strong, and surprisingly smooth. Well, why not; he played soccer, after all, not baseball. "I'm Dahliah Norman. I'm working with Mr. Burr, trying to get a story. And I'm pleased to meet you." The waitress had come over, and Dahliah pointed to Cuffy's plate. "I'll have one of those, please." She glanced at Marc. He nodded. "Make that two." She turned back to the big forward. Cuffy was of average height but, unlike the other soccer players she had seen, his shoulders were those of a man six inches taller. "Do you really feel that way, Cuffy? You're paid well to play a game you must enjoy, and you've been picked to represent America on the World Cup Team."

"Four year ago I sign that contract, Miss Norman, and that time was no choice. It not like you a baseball player; lot of opportunity, all different kind. In soccer, professional soccer, got only this one place to go. Either that or coach. Even then, for good coach job, you need the college degree, even doctor. For me? Forget it. So what is left? The private soccer school for the little kids? How many of them? And what they pay?"

"You make a good living, don't you? And you can walk away any time."

"Sure, a good living. But when you are starter, one of the best, pick for the World Cup Team, that be the time . . . see, Miss Norman, an athlete, he got a very short life. The time he must make the money is when he is at the top peak. You think they gonna select me for the next World Cup Team? Four year from now? Hey, I be lucky if I be regular on the team then."

"So you wanted to renegotiate your contract with Mr. Ragusic?"

"All I ask was little—hey, I be starter forward four year. On the Booters, I be big star. Only black man on first team. You know what that mean? You think all my people come to see just Boni? You look up in the stand someday. You know what you see? Half the people, more than half, they be from my side, or José's. I bring in the money, and I deserve more than beginner salary. Some kids he hire last year, they getting more than me."

"What did Ragusic say to that?"

"Says he pay market price. Like for piece of meat. When contract is up, we talk again, okay Cuffy? Sure. Yes, Cuffy, nice boy, pat on head. Like dog." Cuffy had stopped eating and was staring straight ahead, jaw clenched. Marc remembered the forward's massive thighs, strong enough to take the head off a horse. Certainly strong enough to crush Ragusic's skull. But was that significant? Even little José Velez—any professional soccer player—could kill a man with one kick. "All the time wait, wait, wait. Always tomorrow; never today."

"Can't you wait one more year?" Dahliah asked.

"I already make the dollar for him. Why he have to wait a year? Can't afford the money? Hey, he got so much, wouldn't even notice. Next year, if I have real bad year, you think he remember how much money I make for him? What happen if those bastards break my leg Sunday?

What happen if I can't play again, ever? Be shoeshine boy?"

Dahliah hesitated, then asked, "Do you think he was prejudiced against you?"

"Think? I *know*. My substitute—O'Rourke; Irish—he get more than me. Why?"

"It can't be that," Dahliah said. Marc knew she was being provocative. "Boni is half black."

"Wrong, miss. Sorry. Boni half *white*. The other half mixed. White, black, Indian, everything."

"And Grilho?"

"Grilho is Grilho. Not black; all mixed. Grilho don't count."

Marc thought it time to take over. "When did you have this fight with Ragusic?" he asked.

"Fight? Wasn't no fight; just talk. He don't need to fight; he just sit there and smile. Big smile. Got nothing to lose. He hold all the cards; what could I do?"

"You could have killed him; kicked his head in."

"That how he did it? Nobody tell me." Royal didn't even quiver. "Don't talk foolish, mon. Why do that? I want money—for my family—not make trouble. I talk sweet talk, that be all; no threat, nothing."

"Yeah, okay. When was that?"

"Yesterday. Late."

"Thursday? Before the murder?"

"Had to be. Mr. Ragusic, he live and smiling when I leave him."

"What time was that?"

"Don't know exact. Must be seven, about."

"Why so late?"

"To be private. Don't want anybody to know. Somebody find out, Ragusic gonna say hey, I love to give you big raise, but if I give you, I gotta give everybody. Too bad, mon."

"Where'd you go after that?"

147

"Home. Where else? To eat."

"Anybody see you?"

"Thousand people, but who gonna remember black man on subway. Without soccer uniform, nobody know me."

"Your wife will vouch for when you got home?"

Royal's face cracked in a wide smile again. "What wife is for. But police—they don't believe nothing. Better ask Security; they got exact time I leave."

"What time did you get in this morning?"

"Don't know exactly. Right after Jason. Saw him go in when I come to near the entrance."

"Isn't there a way to get into the stadium without Security seeing you?"

"Must be some way, but for sneak thief, not for soccer player." He began eating again. "Don't want let this get too cold; bad for digestion."

Time to change the subject. Marc still had to turn in stories. "What do you predict will happen at the big game?"

"Nobody gonna bother with me; think Cuffy Royal not good enough. Beside, they know, if they hurt me—if my kids gonna starve—I kill one of them. Don't care if I get red card; nobody *go* to hurt me. Accidental foul, okay. Happen. But with them? No, I be okay. They gonna pick on John Geis, last starter. That is *all*. Get John and we got no forward starter left. They gonna walk all over us. Three goal, sure."

"The score's going to be three to nothing?"

"If we lucky. Why? You think *we* gonna score?"

Marc had no place to go after that, so Dahliah spoke again. "If you had to pick the most likely person to be the murderer, who would that be?"

He gave her a crooked smile. "Seem to me you already pick that one."

"At this stage. I don't have the slightest idea who . . . what gives you that idea?"

"Why you chase me all the way to here? You like to watch me eat? Or because you think I could be the one?"

"Well, I . . . everybody's a suspect."

"For real? Okay, who you gonna talk to next? José Velez? Boni? Jason Benjamin? Grilho?" Dahliah nodded reluctantly. "Just us poor minority? No *real* Americans?"

"We did speak with Steven Vanderhook."

"Oh, sure, must talk to *Mr.* Vanderhook. For background. Ask about *us.* But he don't count, you know. He not a *real* suspect. All the *real* suspect must be minority."

"It's just a coincidence, really. We're sure it has to be someone from the Booters and it so happens . . . who would you pick?" she challenged.

"No problem, ma'am." Royal smiled widely again. "Not one person, either: whole United States Soccer League." He thought for a moment, then added, "And anybody else do business with him. With that smile."

# 16

"Will you please hurry," Dahliah urged. Anxiously, she pulled Marc along, but the narrow gray street leading to the plaza in front of the stadium was crowded with people returning from lunch and, weaving in and out, they couldn't move very fast.

"What's the rush?" Marc complained.

"I want to get in one more interview before practice starts."

"It's one-thirty already and practice starts at two. Let's leave the interviews for after practice."

"I have a faculty meeting at four. By the time I get back here all the suspects will be on their way home."

"That's okay. I'll interview them and tell you all about it when I get home."

"That's what I was afraid of," Dahliah said.

"I only got a few minutes," José Velez said, glancing nervously around the empty corridor. He looked too slim and dapper to be a professional athlete; more like the popular conception of a Latin dance instructor than one of the best forwards in America. "Mr. Grilho, he likes us to be on the field real early."

"This will just take a few minutes," Marc assured him. "All I want is to ask you a few questions about the murder."

"Yeah, just what I figured. You're buddies with that lieutenant, right?"

"We're not buddies, but Danzig does listen to me. He doesn't always do what I want—" never *does what I want, but if it helps get cooperation from the suspects* "—but he respects what I tell him."

"Yeah, okay, tell him to leave me alone. I got enough problems as it is, and I got to concentrate on the game."

"I can't tell him that, but if I tell him you've been helpful to me, maybe he won't bother you."

"Help? Sure, Marc, you know me. I got nothing to hide. You can level with me, too. You're working tight with Danzig, ain't you? Everybody's talking about how you're going around like a cop."

"Not like a cop; like a good investigative reporter. But if I happen to find out anything useful, I have to tell the police." Velez looked so twitchy that Marc decided to go the long way around. "How do you think the game's going to go?"

Velez, after a moment's surprise, grabbed the opportunity to get off the murder. "The game? I don't think about the game. I watch the movies, see how their fullbacks work, figure out how to get the ball down the touchlines so I can feed a good one to John Geis or Teddy Pangos in front of the goal. Us flankers practically never get a chance to score; only the stars."

"Yes," Marc sympathized, "it's a shame the guys who

boot in the goals get the big money and the guys who make it possible for them to do it, get peanuts. You ever discuss this with Ragusic?"

"Yeah, once or twice. Waste of time. He just smiles and says he'll take care of me when the contract renewal comes up. Next year."

"You've been with the Booters four years now?"

"Yeah. Same time as Cuffy."

"And in four years, you asked Ragusic for more money only two times?"

"Well, maybe a couple more times. I knew it wouldn't help, so save your breath."

"It's a shame the way he treated you and Cuffy. Two of the best flankers in the league, the guys who make it possible for Boni to score so high, getting so little money. Cuffy says he asked Ragusic lots of times."

"Cuffy, he's very stubborn. Also he got a big family. I manage."

"So you were sore at Ragusic?"

"Business, man. You don't get sore in business. Next year—I was figuring on getting a damn good contract, a hell of a lot more bread. Back when I signed that contract, I was a kid, and I was damn glad to get it. It looked like a lot of money to me, then. I keep my word and Ragusic keeps his."

"Not sore at all? Okay, Saint José, let me give you a tip. When you talk to the police—Danzig—don't tell him that. Say, sure you were sore, but there was nothing you could do about it, so you swallowed it and went on, figuring to get a big raise next year. Now, what else have you got for me? I need news."

"I got nothing new for you; didn't Danzig tell you? I already told them everything I know, 'cause I don't know nothing. I told them ten times at least. They kept asking me over and over, same thing."

"Tell me," Marc prompted. "Just once."

Velez looked highly put upon. "Okay, but just one time," he said. He smoothed his narrow moustache and began, in a bored voice. "I come in about seven o'clock—maybe a little before—and went right to the locker. I got dressed. Didn't do no stretching 'cause Mr. Grilho, he always starts with stretching. I loafed around, resting. Then the cops came and made us all wait around, miss the beginning practice, and asked a lot of questions. That's all."

"Anybody see you?"

"Oh, sure, everybody."

"All the time?" Marc had long experience interviewing owners, managers, and even some politicians, so he had a nose for liars. Funny how they all used the same faces when they were not telling the whole truth. Right now, he smelled that José was holding something back. "Some of the other players said you were missing from the locker room for some time." This had to be true; what could he lose?

"Well, sure, go to the toilet."

Marc was positive now. "Longer than that, José. The cops are going to wonder why you didn't mention that."

"Well, they never asked me where I was resting. I would've told them if they asked me."

"Where?"

"Well, you know, it's a lot of noise in the locker room. Happens, sometimes, I was up late the night before and Mr. Grilho, he likes everybody rested. So I found a place, quiet, nobody bothers. . . ."

"The offices on the second floor?"

"They don't come in till nine. No problem. Got a soft couch, set my watch, lay back, get another little rest."

"Why didn't you tell the police this?"

"Way they look at things . . . I didn't want them to think I could've gone near Mr. Ragusic's office. Don't have to *look* for trouble."

"You were in the office next to Ragusic's?"

"Oh, no; I don't take them kinds of chances. Mr. Ragusic could walk in and get mad."

"So you were at the other end? Next to Mr. Vanderhook's office?"

"More like in the middle, near the elevator, the one by the locker room."

"You see anyone up there?"

"Hey, I was sleeping. I told you."

"When you were going in, I mean. Or out."

"Didn't pay no attention. Just wanted to get across the hall fast."

"You didn't even take a quick look around before you left the elevator?"

"Well, yeah, make sure nobody's in the hall. Didn't know what you meant. But just a quick look, know what I mean? Real fast."

"Yeah. Speedy Gonzalez. Fastest man in soccer."

"It's a fact," Velez said, smiling modestly.

"So you didn't see anything at all?"

"I didn't say that. You asked me did I see any*body*, right?"

"Why do I feel like I'm pulling teeth?" Marc was irritated. "Can't you just tell me—"

"Hey, Marc, I'm telling you, ain't I? Everything you ask. You gotta understand where I'm from. South Bronx—you get in real *big* trouble just for *knowing* some things. So, even when I'm a little kid, I learn . . . you know something, Marc, someday maybe you got to cross the Caribbean in a little boat, water full of sharks, just to get away. Then let's see how you answer questions to the police."

"I do understand, Mr. Velez," Dahliah said softly. "And I do know what it feels like. But this is not then. Or there. The police may be slow, they may not ask the correct questions right away—it's only a half a day since the murder—but they are very thorough. And after they get through comparing stories, they're going to get back to you and ask why you didn't tell them the *whole* truth. Then they're going to wonder if you're now telling the truth and, before you know it, they're going to start looking at you as a suspect. And into your background. And at your family. Even check for green cards. You'd be better off if you tell us now what you saw. Marc will tell Lieutenant Danzig that *you* want to tell him something, something you were too flustered to think about. He won't believe that, but he'll accept it, if you go to him voluntarily."

José Velez looked deeply into Dahliah's eyes, studying her, assessing her, for a full minute. Then he spoke. "Maybe you're right. Okay. When I went upstairs—it was right after I come in, street clothes. See, if I got dressed first, they'd know how long I went out of the locker room and besides, on the second floor, in uniform, I'd stick out. Street clothes—from behind, they don't know who I am— I could be somebody coming in early. Also, I got here too early. Subway was on time for once, I got here right after Cuffy. Saw him go in so I waited a minute. I didn't want to go in the locker room, let anybody see me. So I hung around behind that corner across from the elevator, wait till nobody's in the hall, maybe five minutes, maybe ten, and I went upstairs. When I stuck my head out of the elevator, make sure nobody's around, I saw the door to Ragusic's office—not his office, the one outside, for his secretary—was just closing." He stopped, then added, guiltily, "Heard it, too. Very soft, but I heard it. One click."

"That was the murderer," Dahliah said, "going in to kill Ragusic."

"Yeah, what I figured later. Why I didn't want to say nothing. The cops might think I saw him. And *he* might think I saw him."

"But you didn't see anything?"

"Just the door close, I swear. Tell the cops they gotta believe me."

"You tell them," Marc said. "It'll sound better. I'll tell Danzig you want to see him."

"Make sure you tell him I didn't see nothing. *Nobody.*"

"Who do you think it could have been?" Dahliah asked.

"Don't have *any* idea," Velez said vehemently. "Just it wasn't me."

# 17

The pressroom was filled with reporters sending in stories about the latest developments in the Ragusic Murder Case. Not that anything new had come to light since Marc was last there, but the demand for different headlines for later editions made minimally reworded rehashes necessary to give the reader the feel of ever-changing developments. Marc and Dahliah sneaked into the TV room, where they could have some privacy. Dahliah had never been there before. Looking down, she was entranced at the shifting patterns the twenty-two blue- and red-uniformed players made on the field, the flickering kaleidoscope of primary colors against the green background momentarily bringing to life the infinite variety of designs and formations as the ball passed from the control of one team to the other. She watched, fascinated, her first comprehension, internalization, of the beauty of the sport, and began to understand the allure of the game for its billions of fans throughout the world.

"It is fun, isn't it?" Marc broke the silence.

"Yes, yes, I hadn't realized . . . the bitter way you've been talking about your job the past year, I had the feeling you hated sports."

"No, it isn't that. I love sports; it's the phoniness of much of sports reporting I hate. And the commercialization. It's unavoidable, I suppose; people always want to see the best athletes perform. I do, too. There are moments of such beauty that my heart stops, moments that I can't capture on paper or with my camera. But I also feel that the watchers should be playing themselves. Yes, watch the greatest, and play with your peers. Enjoy the participation, the challenge, the beautiful game. Soccer can be played anywhere, by anyone, at any time. Three-year-old kids and ninety-year-old grandmothers. In a nearby field or in your backyard. Even on city streets. Don't just watch; play, too."

"Why don't you do a column on that?"

"I tried, once. Julius Witter pointed out that if I wrote anything that would encourage a drop in ticket sales, I might not have a column the next day, or even a job. So I sell out, and hope, someday, to become an investigative reporter—in politics or some other criminal activity, not in sports—where I can write the truth and not get fired. Maybe even get a medal or a prize."

"Do you really think it'll be different in another field?" Dahliah put her hand over his, warmly. "The discontent is in you, Marc; you want to move the world but you don't have a lever big enough. Or a place to stand. Not now. Accept that. Stop fighting the system openly for a while and be prepared to take the opportunity when it develops. If it develops. Or even to make the opportunity, if a crack opens up." She looked down at the field again. "Meanwhile, enjoy the good part of the world, take strength from it. It isn't all bad."

"Yeah, I guess you're right. Maybe I'll read some of the *Meditations* tonight, the original ones. Old Marcus Aurelius had a way of looking at things. . . ." Marc looked down at the field, too, unable to look at Dahliah, afraid he'd melt into tears. The pressure: Ragusic's murder; Harvey Danzig; Julius Witter; Dahliah's continued refusal to marry him; her obvious attraction to Vanderhook; the World Cup Game; tomorrow morning's breakfast with Danzig, which would bring more nasty threats and even greater pressure; the deadline that he couldn't possibly. . . .

Dahliah broke into his brooding. "Shouldn't we be analyzing what we found out just now? I have to get back to school soon."

"Yeah, I guess so," he said, still down. "I have a couple of stories to send in, too, for the late edition."

"Start with José Velez?" Marc nodded. "He's lying, isn't he?"

"Oh, sure; they're all lying, to some extent. But José— I don't think he's lying when he says something that can be checked up on; he's too smart for that. He's just lying about his motives and his actions, things that only he knows."

"He didn't go upstairs to rest, did he?"

"Obviously not. He had to admit that he went upstairs, because there was always the possibility that someone had seen him and told the police. But what else could he say? What other reason could he have had to be on the second floor?"

"He didn't take the elevator, did he?"

"He took the stairs. I can't believe he hung around in the main corridor—which is near the locker room—for five or ten minutes. Trying not to be seen? Ridiculous. No, he ran up the stairs as soon as he got in; the less time he spent on the first floor, the better the chance he would not be observed. The only reason he said he took the elevator was so he could say he saw the door to Ragusic's outer office close. The elevator is across the hall from Ragusic's office; the stairs are on the same side. If he admitted he took the stairs, he could never have said he saw the door close."

"Did he see the door close?"

"That I believe. The question is, did he see it close from the outside or the inside?"

"From the inside," Dahliah said firmly.

"You sure? How?"

"Positive. He went upstairs for only one reason: to see Ragusic. No other explanation is possible for his coming in unusually early—he admitted that himself—or for his need not to be seen going upstairs. Either he had an appointment to see Ragusic, in which case he wouldn't have tried to sneak up, or he wanted to grab Ragusic at a time when no one was around. For what? To insist on more money now, before contract renewal time. At a time when he was to play as a starter in the World Cup Final Game. Psychologically, the perfect time."

"Did he kill Ragusic?"

"I don't think so, Marc. But he did find the body. Or, at least, saw it when he opened the door to Ragusic's office. Remember how frightened he looked when he insisted that he didn't see anything or anybody? He's afraid the killer might have been hanging around the office area and saw him; that the killer might think Velez knows something and kill him next."

"Velez is street smart. His family lived under a dictatorship. He's perfectly capable of acting that way to throw us off. And the police, too. If he's the killer, and he doesn't know if he was observed going upstairs, and maybe even into Ragusic's office, this might be the smart way to play it. What do you think, Dahliah? Could he have killed Ragusic?"

"Could? Yes, of course. Any of them could. But did? I don't have enough to work on yet. Over a refusal to raise his salary? Seems like a poor motive."

"On the other hand, Cuffy said Ragusic was a bigot. Bigots are not always very selective. Maybe Ragusic, in turning down Velez, said something about his ancestry? Hispanics are strong family people, and proud; one does not insult the family with impunity. What do you think?"

"It could also be something we don't know about. I agree; Velez is still on the list. What about Cuffy Royal?"

"Same thing, I guess. We know Cuffy came in before Velez, so even if Velez did find the body, Cuffy is not off the hook. As for motive, do you believe that Cuffy saw Ragusic Thursday night only?"

Dahliah thought for several seconds, then said, "I'm sure he did see him then. He had no way of knowing if Ragusic made a note about their meeting, or said something to his secretary or left some dictation on a machine. Motive? Probably same as José's. What we don't know is whether or not Cuffy went upstairs when he came in, and if he did, why? He could easily have gone in to see Ragusic and, if most of what Velez says is the truth, he had time to kill Ragusic. The whole thing couldn't have taken more than two minutes. Less."

Marc sighed. "True. But if it happened that way, we'll never get him to admit anything. If Royal did it this morning, it had to be premeditated. Otherwise why come back? To plead for money? He seems too proud to do that. And it fits something else, too. Black people have long learned to smile for the boss, but if pushed too far, like a member of any downtrodden group, Cuffy might take advantage of an unexpectedly favorable situation to balance the scales."

"So we still have the same suspects?"

"Yeah," Marc smiled wryly. "But now we know for sure that they're suspects. A great improvement." And he hadn't even spoken to Grilho about the murder, or Jason Benjamin. And there was no way he could do it today, with Dahliah at her faculty meeting. If he spoke to them without her, it might be just the kind of thing she'd misunderstand. *Understand*. Lack of faith, bad faith, lack of trust, God knew what. And early tomorrow he had to see Danzig. With nothing solid to report. And this evening, he had to see Witter. To get flayed for stupidity. Also with nothing to report. Another joyful occasion.

"I have a couple of stories to send in," he said. "Why don't you go to your faculty meeting a little early? I'll see you tonight and we'll discuss what we're going to do tomorrow; maybe you'll have time to think of something I missed. And, oh, I'll probably be a little late for supper. Meeting with Julius." He kissed her lightly. "Figure I'll be home about seven-thirty." *On my shield.*

# 18

When Marc hit the first floor, all the reporters were moving toward the press conference room. He grabbed Eli Rosen, a bored old-timer from the *Post*. "What's going on?"

"The Commissioner's called a conference for the Commies and the striped-pants boys." Rosen looked highly unimpressed as he pushed his way into the elevator.

Marc followed. "What's the State Department doing here? Was Ragusic a spy or something?"

"Who the hell knows? We'll find out soon."

"From them?"

"Sure, if they say anything of substance. Whatever they say, the opposite is the truth. I had my story written an hour ago. 'It was announced today by a press representative of the German Democratic Republic that the international socialist sports world deeply regrets the unfortunate death of one of the world's greatest sports pioneers, Mr. Gregor Ragusic, the former Yugoslavian World Cup player, who scored a goal in the 1966 World Cup Games. Ragusic gave up a promising sports career in his native land in order to bring the truly collective game of soccer to the oppressed masses of the crime-ridden capital of capitalism. He gave his life, like a true socialist hero, in the cause.' In five hundred words."

"You're kidding. They wouldn't dare. He hated them."

"Sure, you know it and I know it, but who's going to print it? What the hell do you think the cookie pushers are there for? Kiss, kiss, and is your shoe licked clean enough, Sire? How long you been in this business, kid?"

"Sixteen years, but only in sports."

"Yeah, that's the trouble. Soccer ain't sports, kid; it's war."

---

Standing, leaning on the lectern, now formally and, Marc had to admit, beautifully dressed, Commissioner Steven Vanderhook graciously introduced the press representatives of the United Nations, the German Democratic Republic, and the Department of State, as well as the *Staatssicherheitsdienst* representative, the SSD officer who was responsible for the safety of the East German Team and their entourage, all of whom had come to express their sympathy to the American public and to soccer fans all around the world for the tragic loss of Gregor Ragusic.

"What the hell's an SSD big shot doing here?" Irv whispered excitedly to Marc. "And only half a day after the murder. This could be interesting. Look at those guys." With a slight tilt of his eyebrows, he indicated two thickset, bulky men standing stolidly at each side of the platform, their eyes coldly scanning the audience of reporters. One of them seemed to be looking directly at Marc. He was a hairless, middle-aged, lumpy-faced man with pale eyes, wearing a dark-brown overcoat and a brown leather cap. The man kept both hands in his pockets. Marc looked away, then back, and the lumpy man was still looking at him. Staring. Definitely staring.

Pierre L'Oiseaux, the plump, beautifully dressed United Nations press representative, explained that the Secretary General had been asked by the honorable Ambassador to the United Nations of the German Democratic Republic to use his good offices to ensure that the final game for the World Cup would not be interrupted by any demonstrations resulting from the tragic demise of Mr. Gregor Ragusic, either prior to the final game, during the game itself, or after the game. The Secretary General had assured the Ambassador that the press would cooperate in every way to avoid inflammatory, baseless conjectures that might lead some people to assume that the GDR was interested in the unfortunate matter other than as a sympathetic observer who desired that the international standards of justice be upheld. No questions, please.

At the far corners of the big room, Marc saw two other pairs of chunky, hard-faced men in black overcoats and black fedoras, right out of the forties private-eye movies, standing erect, alertly examining the crowd. One of them seemed to be looking straight at Marc. It wasn't his imagination. When Marc turned his head to look at Brown Coat, then turned back, Black Coat was still staring at him. He didn't seem to mind that Marc saw him, either.

In perfect, precise English, Heinrich Kunstler, the slim, beautifully dressed press representative of the GDR offered his regrets and sympathy to the United States on the loss of a great sportsman who had been trained in soccer in a socialist country. He hoped that the person who committed the cowardly crime would be brought to justice by the proper authorities as soon after the Final World Cup Game as possible, as a fitting tribute to the international amity fostered by these games. He further wished that the games might continue to serve as a bridge of understanding between the socialist world, whose people desired only peace, and the imperialist powers, so as to reduce the danger of nuclear war. It would be highly regrettable if some misguided people, inflamed by the pernicious propaganda of antiprogressive elements, misinterpreted the energetic socialist style of play, which had brought the great GDR Team to its present championship stature, and attempted to slander the world's best team and to besmirch in advance its justly anticipated victory over its worthy opponent. In deference to the solemnity of the occasion, there would be no questions.

Suspiciously, Marc turned his head to the back of the room. There were two pairs of massive, stony-faced, blue-coated men, tall ones, watching the proceedings from the back corners of the room. No, not what was happening on the platform. They were watching the reporters who were watching the platform, and one of the blue coats was clearly watching him. Marc turned back and took a quick look around. Brown Coat was still watching him, Black Coat was still watching him and, with a quick partial turn and a sideways glance, he saw that Blue Coat was still watching him, too.

"What the hell is going on here?" he asked Rosen.

"Later," Rosen said, and turned to a new page in his notebook.

Harriss Lamont Burnsides, the perfectly groomed, beautifully dressed representative of the State Department, noted that the passing of Mr. Gregor Ragusic was a great loss to his country and to American soccer. In these troubled times, when the representatives of the Department of State were working diligently to defuse any situation which might have an adverse affect on the slow, steady march of standard diplomatic procedures toward a greater understanding between our great country and the other countries with which we share the world and with which we must live in peace, any implication that the World Cup Games had any connection to political matters or to the unfortunate loss we were all mourning today, would be counterproductive and should be avoided. *Abjured,* even. And since he had urgent business in Washington, he regretted he could not stay for questions.

"Take a quick look around," Marc asked Rosen. "Am I crazy, or are there three guys watching me? Or could they be looking at the guy behind me?"

Rosen stretched and glanced around "You," he whispered. "What the hell did you do?"

"Nothing. Absolutely nothing. Why me? Who are they?"

"Later," Rosen said.

Karl Jaeger, the SSD officer in charge, beautifully dressed in a simple, soft, Italian tailored suit, explained that he had offered his services and those of his associates, who were highly experienced in the apprehension of criminal elements as well as in the prevention of criminal activities, to the local authorities in charge of this case, as well as to those federal authorities who had an interest in the interstate and, possibly, the international aspects of this crime, in order to prevent any unwarranted disturbances which could mar the dignity of the coming championship game and to ensure that the perpetrator of this senseless, unnecessary, emotional crime would soon be found. In the interim, he and his associates would be highly interested observers of the situation who would not, of course, interfere in any way with the work of the local forces but would call to the attention of the proper authorities, after satisfying themselves of its authenticity, any information which might be useful in the apprehension of the criminal group which was futilely attempting to poison the atmosphere of friendly competition which existed between the socialist champions and their opponents. In his position, he could not, of course, answer any questions. At this time.

When Commissioner Vanderhook announced that the press conference was over, the crowd started for the doors in the back of the room. Marc kept Rosen back. "How'd you like to interpret for me? They were all lying, weren't they?"

"I'd like to get to a phone," Rosen said, "and sure, they were lying. But actually, if you understood the code, you'd see they were all telling you the truth. From the moment the Commissioner introduced them. Him, too. If they wanted to express their sympathy, all they had to do was send a card and some flowers to Ragusic's family. None of whom, you may have noticed, were present today. And why was the UN guy there? And why here? A short statement by the Secretary General, a handout issued at the Secretariat, would have been appropriate. More than enough. I mean, Ragusic is important enough to interest the UN? Then the East German Ambassador asked the Secretary General to make sure that the final game shouldn't have demonstrations? What the hell can the UN do about that? Inflammatory, baseless conjectures? They have no interest other than justice? They're going to an awful lot of trouble for something they have no interest in. It's clear they're worried somebody will write that they had something to do with the murder."

"Isn't that a clumsy way to handle things? Shouldn't they have just kept a low profile?"

"Aside from being stupid and clumsy, there has to be something else. Maybe they're trying to set up an excuse if they lose, which doesn't seem likely. Maybe they're trying to *encourage* demonstrations, though who's going to demonstrate, I don't know. Maybe they're going to repeat what the Bulgarians did, and cripple the rest of our team and they don't want any complaints, so they're going to blame whatever happens on the Ragusic murder."

"That's crazy. The fans would tear them to pieces, along with the referee."

"Yeah, but then they can blame it on the inflammatory, baseless conjectures, instead of dirty play. Did you get that part about antiprogressive elements misinterpreting their aggressive style of play? It looks to me like they're going to pull out all stops. This is going to be the dirtiest final game of all time."

"Shouldn't we warn Grilho? And Vanderhook."

"They know. Believe me, they know. But what the hell can they do about it? After this press conference, anything they say will be misinterpreted by every columnist and editorial writer as inciting to riot against the poor misunderstood East Germans."

"Then why is the State Department helping them? I should think—"

"Do you ever read anything but the sports pages, kid?" Rosen looked disgusted.

"The front page, when I get a chance."

"Yeah, well, the important news—if they print it at all— is usually buried on page eight or ten. Lower left-hand corner, where nobody will see it. State has to be working a deal with the East Germans and they don't want to upset the apple cart, get the GDR mad at them. Probably the ransom business for letting East Germans get across the Wall. Some of those people must be pretty important to the West Germans, so State wants to cool the atmosphere. Did you get what that SSD guy said about a senseless, *emotional* crime? Keep people's minds off a planned crime, that's for sure. And that they were keeping an eye on the situation in order to help the local authorities?"

"He's going to make sure the police don't find any political connection?"

"You're learning, kid," Rosen said approvingly, "Though I don't see how there can be any political connection."

"Well, Ragusic did most of his export-import with the Eastern Europeans. Could he have been involved in spying? Selling them our technology?"

"Anything is possible, but I never heard anything along those lines. On the other hand, sports is my beat, so I wouldn't know anyway." Rosen made another note in his little book, then got up. "I got to go now, call in. Don't want them to find out how slow I am getting a story in."

"I thought you already sent in your story, Irv."

"Wrote it, not sent. Have to make a few changes. Stick in a few subtle hints as to what might really be going on. Just in case I got a reader or two who looks at page eight once in a while." He took off, moving surprisingly fast for a man his age, through the now-empty press conference room.

Almost empty. At the door, Marc was blocked by Black Coat, the one who had been staring at him, and his equally hard-faced associate. "Mr. Burr," Black Coat said. It wasn't a question. "One moment, please." It didn't sound polite. The other black coat stepped out into the hall and returned a moment later with the UN press representative. "So nice to meet you, Mr. Burr," Pierre L'Oiseaux said. "As a fellow news reporter, former reporter, I must tell you I have admired your columns very much. I really must rush back, but I did want to exchange a few words with you."

"On the record?"

Pierre shrugged. "If you wish. I understand you are very close to the police officer in charge of the Gregor Ragusic case, no?"

"Well, not really close. I sometimes—as a good citizen—help him. The police."

"Excellent. I assume he realizes the importance of not providing incomplete information to the public? As you do?"

"Lieutenant Danzig is very careful not to provide information to anyone." *Especially me,* Marc thought. "Only to his superiors, when the case is closed."

"And you, Mr. Burr, surely you do not act irresponsibly either? Or write irresponsibly?"

"Me?" Marc tried to look as innocent as possible. "If I ever—accidentally, of course—gave my editor the slightest cause for concern, I'd be fired." Even without cause, if Witter had his way.

"I was certain I could count on you," Pierre L'Oiseaux smiled sweetly. "My superior will be having dinner tonight with Mr. Heisenberg, the owner of your estimable paper. I will ask him to be sure to inform Mr. Heisenberg, in detail, of the highly responsible people who are watching out for his interests, both professional and financial." He grabbed Marc's right hand, gave it a quick but warm shake, and left abruptly.

"Hey, wait a minute." Marc tried to follow, shouting, "What makes you think the East—"

Black Coat was in his way. Black Coat's partner closed the door to the corridor, leaving the three of them alone in the big room. Black Coat took one quick look around. No one there to see. He grabbed Marc by the coat front with both hands, pushed him back against the wall, and carefully placed his right knee in Marc's crotch. One quick jerk and Marc was pinned against the wall, a foot off the floor. Although Black Coat was clearly trying not to cause him *great* pain, Marc felt as though the top of his head were coming off.

"You understand?" Black Coat said. He had a vaguely foreign accent. "Everything?" Marc nodded, gritting his teeth. "Good," Black Coat said, and jerked his knee upward a bit. Marc jerked his head back in reflex, slamming it against the wall, sure that the top of his head had come off. Black Coat let him down gently, still holding him so he would not fall. "Just make sure you remember. . . ." Black Coat let go suddenly and Marc crumpled to the floor, still, unfortunately, fully conscious and still able to feel the pain.

When the agony in his head—no, groin—no, the head was worse—had subsided a little, Marc got to his hands and knees. The bastard had kneed him in such a way that there would be no evidence anything had happened. Slimy Pierre would swear he knew nothing about what had happened—could even take a lie detector test, because he didn't know any of the details. He would swear that his security people had left with him, and that he had merely told them he hoped Marc understood the importance of avoiding inflammatory, baseless conjectures and that his superior had excellent relations with the owner of the *Sentry*. The bastard.

Marc got up very slowly, dusted off his pants, and as slowly made his way out of the stadium. Just as he left the entrance, he saw fat Harriss Lamont Burnsides waiting at the curb as his official stretch limousine pulled up. As Burnsides moved aside to allow one of his men, Blue Coat, to open the door for him, he noticed Marc. "Ah, Mr. Burr," he purred, "how convenient. Which way are you going?"

"To my office," Marc said, moving to the curb so he could signal a taxi.

"Would you like a lift?" Burnsides offered.

Marc looked at Blue Coat suspiciously. "I think I'll take a taxi. Thanks anyway."

"As you wish." Burnsides ducked and entered the limousine.

As Marc started to move off, he félt another blue coat behind him—it had to be blue—forcing him forward. As soon as Marc got in front of the open car door, Blue Coat took over and push-kicked him inside, following up with a knee—carrying the full weight of the massive guard—in the small of his back.

"Mr. Burr changed his mind, sir," Blue Coat said. "He'd

like a lift to his office. But he tripped getting in." The limousine started moving smoothly.

"I'm very pleased, Mr. Burr," Burnsides said."I did want to talk to you. Will you help him up?" he asked the guard.

Blue Coat grabbed Marc's hair from behind and pulled, slowly, so as not to rip off the scalp, but with enough force to make Marc scream. "It's very crowded in the back here," Blue Coat apologized. "Maybe by the arms?" He grabbed both of Marc's wrists and, with his knee still in Marc's back, pulled backward. Marc felt as if his shoulders would tear open and his arms would come off. And his back break. He screamed again. Blue Coat let go. "Gee, sir, I don't know how to help him. He's very clumsy and uncooperative."

"Why don't you sit down," Burnsides said, in the corner, and I'll try." Blue Coat got up fast, giving Marc's back an extra kneeing in the process, and sat on the seat, digging his heels sharply into Marc's calves. Burnsides put out his hand to Marc, who grabbed it desperately. Slowly, inch by inch, struggling against the resistance of Blue Coat's feet, he lifted himself to the seat between the two men. "There now," Burnsides offered, "isn't that better? Always ready to help a fellow professional; just call on me. Anytime."

"Hurts," Marc said, drawing in a shuddering breath. "My head."

"From the fall?" Burnsides asked solicitously. "Or did anything happen inside before you came out? I was getting worried; it took you so long to come out."

"You were waiting for me?"

"Not per se; the traffic must have been very heavy. But I did notice . . . and I'm glad it took so long for the limousine to come. Gives us a chance to exchange views." He took a huge cigar out of a case and lit it slowly, making a big ceremony out of the process. "Mind if I smoke?" he asked, blowing a cloud of smoke into Marc's eyes. "No? Thanks." He took another long pull and said, "I understand, Burr, you have quite a reputation as an investigative reporter. Almost a detective, it seems. And that you have been looking into the inopportune demise of Gregor Ragusic quite diligently, although it happened only some nine hours ago."

"That's all?" Marc waved his hands in front of his face, trying to dissipate the clouds of smoke. "Seems like so much has happened." He tried to take his mind off his aching head, groin, shoulders, arms, scalp, back. It didn't work. Too many things to concentrate on at once, what with an aching head, back, scalp . . . enough. "How is it you were able to get here so quickly?"

"Oh, I was on my way up anyway, and sometimes they give my plane priority. An old friend asked me to drop by and talk to the press, so . . . I never forget an old friend. Always try to be helpful. To friends." A big smile spread across his fat face. "Friends should help each other, don't you think? I could help you, if you want to be friends. Give you some useful advice, if you want. Do you?"

"For the record?" Marc asked suspiciously.

"I never speak for the record, Marc. I am taping our little talk, however, just in case someone should misconstrue what I said." Burnsides looked out through the darkened windows of the limousine. "It's a lovely day, but we don't really have time to discuss the weather. I think it would be helpful to analyze the situation, helpful to you, make your job easier by eliminating some of the possible suspects."

"At this stage? I don't know enough; haven't even spoken to all—"

"It's really not necessary to speak to everyone in Brooklyn, you know. For example, it is certain that the crime was committed by an American, isn't it?"

Marc was acutely conscious of Blue Coat leaning on him

harder. Much harder than the closeness warranted. "Well, yes, I never considered that—"

"Good," Burnsides beamed through the thick cigar smoke. "That's the main point. As was mentioned earlier, this was clearly a crime of passion and couldn't possibly have any connection with international politics."

"Well, Ragusic was a major importer and exporter to the Warsaw Pact countries."

"Irrelevant, Burr. His interest at this time was concentrated on the World Cup Games. And he was killed in his soccer office just prior to the final game. Given that, it's obvious it was connected with his major interest, soccer."

"Well, still, maybe one of the other teams? The East—"

"Ridiculous. What could they possibly have to gain by it? No, no, not even worth discussing. The only question is, which American? Let's start by eliminating Mr. Grinell Hollingsworth's grandson, Cabot."

"Boni? But he's—"

"He isn't," Burnsides said flatly. "You couldn't possibly imagine that a Hollingsworth would stoop to . . . whatever you were about to say . . . I am sure you can persuade Lieutenant Danzig that he need not look in that direction."

"But the shoe—"

"Mr. Burr. My dear Marc. There is no evidence of any kind that could possibly connect Cabot to . . . none at all. You will see that Lieutenant Danzig understands that, won't you?"

Marc didn't answer. Blue Coat increased the pressure on Marc's shoulders. Then a little more. And a little more. It was getting hard to breathe. "Yes, sure," Marc gasped. "Is Grilho okay?"

"Grilho? Mrs. Kimberly *Hollingsworth* Vargas' husband? And a national hero, both here and in Brazil? I hardly think so, Marc. Don't you agree?"

175

"Oh, yes, sure." The pressure eased off somewhat. "How about Cuffy Royal? And José Velez?"

"Isn't Mr. Royal black? And a good family man with a perfectly clean record? And the only black player on the Booters? This would be an inappropriate time for a black of his stature to be accused, isn't that so? Or even suspected. And what possible motive could he have? As for Mr. Velez, he and his family are known to be anti-Castro, so he certainly is not of the caliber to do anything which might bring opprobrium upon the movement. No, I'm afraid you're barking up the wrong tree, Marc. Try another."

"Jason Benjamin?" By now, Marc would have offered up Julius Witter if he thought it would get him out of that car and away from Blue coat.

"Jewish, isn't he? Personally, I would like to have seen . . . however, lately we've been giving Israel a hard time so, at this particular point in time, it might be misunderstood if . . . surely, Marc, there is at least one suspicious character who had the motive, means, and opportunity, to speak technically?"

Marc cast about desperately, floundering. Finally, "How about Francisco Guzman? The kid who takes care of the shoes? He could have. He knows soccer and he could have worn . . . he's tall. And he came in early enough."

"Guzman?" Burnsides considered the name, puffing slowly, as though it had not occurred to him before. He made such a show of it that Marc was sure he had decided on Guzman before he had even entered the stadium. "Guzman? And you say he had the means, motive, and the opportunity?" Marc nodded. "Poor?" Marc nodded again. "Unaffiliated?" Marc nodded a third time. "Puerto Rican?" Marc nodded, and suddenly all pressure was removed from his back and shoulders. "He's not dark-skinned, is he?" Burnsides asked.

"No, no, very light."

"Family?"

"Single. About nineteen or twenty."

"A record?"

"I don't know. I think he's clean."

"No matter. John, here, has a photographic memory."

"Three juvenile arrests." Blue Coat's voice now had muscles showing. Flexed."Misdemeanors. One conviction. No time served. Plea bargained to parole on a first-conviction basis."

"Sounds like a prime suspect to me, wouldn't you say, Burr? Yes, I think it would be very helpful in closing this case if it turned out that Mr. Guzman was charged and arrested. Immediately after all the foreign teams left the country, of course; speed is important in capital cases. Avoids all sorts of rumors and wasted investigations. Of course, if he turned out to be wrongly accused, we would want him to be acquitted. Possibly with some recompense for his troubles." The limousine drew to a stop. "Well, Marc, I do believe we're here. Just in time. May I say what a pleasure it was talking to you; you seem to have such a quick grasp of foreign affairs. John will help you out."

"Don't bother," Marc said and started to get up.

John opened the door and got out. He took Marc firmly by the arm. Very firmly. "No trouble at all," he said.

# 19

"Why Marc," Julius Witter looked genuinely pleased. "How nice to see you again. It's been such a long time."

"I was here late Wednesday, Julius," Marc said sourly. "So I didn't come in Thursday; don't make a big deal of it. Sent in my stories, my column, everything. I was working."

"Why yes, so you were. If you can call that working. And you did send in some stories, true. As you are paid to do. Overpaid, so don't expect any gold stars for that. But you did allow yourself to be scooped by a rank amateur. On the most important story of the month. Which you had in your control. The *Sentry* could have been on the streets with an exclusive a half hour earlier if it hadn't been for your pusillanimous refusal to perform your normal, simple duties." He took out his pipe. "Such as calling your editor at once."

"Please, Julius," Marc begged. "Not today. I've just come from being locked in a car with a bad cigar, a *big*, bad cigar. I've been beaten up twice and threatened and I've just about had it. You know why I didn't call you from Ragusic's office; it was to save myself—and you—from being harassed by Danzig. And I did call you, remember? From Borough Hall. And you deliberately sent me back to Danzig to put my neck on the block."

"That isn't very chivalrous of you, Marc. Would you rather have left Dahliah to the tender mercies of Lieutenant Danzig? I didn't force you, you may recall; I even suggested you could go to New Jersey. It was you who decided to go back to Danzig and confess voluntarily. How much time did he give you?" he asked casually. "Just as a matter of interest, you understand. And efficiency. So I'll know when to have the obit ready. I'll write it myself, make it very flattering; leave out all the trouble you've caused. After all, *de mortuis, nil nisi bonum*, don't you agree?"

"You set it up so that . . . are you the one who told everybody I was working on the case? As a detective? For Danzig?"

"Some people did ask, but I never said you were a detective. I told them you were our ace investigative reporter—a forgivable exaggeration—for sports matters and had the confidence of Lieutenant Danzig. Haven't you been imploring, begging me, for years, to allow you to do investigative reporting? Well, now I'm not only allowing you, I'm officially *encouraging* you. Some gratefulness would have been in order, but this younger generation. . . ." He sighed loudly. Falsely.

"It was your telling them that, that got me beaten up, Julius. And threatened with worse."

"Excellent, Marc; shows we're getting someplace." He reached for the intercom. "I'll get a photographer on it right away." He looked Marc over carefully. "You don't look beaten up, but we have some film now that will pick up deep bruises before they fully develop. Very contrasty. We can touch you up with a little makeup if the marks aren't clear enough. Or if you're a stickler for accuracy in the media, I can get a couple of boys from distribution to work you over—in the sensitive places only; won't take long—and we'll have a strong editorial as well as a good story. We haven't had a good case of police brutality for months. You did have the presence of mind to record the names of witnesses and the shield numbers, didn't you?"

"Forget it; nothing will show. These guys were experts."

"Don't tell me our police have caught up with the rest of the world and hired specialists in obtaining confessions? Wonderful. You can write the story yourself. *'Sentry Reporter Brutally Beaten by Torture Squad.'* With a by-line. Should make you very popular with Danzig."

"It wasn't the police; it was the UN and the State Department."

"Even if I believed that ridiculous story—which I don't—you know that Mr. Heisenberg doesn't like criticism of his two favorite institutions. Now let's get on with the important news. How much time did Danzig give you? Sunday night?"

"Six o'clock."

"Lieutenant Danzig is so predictable. And yet, somehow he does accomplish what he sets out to do. Which is to get *somebody* arrested. Have you come to any conclusion yet? Know who did it? I don't mean grand jury evidence; just your *feel*."

"Not the slightest idea. The State Department would be very happy if it was the kid who takes care of the shoes. But they want me to solve the case, that is, to frame Frankie Guzman, only after everybody goes home."

"Understandable. Let me think." Witter sucked on the unlit pipe for a moment, then said, "To fulfill both requirements, Danzig's and State's, we could let Danzig arrest you and we—our lawyers—would not get you out on bail till Monday. By then, all the players will be gone, and you can come out and frame whomever you have to frame. It will make a good story too; an inside story—what it feels like to be jailed with murderers, muggers, and drug addicts. By-line, of course."

"I don't want to go to jail, Julius; especially not the way Danzig is going to arrange it. And I don't want to frame anybody. Besides, Danzig isn't going to send only me to jail this time; he's going to send Dahliah, too."

"We can't let him do that; I *like* Dahliah. Does her job, more than her job. She'll be a big asset to Nelda Shaver's page someday. No, Marc, my boy. The way I see it, your only hope is to confess."

"I already confessed. Danzig would rather have Dahliah."

"No, no, you don't understand, Marc. I mean confess to the murder. A brilliant solution to the problem, if I do say so myself. We'll put your confession on the front page; a real exclusive. My by-line, of course. You understand."

"You're against me, too, Julius."

"Naturally, but only professionally and personally, and you are in no danger of physical harm from me. Directly. What did the others threaten to do to you? State, the UN, and Danzig?"

"They weren't specific, but what they did while they were explaining things to me was enough."

"You realize that you have only tomorrow to complete your investigation? Sunday you're going to do the play-by-play of the big game and I doubt that Grilho will let you even see his players Sunday morning, much less talk to them."

"Thanks for explaining my problems to me, Julius. I wouldn't have known without your brilliant analysis."

"It always helps to have a disinterested observer put things in proper perspective. If you won't confess to the murder yourself, there is an alternative." He studied Marc calculatingly. "Do you think you can frame Frankie Guzman in only one day? It's a very short time for a truly inept investigator. And you will still have to send in your regular stories. Which reminds me: You haven't sent in a word about the East German Team."

"I offered to go to the Meadowlands this morning."

"Shirking your responsibilities doesn't count, but I did nothing to prevent you from running away, if you recall. I want a color story and a news story on the GDR team early tomorrow morning for the Sports Final."

Marc remembered his date for breakfast with Danzig. "I'll be there early, but this will kill my interviews with Grilho and Benjamin before practice tomorrow."

"I am not the least bit interested in how you do your work; just get the stories in on time. And I will not approve taxi fare to New Jersey; your pathological fear of trains is not the responsibility of the *Sentry*."

"I have no problem with the PATH train; it's the subway that's scary. But I'll have to take a taxi from the PATH station to the stadium."

"From where you live, you can take a bus to the PATH terminal. One local trip to work, and one from work, is your responsibility. I will approve a round-trip PATH fare and a taxi to the stadium." Marc felt it best not to mention that he would be going to New Jersey from south Brooklyn where, according to Danzig, the best diner in Brooklyn was located. Another big bite out of his income, but better than explaining to Witter, who would no doubt tell everyone—publish—that Marc would soon expose the murderer, envisioning big headlines proclaiming the murder of the *Sentry*'s ace investigative reporter.

"I'm also," Witter continued, "going to put out a special World Cup edition for early Saturday evening, for which I'll need more color stories, and I want a long column, a thousand words, analyzing the comparative strengths of both teams for the Sunday Sports Section. Clear?" Marc nodded. Witter stared at him judiciously. "Will Lieutenant Danzig accept your clumsy attempts at implicating a presumably innocent young man? Or will he see through your scheme and arrest you for obstructing justice? He's not completely stupid, you know."

"I'm not going to frame anyone," Marc muttered.

"If that's your attitude, I'll get to work at once and prepare for a special edition for Sunday night, with big headlines accusing the police of harassing the press and violating the First Amendment. Given their natural response, I can make the story last for three days." He smiled benevolently at Marc. "I want you to know, my boy, that I accept your sacrifice as an expiation—a *partial* expiation—for your not calling me directly from Ragusic's office. And in return, I will use all the *Sentry*'s power and legal staff to ensure that when Dahliah is arrested, too, she will not be put in with the common prostitutes and drug addicts."

Marc's scalp was still hurting when he left Witter's office, so he didn't slam the door.

# 20

Although the bus home from the office took longer, Marc, like many New Yorkers, never took the subway. It was prudent to take taxis during working hours, even though some of the cost was not reimbursed by the paper. For going home at night, the bus made sense. It also let him off one block nearer to the loft building where he and Dahliah lived. And it was safe. For the first half block off the avenue, there was sufficient light and activity to keep the mugging rate very low. After that, the area turned completely industrial, and the streets were deserted. A mugger could starve to death there, so except for an occasional wino who got lost, there were no real problems. Even so, Marc didn't like Dahliah walking there alone at night, and the few times she had a late meeting or a special event at the school, he tried to get her to take taxis directly to the door. Dahliah took this as a personal insult from an insecure male, pointing out that she was an accomplished student of karate, had served in the Israeli Army for two years, and could lick Marc with one hand tied behind her back anytime he wanted to try. He could not persuade her that there was a difference between tussling on a gym mat with a man who loved her and fighting three muggers with knives who wanted her bag. And since she was such an attractive woman, rape was not inconceivable, either. If she struggled, she might end up . . .

He didn't want to think about it. As usual, he was walking along the curb. Who knew what evil lurked in the dark doorways of the loft buildings that lined the street. He looked ahead and tried to move with confidence to signal to a possible predator that he would not be easy prey.

So although Marc heard the car pull up behind him, it didn't really register until he felt the heavy plastic go around his face, pulling his head back hard, and the knee in his back forcing him to the ground. The wind knocked out of him, he tried to draw a breath, but his nose and mouth were completely covered. The man on his back was heavy and kept pulling his head back as far as it would go, trying to get it back even farther, farther, and he couldn't breathe and he couldn't move and the lights were exploding and he was getting dizzy and then it was dark.

---

"Are you all right, Mr. Burr?" Karl Jaeger asked. The SSD officer was now dressed in a uniform that looked more like a general's than a spy's, but his slightly accented voice sounded, to Marc, like the voice of angels. His smooth, angular face looked down on Marc, sprawled on the backseat of the limousine, with what appeared to be concern. On the other hand, Brown Coat, the same ugly Brown Coat who had been staring at Marc during the press conference that afternoon, was looking down on him from the front seat of the car with a smile that clearly told Marc who had almost killed him. "Will you check your wallet, please, Mr. Burr," Jaeger continued. "I think we frightened off your assailant in time, but I am not certain."

Marc drew another deep breath and struggled up on the seat, leaning his head against the back and filling his lungs deliciously. A few more breaths and he was able to speak. "I'm sure it's all right, thank you." If they let him live, they wouldn't bother stealing his few dollars. And why all this knees-in-the-back stuff? Did they all go to the same school? He'd be walking bent over for a week, if he didn't already have some ruptured discs. No, these were professionals; they'd leave nothing that would show Marc had ever been attacked. "It was very fortunate you were here, sir, at just this time." He tried to make it sound nonsarcastic.

"Yes, very, but it was no accident. I wanted to talk to you and when we saw an innocent citizen being attacked, we rushed to the rescue. Unfortunately, the perpetrator got away." Jaeger clucked regretfully. "Imagine my surprise when I saw it was you."

"Yes, imagine. Well, I live just down the block; you can let me off here."

"No, no, we will escort you to your door. I insist." It sounded very polite and considerate. Brown Coat looked as though he would be pleased if Marc disagreed. "And while you are regaining your composure, let us talk for a moment." Jaeger thought for a moment, trying to choose the exact words to use. "It is my understanding that you are very close friends with the lieutenant in charge of the Ragusic case. Is that not so?"

"Not friends. No."

"But you have worked together successfully? Twice?"

Marc knew what was coming and tried to forestall it.

"Only in the sense that, as a reporter, I came across certain information which was useful to the police. Accidentally came across it. In the course of my normal work. As a sports reporter. Which is my job."

"You are being overly modest, Mr. Burr." Jaeger sounded almost jovial. Almost."My sources tell me that you were the brilliant detective who actually solved the case and gave Lieutenant Danzig the credit. Very astute of you. So that he would be obligated to you. It is always a good idea to have the authorities in your debt. And conversely, it is always a bad idea—a very bad idea—to have powerful security authorities working against you." A thought seemed to strike him. "Is it possible that this assailant we chased off was not an ordinary robber, but the agent of some organization who wished to do you harm? In which case, we might have, fortunately, saved your life. And if that is the case, is it not possible that he— after killing you—would have made his way to 'just down the block' as you put it, and harmed Miss Norman?"

"It's not possible. Definitely not. I always cooperate with the police. And," he added as an important after-thought, "with all authorized security agencies. Organi-zations. Whatever."

"It is a great pleasure, I assure you, Mr. Burr, to deal with such a public-spirited citizen. While my little organi-zation is not strictly a police department, it does have some of the functions of the police, as well as the functions of your FBI and your dread CIA. Would you consider giving me a bit of cooperation, too? I did make the promise, at the press conference this afternoon, that I would assist the—how do you say it?"

"The duly constituted authorities?"

"Yes, exactly, I do love to practice speaking English. Such a rich language. So in order to assist the duly constituted authorities, I would appreciate your help." He checked his watch. "Unfortunately, I do not have the time to have a *lengthy* conversation with you concerning all my responsibilities, so we will discuss only the Ragusic case. For now. According to my sources, this day you have spoken about the murder, in order, to Lieutenant Danzig, Miss Norman, Cabot Vargas, Francisco Guzman, Commissioner Vanderhook, Miss Norman again, Guzman again, Cuffy Royal, José Velez, and Mr. Witter. Is that correct?"

"Very. And very complete."

"Yes, of course. My sources do not wish to give me incomplete information. And they *never* give me inaccurate information. Never. Now, it seems to me that you have been concentrating on people from Ragusic's team, the Booters. Why is that?"

"It seems to me that the murder had to come out of Ragusic's relationship with people who knew him in his capacity as owner of the Booters, rather than from his foreign—that is, his business—relationships outside of soccer."

"Excellent. You do remember that in my little talk, I mentioned that this was a crime of passion. It is obvious to me—and I have had a great deal of experience with murder—" *that* Marc was sure of, "—that this crime was directly concerned with soccer, and not just soccer, with the Booters. So it was puzzling to me why you did not interrogate—interview—the other two members of the team who were involved."

"Grilho and Benjamin? I was very busy. I think I did a hell of a lot for one day."

"But you will interview them tomorrow, will you not?"

"Oh, sure, as soon as I get a chance."

"A good investigator makes his chances, don't you agree?"

"Oh, sure. Definitely."

"Good." Jaeger seemed to have come to a decision. "Originally, before I knew how astute you were, I thought it might take some time to arrest the murderer. I assumed that this would happen several days after the final game, so that the GDR Team, and I, would be gone when it was finally determined that there was no possible connection between the murder and international events. However, if the murderer were still at large by the time of the final game, there might be—you do understand crowd psychology, do you not?—a tendency on the part of the spectators to transfer the blame for the crime to the GDR Team and even to attempt to influence the referee to act in an improper manner. This would be unsportsmanlike, and conceivably could even be harmful to current events. Don't you agree?"

"Oh, yes, sure. Very unsportsmanlike."

"So you will have Lieutenant Danzig arrest the murderer *before* the game."

"But I don't know who . . . I haven't even spoken to Grilho and Benjamin."

"You did say you would interrogate them early tomorrow. You will then know who the murderer is and you will give the evidence to Lieutenant Danzig and urge him to arrest the criminal."

"Danzig doesn't do—doesn't always listen to me."

"Make him. The press is very powerful here in the United States. He won't dare oppose you. In fact, when you give him the evidence, he will be very grateful."

"What evidence? I don't have the slightest—"

Jaeger sighed. "You are just upset from the . . . mugging. I will give you the benefit of my experience. I have found that it is useful to know who the criminal is. Intuitively, one knows. You then arrest him, interrogate him vigorously, and find the evidence that shows that person is the criminal. Simple and quick, don't you agree? Now, think. This is a very tricky crime, is it not?" Marc nodded. "Based on emotions, no?" Marc nodded again. "Derived from soccer and the Booters, correct?" Marc knew when to nod. "So, who is the most intelligent player on the World Cup Team, who is also a Booter, and is a member of a highly emotional race?"

"Jason Benjamin?"

"You see? I knew you could do it if you analyzed it properly."

"Isn't he also the one who is most likely to prevent a lot of goals by the GDR Team?"

"I hadn't really thought of it that way," Jaeger mused, "but I do believe you are right. However, we shouldn't let nationalism stand in the way of justice, should we?"

"Oh, no, never. Absolutely not. 'Let justice be done, though the heavens fall.' You can count on me."

Jaeger stared hard at Marc for a moment, then relaxed. "Yes, I do believe I can. Before the game starts, remember." He signaled the driver and the limousine pulled up in front of Marc's loft building. "Please transmit my highest regards to Miss Norman," Jaeger said. "Metzger will escort you to the door."

"Don't bother," Marc said. "I can do it myself."

"It's really no bother," Jaeger said. "We'll do it my way."

# 21

"Y ou're late," Dahliah said as Marc wearily closed the elevator door. "I made a special super supper to celebrate our working together, so do your exercise fast and sit down. I laid out your sweat suit."

"I think I'll skip the exercise and just take a hot shower," he said. His neck, where Brown Coat had pulled his head back, was now beginning to hurt more than his back.

"Not even stretching? No hanging?" Dahliah hurried over to him, her face worried. "What's wrong?"

Marc sat down slowly on the living-area couch, kicked his shoes off, and eased himself down flat. "You won't believe this, but I was just beaten up three times. Three separate gangs."

Dahliah paled and put her hand to her mouth. "On our block? How bad is it? Where?"

"All over the place. Once on our block, once on the way to the office, and once in the stadium. And it's not any one place; it's all over: groin, head, neck, scalp, arms, back. Twice in the back. I think they missed my left pinky."

"Nothing broken? Serious?"

"They were very considerate; not a single mark."

"I'm going to call the police."

"And tell them about the UN, the State Department, and the German secret police?"

"The UN? I don't believe the UN . . . but it's a peace-keeping organization."

"Yeah, sure. Notice all the peace we've been having lately? No, don't bother calling the police. There were no witnesses, there's no evidence, and they'll all claim diplomatic immunity anyway, so what's the use. After that, when they have time, they'll do something really bad to me." *And to you, Dahliah,* Marc thought, *which is the main reason I'll do anything they say.* When you love, you give a hostage to fortune.

"Do you want a massage?" Dahliah asked.

"Anytime, but I'd better take that hot shower first."

"You're getting back to normal," she said, sounding relieved. "I made a carob soufflé and I'm putting it in the oven in exactly ten minutes, so don't spend too long in the shower. And no talking business until later; I want to have a relaxing supper."

---

Marc pushed away the bowl contentedly. For therapeutic reasons, Dahliah had allowed him a second helping of the carob soufflé; happy people don't get sick, was one of her precepts. Carob wasn't quite chocolate, but it wasn't bad, either. Chocolate contains theobromine, Dahliah had told him, one of the xanthines and a powerful stimulant. Not as bad as caffeine or tea's theophylline, but to be avoided. The only good stimulation must come from within, from the joy of living and from a oneness with the universe. She was right, of course, but Marc saw no reason he could not enjoy chocolate and still be one with the universe.

"Now we can analyze the case," Dahliah said, putting a yellow legal pad on the table as Marc cleaned away the dishes. "I'll list everybody in the order we saw them. Grilho, Boni—"

"No," Marc said. "Don't put Grilho down. We saw him, but only before the murder. We haven't spoken to him about the murder yet."

"Okay." She crossed out the top name. "Boni, the boy who takes care of the shoes—"

"Frankie."

"Yes, him. Mr. Vanderhook. Cuffy Royal. José Velez." She drew vertical lines on the sheet. "Motive. Means. Opportunity. That's what my students all tell me."

"I think it would be better if you listed them in the order they came to the stadium. According to what Security says." Dahliah tore off the first sheet and drew another diagram. "First in was Gregor Ragusic. About six-thirty. Then Frankie Guzman, Boni, Grilho, and the Commissioner." He didn't feel like saying Steve's name to Dahliah. Foolish. What difference could that make? "Then Jason Benjamin, Cuffy Royal, and José Velez."

"All of them came before you found Ragusic?"

"Oh, yes, well before. In plenty of time to—"

"Could anyone have sneaked into the stadium without Security knowing? And sneaked out again and come in later through the gate?"

"I'm sure it could've been done, but what for? If anyone tried it and was seen, it would automatically mark him as the murderer. I mean, why bother? It's very easy to run upstairs and into Ragusic's office. The whole thing could take two minutes. Less."

"So any one of them had the time, the opportunity, to

go into Ragusic's office?" Dahliah made a series of checks down the "Opportunity" column. "And kill him?"

"Sure, but the problem is, assuming it wasn't Boni who did it, how did one of them get hold of Boni's shoes? Frankie said he always locks the equipment-room door when he goes out. And what about fit?"

"You can always stuff a shoe with paper to make it sort of fit and Boni—he's tall enough so that any of the others could fit into his shoes. We didn't ask Boni if he had one pair or two pairs in his locker that morning, so maybe the shoes were taken out of his locker instead of the equipment room. And where is the other shoe? The left shoe? Boni didn't mention that there were any shoes missing from his locker. If he didn't do it, and a shoe was missing, he would have mentioned it. I'm not crossing anybody off the list yet."

"I'll ask Danzig tomorrow morning," Marc said. "But if Boni didn't do it, then Grilho didn't do it, either. I can't see him getting his son in trouble. He'd die himself, first."

"You like Boni and you can't imagine him killing Ragusic. And Grilho, too. If you're investigating honestly, you can't let personal considerations affect your judgment. And you're assuming two things, Marc, that may not be true. First, that it was done with Boni's shoes and second, that you can tell whose shoe did it. If Grilho's feet are wide and Boni's feet are narrow, it's probable that the studs are the same in both shoes. And the width of the soles. Certainly they must be close enough that you can't tell such minor differences from a crushed skull."

"The studs are the same for all shoes, but as for the width of the heels, that's another thing I have to ask Danzig. Also if they've matched the wound with Boni's shoes. You know, it wouldn't have been hard for someone to get a pair of shoes like Boni's and bring them in, using a small bag, say, just for that purpose. To frame Boni."

"Which means it was planned a long time ago. As long

as we have to wait to get more information on the shoes, let's follow up that question. Motive for killing Ragusic. Without talking to Benjamin and Grilho yet, I'm sure they all had good motives." She made another vertical set of checks in the "Motive" column. "But who would have a motive to frame Boni?"

"Cuffy Royal and José Velez are jealous that the striker gets the big money and the flanking forwards get peanuts, comparatively, but I don't see that as a motive to frame somebody for murder. Everybody loves Boni."

"Somebody doesn't. His shoes are distinctive; the murderer didn't pick them by accident."

"Yeah, I guess you're right. And we don't have to bother about means; Danzig told me how Ragusic was killed. So where does that leave us? All our suspects are still our suspects."

"Not Steve," Dahliah said.

First-name basis already? Even if it was just in her mind, Marc couldn't help feeling a twinge of jealousy. "Look, we still have two more interviews tomorrow. More, if we learn something that contradicts what one of the others told us. I'll meet you at the stadium at eleven."

"Meet?" Dahliah looked puzzled. "Why so late when we have so little time? And why not go together?"

"I have to have breakfast with Danzig tomorrow at eight and practice won't be over till eleven."

"You'd rather have breakfast with him than with me?"

Marc squirmed. "Not rather. Must. He's ready, willing, and able to put me in jail." *And you, too, darling, but I don't want to worry you.*

"It's not the end of the world if you don't solve the crime," she said soothingly. "He can't put you in jail for that. After all, you're not a policeman."

*No,* Marc thought. *I'm worse off; I can't even resign.* Danzig wanted him to make sure either Royal or Velez was the killer. L'Oiseaux wanted to make sure no one who had any international connections was found to be the murderer. Which, in the case of the World Cup Games, meant that the murderer must not be found, or else had to be a derelict named John Doe. Burnsides wanted Marc to frame Frankie Guzman. Witter wanted Marc to confess he was the murderer, hinting that if he did not, Witter would turn Dahliah over to the police. Worse, to Danzig. Jaeger, the SSD officer, probably the most dangerous of the lot, wanted Marc to provide the evidence so that Benjamin would be convicted. All before 6:00 P.M. Sunday.

"I've got a headache," Marc said. "I need a vacation. While I'm with Danzig tomorrow morning," lulling the bastard's suspicions, "why don't you go to a travel agency and get us two tickets to Tahiti?"

"I can't do that, darling; I've got responsibilities. But it's a lovely thought; we'll go during the winter intersession." She softened. "I'm sorry your head hurts. Come to bed now and I'll make everything nice."

"Can't," Marc said. "That hurts, too."

# 22

"I got here early," Danzig was at his usual corner table near the window of the diner,"so I ordered for you. Knowing you don't know what's good here yet, even though you been here twice already."

"But I. . . ." Waste of breath, with Danzig. Marc gingerly took the seat opposite—his back and neck still hurt—and groaned.

"What're you complaining about? I ordered the best of the best for you, in the best diner in Brooklyn. Real fresh-squeezed grapefruit juice, melted cheese—real Gruyère from Switzerland, browned, not the regular Swiss cheese—with real Dijon mustard on top over real Jewish rye with lots of seeds. A double order. Too much for you, I'll help you finish it. Skim milk and their special cherry cheesecake, a big piece. And a prune Danish."

"I can't eat all that much. And you know I hate prune Danish."

Danzig looked puzzled. "You hate it? Then why do you let me order it for you all the time? Okay, don't worry, I'll have the girl wrap it up and I'll take it for later. I'll tell her to bring you an extra cherry cheesecake instead. You know what I'm having? Plain lake sturgeon plate with Vidalia onions. That's all. On account of I'm not so hungry today. With Jaffa orange juice, fresh squeezed, and poppy-seed bagels, toasted, with butter. And coffee; they now got Jamaica Blue Mountain. You want a taste? Make you change your mind about coffee. You could also have a little taste of my seven-layer chocolate cake. They make it special here."

"Do we have to meet here all the time?" Marc asked. "I don't get reimbursed for this and it's very expensive."

"You want to eat in a *cheap* diner?" Danzig was truly astounded. "You could get ptomained in a cheap place. And you wouldn't enjoy it, so even cheap, it would be wasted money. Besides, even if you don't know how to bury a legit expense in your expense account, figure what it would cost you to get a lawyer and a bail bondsman and the hospital bills and the clothes—some of these guys would kill for a nice suit like you got there—and that's only the beginning. Actually, you're way ahead of the game, the way I see it." The waitress began putting the dishes on the table. "Okay, no more business talk till we're finished. Enjoy."

---

Marc didn't enjoy. He did like the food, but he was able to eat only half of one portion of the melted cheese dish and a forkful of the cherry cheesecake. Dahliah would kill him if he told her he had even looked at that much sugar, so he wouldn't tell her. But the bill, including the taxis he'd have to take both ways, came to enough to feed him and Dahliah for a week. After the waitress had cleared the table and placed a big bag of take-home goodies in front of Danzig, the detective loosened his belt and spoke."Okay, who did it?"

"Have a heart, Danzig; I just started. I didn't even interview Grilho or Benjamin yet."

"Why do you always make things complicated, Burr? Didn't I tell you who done it? Either the black or the PR, right? Didn't I tell you that? Don't you ever listen?"

"Cuban," Marc corrected automatically. "Cuban-American. But you want evidence. I have to talk to them all, don't I?"

"Not evidence like I need for the DA, Burr." Danzig explained, trying to be patient. "Just enough so I can take him downtown and sweat him. You tell me who, I'll get the rest out of him. After the confession, then it's just routine."

"I don't have anything yet. Honest. I have to question them all first, see if there are any discrepancies in what they tell me."

"You're too soft, Burr; that's the trouble with you amateurs. You got a murderer, a killer, you can't treat him like he was a regular human being. You got to put on the pressure till he cracks. Ask tough questions. Make like you know it's him."

"Yeah, so the murderer will try to kill me."

"Now you got it. That's how we get the proof. Why? You worried?"

"Me, worry? Damn right."

"Hey, didn't I protect you good the last two times?"

"You almost killed me."

"Almost don't count. Didn't I save your life? Don't you owe me? Forget what I'm gonna do to you if you screw up; just remember you owe me. It's like honorable, right? You're very big on honor, ain't you, if I remember correctly?"

"Yeah, then where were you when I got beaten up yesterday? Three times."

"He beat you up?" Danzig smiled. "That's great. Why didn't you tell me? Who done it?"

"Why didn't you protect me? Have somebody watching me?"

"Hey, you know how shorthanded the force is; I bet you're probably one of those guys always complaining about taxes. If you told me you was closing in, I would've protected you myself. Which one done it? I bet it was the PR; he got that too-innocent look. And a moustache. Half the guys I take in, they got moustaches. Or beards."

"It was the UN, the State Department, and the East German Secret Police."

"What're you fooling around with them guys for; you know I can't use them. Five minutes after I take one of them in, with the smoking gun right in his hand, the Captain gets a call from Washington and the perpetrator walks. Before I even *start* writing out the report. For Pete's sake, Burr, use your head, will you? Don't waste no time on politicians; go after the two guys I told you." He shook his head in wonder about the stubbornness of amateurs who just wouldn't listen. "Okay, look, we got very little time to waste fooling around. What did you find out about the suspects?"

"Well, all the suspects had the means, the opportunity, and I'm sure, the motive."

"Not *all*, Burr," Danzig sounded weary. "Just the two. Whatsisname and the other guy."

"Cuffy Royal and José Velez?"

"Yeah, them."

"They both had the time and they were both, as far as I could tell, out of sight of any witnesses for several minutes. They're both soccer players and they both—everybody, in fact, as I see it—hated Ragusic. The problem is . . . tell me something; did Boni's shoe match the wound?"

"Yeah, only trouble is, the technical boys tell me almost any shoe of that kind could have done it. There ain't all that much difference in the heels or the cleats, and the victim's head was crushed good. This Royal, he looks tough. He also got strong legs? Real powerful?"

"All soccer players have powerful legs, even skinny ones like Velez. Any one of them could take your head off. Have you found the shoe yet? The one that did it?"

"I got the report a pair's missing from the equipment room. One of the big blond kid's. Vargas. The young one. He says he had both regular pairs in his locker, the ones he's supposed to have. According to the tech boys, it could've easy been them. Him."

"But you're not sure?"

"I told you, the victim's head was smashed in, but good. They can't make a positive identification that'd stand up against a good lawyer. If we had the original shoes . . . They're probably at the bottom of the bay by now. If you had called me right away, we maybe could've found them with the blood on them and everything. Which is another thing I got against you."

"If a pair of Boni's shoes are missing, the killer's shoes weren't brought in from the outside. They had to have been stolen from the equipment room. But that brings up another problem, assuming Boni didn't do it."

"Hey, you trying to make trouble for me? I already told you he didn't do it; I don't want to arrest a rich kid with pull. I told you who it gotta be, didn't I?"

"Well, if Boni didn't do it, how did the killer get Boni's shoes? Frankie told me he always locks the door whenever he leaves."

"Frankie? Who the hell's Frankie? You never mentioned no Frankie to me before."

"Francisco Guzman. He takes care of the equipment."

"The PR?" Danzig's whole manner picked up. "The shoe kid?"

"I believe he's of Puerto Rican descent."

"Okay, the case is solved. He gave the shoes to the other PR. They all stick together, don't they? I'm gonna pick him up and sweat him a little; give him a chance to turn in the other one. Tell him if he didn't know that the other guy was gonna kill the victim, he's in the clear. Almost. Maybe he even made a mistake; gave the other one the wrong shoes, right?"

"Frankie didn't do it, I'm sure. And Puerto Ricans aren't Cubans." Marc was desperate, even though Harriss Burnsides wanted Marc to make sure Frankie hung for the murder. "Velez is intelligent, street smart. If he were going to kill Ragusic, to take Boni's shoes to kill Ragusic, he'd never depend on a kid like Frankie to protect him."

Danzig frowned. "Yeah, maybe you're right. Still . . . okay, I'll do you a favor; I'll lay off the PR kid. Till six o'clock Sunday. But you better have it settled by then. Otherwise, you and the PR are gonna be in the same cell with the animals. And that's another one you owe me."

"Owe you? You get me killed and there's no way you can collect."

"Maybe I don't collect, but it'll still cost you."

"You said you'd protect me. Now you talk like you *want* me to get killed."

"Did I say that? I don't want you to *get* killed; you're an important witness. What I want is the perpetrator should *try* to kill you, with me watching. Then I can take him in and sweat him good about the Ragusic case."

"Does that mean you're going to be watching over me?"

"Absolutely, whenever I got the time." He took his take-home bag and stood up to go. "Okay, meet you here tomorrow morning. Same time."

"Sunday? I can't. That's the day of the big game. I have to do a play-by-play. A lot of preparation. And maybe, if

I can find the time, talk to some of the suspects—yes, yes, I know: the *two* suspects—some more. No way."

"Okay, I'll let you get away with it this time. That's another one you owe me. Leave a good tip for the waitress; I don't want her to think I'm cheap."

# 23

The big red-jerseyed team wasn't as monstrous, or as rigid, as Gregor Ragusic had mimed for Marc Thursday morning, twenty-four hours before he had been killed, but they still looked very, very tough, practically invincible. As Ragusic had predicted, the East German first team was playing a blue-shirted team that, from a distance, could have been the United States first team, or rather, what was now the first team. A broad-shouldered black was the left winger and a slim Hispanic was the right, with a big John Geis type and a short, long-haired twin of Ted Pangos as center forwards in a 4-2-4 formation. The goalkeeper was as tall as Jason Benjamin and as skinny. Where did they get them all, Marc wondered, and how did they play as a team on such short notice? Could the GDR have kept two teams in reserve, to practice against, regardless of whether the Bulgarians or the Americans had won the semi-final game? With a regime that treated sports as yet another political weapon, that was the most likely explanation. Marc recalled how the U.S. Olympic Committee had to go hat in hand, begging, for the minimal funds needed to train its athletes, and how the Olympics were once described as "their professionals against our high school kids." He was determined, when the next Olympics came around, to write several strong columns, a whole campaign, against the phony amateurism some other countries got away with and to push for pitting the best athletes in each sport, regardless of professional status, against each other.

"If you are here to spy," a heavily accented German voice said behind him, "you are quite welcome." Marc turned around to see Heinz Grob, the fat, blond, good-natured Head Coach of the GDR Team approaching, accompanied by a short, slim, elderly man wearing a goatee and wire-rimmed glasses.

"Hello, Mr. Grob," Marc said. "The only spying I do is for my readers. And I doubt they'll understand the fine points of the game, I'm sorry to say."

"The Security Service is instructed to only allow someone in who doesn't look like a criminal. So how is it they permit you inside, Mr. Burr?" He chuckled at this. "Just a *Witz*, Burr. A joke, no?"

"Yes, very funny. But if you don't want me out here, watching—my editor wants me to interview you—we can go inside to talk. Can we do it now, please? I have to be back in Brooklyn by eleven. Meet someone."

"Here is okay. But I would be happy, happier, if you would tell your paper to stop making the talk that we want, like, that Gregor Ragusic was killed and that the SSD had something to do with it. It is very humiliating to my players and it is making them nervous. If this is a way to make them play poor soccer, it will not work. They are well disciplined, but still, to make them think that the CIA will kidnap and torture them over this, it is not nice to do."

"Unfortunately, I don't own the paper, Mr. Grob, but if it'll help, I'll tell my editor to ask the editorial board to tone down the editorials. You must have the same problem, in reverse, in your country, don't you?"

"No, at home there is more control by the people of what is said, so only stories about criminals that are true are allowed to be printed."

"Yes, well . . . I don't know much about politics; I came to interview you about sports. It's okay if I watch how you practice and ask questions about tomorrow's game?"

"Ja, sure, go ahead. Ask. Everybody has films, tapes, of the way we play, the way every team plays, so by now they all know what we have done, even Grilho, so what it matters, eh? Nobody can change their system in time. Besides, our order of battle is undestroyable, thanks to our master theoretician. Allow me to introduce you." He turned to the elderly man at his side. "It is my pleasure, Herr Doktor, to introduce to you Mr. Marcus Burr, a famous newspaper reporter and writer of columns. And this gentleman, Marcus, is the famous Herr Dr. Professor Reinhold Ziegler, who has studied the sport of soccer very intensively and has finally combined the theory of the blitzkrieg with the Marxist-Leninist socialist philosophy by means of the dialectical materialism. For soccer."

"I'm honored to meet you, Professor," Marc said. "May I quote whatever you tell me?"

"Oh, yes, certainly." Dr. Ziegler said. "It will no longer be a secret after tomorrow when two billion people watch the game. Also, I will be publishing my theories and," with a small nod to Grob, "the way they have been excellently put into practice, very soon in the professional journals, and after that, it is possible, in a popular book. Which will revolutionize the game."

"Won't that take away from the advantage you now have? The GDR Team, I mean?"

"Not possible, Mr. Burr," Dr. Ziegler shook his head emphatically. "Even if they know, they cannot practice the principles. Only athletes brought up in a socialist environment, with the proper mental attitudes as part of them, the total gestalt, can apply the principles perfectly. Look on the field, you will see."

The red team had control of the ball and was moving down the field like a machine. Five forwards, spread across the width of the field, were overwhelming the defense, getting the ball closer to the penalty area in front of the goal. The defenders were consolidating as the attackers pushed closer, the fullbacks pulling in to protect the goal area, when the two trailing red halfbacks joined the attack, again outnumbering the defenders. As the blue halfbacks fell back and toward the center, one of the red wingers broke free and dashed toward the left corner of the field. Immediately the dribbler smashed a hard, low pass to him and broke for the near corner of the goal just as his right winger broke for the far corner of the goal. As the defenders split to contain both threats, the two other red forwards dashed straight ahead into the penalty area just in front of the goal. One of them was unmarked by any blue back and the left winger slammed a low, fast pass to him, barely higher than the top of the goalposts. As the blue goalkeeper, caught off balance, dived for the middle of the goal, the unguarded red forward jumped up and headed the ball into the far corner of the goal for a score. The whole operation, from midfield to goal, had taken less than a minute.

"That's amazing," Marc said. "But you're using five forwards. And you have two halfbacks past midfield. Isn't that dangerous? I mean, suppose one of the defenders gets the ball—intercepts a pass or tackles a forward—and blasts it into your territory. Or the goalkeeper kicks it there. You have only three defenders left, and they're spread out on your half of the field. You're very vulnerable."

"Not quite," the professor said. "You were not watching the beginning of the play, obviously. I use one stopper, operating in front of the goal, and two fullbacks, who operate as sweepers, covering in front of the penalty area. The two halfbacks who followed the forwards into enemy territory don't go too far away from the midfield line unless an opportunity presents itself. If the ball comes back toward our castle, goal, they fall back fast, as do the forwards. You see, unlike the normal distributions, four-two-four or three-three-four, we use one-two-two-five, which gives us four lines of defense of the homeland, the goal, instead of three, plus the goalkeeper, and also allows us to send five forwards, with two halfbacks in close reserve, across the border, the midfield line, into enemy territory, to crush the opposition, to overwhelm the enemy. Like a panzer attack, with reserves. A blitzkrieg."

"Still, a fast counterattack will be dangerous for you."

"A fast counterattack is always dangerous, Mr. Burr, but we have ways of preventing that, too. But that, for the while, must remain not discussed."

"I find it interesting, Professor, that you used so many military terms in describing the game. As though it were a war."

"*Naturlich,* it is a war. Just as chess is a war. It was through the concept of war that the Ziegler technique was arrived at. But it is a war that no one else can copy, just as the victorious armies of the *Dritte*—of the past—used the blitzkrieg to overcome all obstacles with great rapidity. We sweep in at great speed, with maximum forces concentrated at one weak point, so that we have the benefits of surprise, speed, and superior force concentration. So we must break through. Impossible to stop."

"Don't all the other teams try for the same combination?"

The professor laughed smugly. "Try, yes, but they cannot. It is a matter of national character, of culture. The American team, you think they can do this? Nonsense. They are not a true *team*; they are a group of eleven individuals. No discipline, no acting as a single unit like the fingers of one hand. The Americans are accustomed to do what they wish, have no concept of command in response to a higher leader. Grilho, you think he is a *leader*? You think he can give *orders* that must be obeyed? Never. He is from the old Brazil school. The carioca system, where everything is *fun*; a dancing, a singing, a *playing* at war. We, the standard-bearers of the German Democratic Republic, we know how to act as one. Disciplined. Uniform. From childhood. This cannot be learned; it must be lived." The professor's face was red; he was breathing heavily.

"As I remember it," Marc said mildly, "those disciplined standard-bearers got the crap beat out of them the last couple of times out."

"On the field of battle, Sunday, they will not be outnumbered!" Ziegler shouted. "Then you will see." He turned away abruptly and walked toward the other end of the field.

"He is an old man," Grob explained apologetically. "With memories. His ideas, you must not take them seriously. About culture, you understand. About soccer, that is different. His methods, they have worked very well. Look where we are, a small country, playing in the final. Our team is well practiced together; for two years we have worked hard. The five-forward system, yes, it is an excellent attacking system. It also has weaknesses, as you said; no system is perfect. But I don't believe . . . I ask you, Marc, what do you think? Perhaps if Boni and the others were there, perhaps . . . but they are not. Royal and Velez and Pangos, they are adequate. But do you see any of them—tell the truth, Marc—taking the ball away from Bauer or Schotz? Dribbling through our many lines of defenses?"

"Truthfully, Grob, I don't. But soccer is not played on a computer. It's played by human beings on a big field. In one game . . . I have found out, since I became a sports reporter, that in a short series, anything can happen. Upsets are not uncommon. And in one game, one bout, one anything . . . I wouldn't bet against the American team."

Grob looked Marc in the eye. "Yes, but would you bet *on* them?"

# 24

Marc's taxi pulled up in front of Koch Stadium just in time to see Dahliah entering the players' entrance. He hurried after her—it was hard to run carrying the portable computer terminal, light as it was—and caught up with her at the Security gate. Leaving Dahliah outside, Marc went into the locker room, collared the already-showered Jason Benjamin, and arranged to meet him on the field at the substitutes' bench when he was dressed.

Marc sat back for a moment, leaning against the wall of the stands, closed his eyes, and relaxed under the warm sun, letting its comfort seep into his aching body. Dahliah let him stay that way for a while, until she couldn't hold back. "Did you find out anything from Danzig that I should know? Or the Germans?"

"The *East* Germans are going to beat the pants off us tomorrow," he said, without opening his eyes. "Danzig says it's probably Boni who did it, but with Ragusic's head smashed in so badly, he can't make an absolutely positive identification, so he wants me to make sure it was either Royal or Velez."

"What do you mean 'make sure'? Frame them? *Minorities?* Because they're minorities?"

"Because the other suspects are either rich or troublesome. It isn't that he's against minorities—Danzig is an equal-opportunity hater—he just wants somebody who won't give him trouble. He'll settle for Frankie, the equipment kid, if he has to."

"And you agreed?" Dahliah couldn't believe it.

"Of course I agreed. Actually, I didn't *disagree*. Why should I fight with Danzig now," he visualized Dahliah thrown into the tank with prostitutes, "and get into trouble and never get a chance to even look for the real killer? If Danzig gets mad at me, I'll be in jail," *and so will you, Dahliah,* "and never have a chance to find the killer. If I find—*when* I find the murderer, I'm going to turn him over to Danzig and then what choice does he have? And if I'm lucky and it turns out to be Royal or Velez or Frankie, then Danzig will think I did what he wanted; who's to know?"

"Then you have to find the real murderer," Dahliah said with finality. "Make sure it isn't Royal or Velez or Frankie."

Before Marc could point out that there was a slight inconsistency in the logic of her statements, one that no professor should have permitted, Jason Benjamin joined them, automatically taking the seat next to Dahliah. Naturally; she was a nice Jewish girl, but Jason should have noticed she was old enough to be his mother. If she had married young. Twelve? Okay, sister. Older sister.

"I didn't do it," the tall young man said, smiling warmly at Dahliah. Couldn't have been a day over twenty-five; why didn't he pick on someone his own age?

"Do what?" Marc jumped up and moved to the other side of Benjamin so the skinny goalie would have to turn away from Dahliah.

Still smiling at Dahliah, Jason said, "Kill Ragusic, what else? Everybody knows you're working for Lieutenant Danzig."

"I am not working for Lieutenant Danzig," Marc insisted. "I am working *with* him. That is, as I go about my normal reporting job, doing investigative reporting, if I should happen to come across any information that would assist the police, like any good citizen, I would inform the police officer in charge. Who happens to be Lieutenant Danzig. How do you know I didn't want to talk to you about tomorrow's game?" Why did he feel so insecure? About *everything?* Well, there was a reason. Such as three different groups wanting to make sure that he picked, *framed,* three mutually exclusive suspects. Or else. And Danzig. Who gave him a choice from Column A or one from Column B. Or maybe one from Column C. Or else. And Witter, who was just waiting for—looking *actively* for—a chance to "or else" him, too. All by tomorrow night. Evening.

"Okay," Benjamin said, still not looking at Marc, "what do you want to know about the final game?"

"Forget it," Marc said. "Tell me what you know about the murder."

"Same as I told the police." *Now* Benjamin tore his eyes away from Dahliah and looked at Marc. That was the way to do it. Like with mules; first you have to get their attention. "I came in around seven, got into uniform—makes Grilho happy—went to the toilet, went into the gym for a rest, and when the whistle blew, I went out on the field and worked out. Practiced. Until the police got me."

"Anyone see you?"

"Of course not; that's the idea of hiding out. Grilho sees

me, he forgets he called the practice for eight and wants to know why, since it's already seven-ten, I'm not throwing myself to the ground heavily, breaking ribs, to warm up for the warm-up.''

"Did you see anyone?"

"In the locker room, everybody. In the toilet, one or two guys, for a minute. In the gym, nobody.''

"Where do you rest in the gym?"

"Depends. Sometimes on the tumbling mat—it's not soft but it's a lot less hard than the ground I spend half my time picking myself up from—or the quadriceps machine. That's harder than the mat, but it has a bend at the knees that's very relaxing. Thursday I was on the mat.''

"What size shoe do you wear?" Marc asked suddenly. Benjamin was supposed to flinch at this.

Jason looked amused. "The cops asked the same question the second time around. Same size as Boni, to shorten the session. So the cops think he did it, do they?''

"No conclusions have been reached yet.''

"Why don't they arrest him? For the good of the game, I mean. It's logical. He's out of action anyway; I'm the first-string goalkeeper. Without me, the score will be ten-zip instead of five-zip. And with his money and pull, he'd be out on bail in two hours and Lieutenant Danzig would be a school crossing guard in the far end of Staten Island in four hours.''

"You *want* them to arrest Boni? You hate him that much?''

"Hell, no, I like Boni. Everybody does. But if they arrest him, nothing bad happens. Not even in the papers. Even in your rag. His grandfather gets on the phone, and your boss, your *owner*, kills the story in one minute. You think if I wanted to frame somebody, I'd pick Boni?''

"From what you said, it makes sense. Would you rather frame somebody defenseless? Like Frankie?''

"On second thought, Marc, you're right. Boni would be

perfect to frame because even if the police believed the frame—especially if they bought it—nobody'd get hurt. Any murderer with heart would pick Boni as the perfect frame; Boni is untouchable."

"You're the first one who thought that way. Maybe you thought of that before; that's why you wore Boni's shoes?"

Jason smiled. At Marc, this time. "Come off it, Marc. I happen to be the most intelligent guy on the team, that's all. Whoever values intelligence," he turned to smile at Dahliah again, "would appreciate that. If I wanted to murder anyone connected with anything I do, anything I'm interested in, particularly soccer, would I do it here? With soccer equipment? You know me better than that."

"On the other hand," Dahliah responded, before Marc could answer, "might you not have done exactly that because no one would suspect you of doing something that obvious?" *Well*, Marc thought. *At last, Dahliah is on my side.* Smiles don't always work.

"I might," Jason conceded. "But that puts me in a position of having to decide how many cycles of 'he thinks that I think that he thinks that . . .' it takes to fool a Lieutenant Danzig. My guess is that it takes no cycles; I've spoken to the man twice. Danzig looks for the obvious, that's all. Anything subtle would pass him by completely."

"You had no way of knowing Lieutenant Danzig would be assigned to the case."

"So now, Jason Benjamin, the Professor Moriarity of the Brooklyn Booters, is put into the position of having to figure, mathematically, the odds for the officer in charge of the case to be within a certain range of intelligence and intricacy of thought so I can add that uncertainty to the choice of how many cycles of subtlety to follow." He looked at Marc mockingly. "You want to try explaining that to Danzig?"

"Forget it," Marc said. "Tell me something: Who do you think did it?"

Jason thought for a moment. "If it was a crime of passion, it was one of us players. That includes Boni, much as I like him. Probably a Booter; the other members of the World Cup Team have had too little exposure to Ragusic to want to kill him. Boni gives the impression of being cool, but I've seen him when, big as I am, I'd be afraid to say hello to him. He has a very strong sense of fairness, of sportsmanship, and if someone violates what he considers . . . he keeps good control over himself, but if driven too far . . . well, anyone, everyone, has limits. For that matter, I wouldn't exclude Grilho, either. He has the reputation of never having received a red card, of never being taken out of the game. Well, that's true; he even gives a hand to lift up the man who fouled him. He's a great team player; would never leave his team short-handed, and he wants to win more than anyone I've ever met. But have you ever noticed, even in practice—which he takes very seriously—that the man who fouled him is very often tackled hard, real hard, shortly afterward and ends up with, at least, severe bruises?"

"And if it was a planned murder?" Dahliah asked.

"Then someone is trying to frame Boni, and I can't imagine who. There is one other thing you haven't mentioned. That maybe this murder had nothing to do with the Booters; that maybe it had to do with some of Ragusic's other interests. He was not the straightest guy in the world, you know."

Marc was not about to let the talk take this dangerous turn. Dangerous to him, of course. And to Dahliah. The SSD—and probably the other two—knew where he lived and how vulnerable he was. "You hated Ragusic?" he asked. "Why?"

"Why? No reason, just a whim. Why should I hate a guy who conned me into signing a peonage contract? Who immediately forgot every promise he made to me? Who yells at me, insults me, in public, even though I'm the best goalie in the league? Who threatens to sell me down the river to Jackson, Mississippi, for two million, of which I won't see one penny? Who happens to be a liar, a cheat, a bully, and not incidentally, an anti-Semite?"

"You had a good motive to kill him, then."

"Me and half the world; I'm sure everyone who knew him hated him. So? Does that mean I wanted to kill him? I don't hate anybody that much—I don't mean to kill some bastard; I mean to risk my own neck in doing it."

"But if you could get away with it by framing somebody else?"

Benjamin got up. "If you think I was capable of doing that, what good is my answering anything you ask?" He stalked away on his long, thin legs.

# 25

The waitress brought their hot-and-sour soup and took their order for dry-fried string beans and Hunan spicy eggplant. "Why didn't you want to talk to Grilho now?" Dahliah asked, dipping a broad fried noodle into the mustard.

"He likes to eat alone at lunchtime," Marc said. "That's when he thinks, plans, how he's going to torture his players in the afternoon practice."

"I don't think he deliberately tortures the players; I feel he just wants them to operate at the maximum they're capable of."

"Same thing, from the players' point of view." Marc concentrated on his soup; it was as good as any he had ever had. Next time he had to meet Danzig, he would bring him here. It would save a lot of time and money. Only trouble was, Chinese restaurants don't serve breakfast. And Danzig wouldn't listen, might even take it as a personal insult that Marc didn't want to go to the best diner in Brooklyn. "Did you finish your psychoanalysis of Jason Benjamin yet?"

"I keep telling you, I'm a psychologist and I don't do psychoanalysis, and even if I did, a ten-minute conversation about soccer and murder doesn't quite lend itself to much more than broad superficial generalizations."

The waitress brought two covered dishes. Marc served Dahliah the best-looking, most frizzled string beans and the juiciest chunks of eggplant. "Okay, I'll accept that. So did he murder Gregor Ragusic?"

"If I didn't think you were kidding. . . ." She ate for a while, thinking, then said, "Benjamin could have done it, of course. He makes decisions quickly and carries them out. Like the abrupt way he told you off and just walked away. He's also intelligent enough to have done it in a way that makes it appear Boni did it and his choice of Boni to frame—on the assumption that Boni would never be arrested—may very well be a sensible solution to the problem. Tell me something, how important is the World Cup Game to Benjamin?"

"Very. If he holds the GDR Team down to a reasonable score—say three goals or less, given the conditions—it would class him one of the best in the world. Fame, big salary—renegotiate his contract, especially with a new owner—endorsements, prestige . . . very, very important in every way. Some people would kill for less."

"Then if he were the murderer, he would try very hard not to hurt the team. Boni is injured, so if he were arrested, it would not affect the big game. And, as a decent human being, Jason would not want to hurt an innocent person. So for Benjamin, putting it all together, the only possible person to frame would be Boni."

"Decent human being? If he's a murderer?" What was this obsession Dahliah had with tall men, Marc wondered?

219

Wasn't he taller than her if they were both in stocking feet?

"Decent human beings can be driven to murder. It happens all the time."

"Driven, yes. But he stole a pair of Boni's shoes. Not for a joke; he wore them to kill Ragusic with. That's premeditation."

"You're putting it backward. The murderer stole Boni's shoes. That doesn't mean Jason is the murderer."

"Benjamin has big feet. He wouldn't have to stuff paper in the toes."

Dahliah put down her chopsticks and looked at Marc with concern. "What have you got against Jason Benjamin? Why the concentration on him? I thought you were supposed to frame Royal or one of the other poor minority suspects."

*Yeah, for your sake,* he thought, but he couldn't say it. If Dahliah only knew . . . to save her, if all else failed, he would have to confess that he was the killer, if he could figure out a way to convince Danzig it was true. Which shouldn't be too hard; Danzig wanted to arrest somebody, and it didn't really matter who. But Dahliah would take this as another manifestation of the male ego, not as a sign of true love and sacrifice. "I'm not going to frame anybody," Marc said. "I'm going to find the murderer."

They finished eating in silence. The waitress brought the check and two fortune cookies. Dahliah's said, "Fortune smiles on one who is alert."

"Let's go," Dahliah said. "On to Grilho. To grill Grilho." She smiled. It wasn't that funny. If only she knew what Marc's cookie said. "Women are born to deceive. Beware of a tall, dark man." Marc told her it said, "Move forward with confidence today." He tried to look confident.

220

# 26

Although it was only one o'clock and practice wasn't scheduled until two, Grilho was already on the field, in uniform, stretching and limbering up in preparation for the stretching and limbering-up exercises with which he started every practice session. He also kept looking around, clearly irritated that none of the players were on the field with him, getting ready for the practice. Though he was turned a full ninety degrees away, he noticed Dahliah and Marc approaching and stopped exercising when they were close. "I am sorry, Miss Norman," he said, "but as I have already informed you, I never discuss my family." He went over to the home team touchline, where he had a dozen balls lined up, picked a ball up with his foot in a single maneuver, and began juggling the ball from knee to knee, dancing in rhythm with the ever-present "Tico Tico" on the PA system.

"I'd like some information about the game," Marc said. "Why are you calling a practice the afternoon before the big game? Shouldn't your players be resting?"

"It is not a real practice," Grilho explained. "One half hour of bending, stretching, and twisting. To prevent injury. Then one half hour of calisthenics, for the cardio-vascular system. Then one half hour of juggling the ball, as I am doing, and finish with one half hour of fundamentals. Then we go into the conference room for more resting: plans, analysis, movies. No more than two hours, then go home to rest some more."

Two hours of hard workout? A Grilho workout? Not a real practice? "And tomorrow morning?" Marc asked sarcastically. "Another light practice?"

"Exactly." Grilho didn't smile. "But I have hired extra trainers to give a massage to each starter after practice. We will have a light meal at noon served in the conference room. After that, there will be resting, sleeping, concentration, prayer, until one hour before the game. Then a little stretching, a little shooting, and that is all."

"Can I ask you some questions, too?" Dahliah asked.

Grilho looked at her suspiciously. "About family?"

"I really came to talk to you about the murder of Gregor Ragusic," Dahliah said. "Unfortunately, the police believe a member of your family is deeply involved so I don't see how we can talk about this without discussing your family a little. But I believe that Marc and I can help in this matter." Marc was pleased at how quickly Dahliah had picked up the technique of getting a lead-in to an interview. On the other hand, who should know better how to use psychology than a psychologist?

Without stopping his juggling, Grilho turned to face her fully. "I wanted to talk to you about that, and to Marc, too. What I meant about my family . . . personal matters is what I had in mind. When Kimberly and I were first married, the reporters gave us no privacy at all. Not only that, all they were interested in was color. There is much more to a human being than the color of one's skin."

"It must have been awful," Dahliah said sympathetically, "to have reporters following you around on your honeymoon."

Grilho glanced at her wryly. "Miss Norman, they have tried every technique that exists to get me to talk about my family. Including your empathy which, though no doubt sincere, does not work. My family is private. You wish to discuss my profession, I am at your disposal. You want to discuss the murder and tell me what the police lieutenant is doing and thinking, I will be most grateful." He switched the ball from his knees to the inside of his instep, tapping the ball in front of him while quickly rotating in place.

"I have some information for you," Marc interrupted. When Grilho was in his formal mode, you got very little that was useful from him. "I was at the Meadowlands this morning, watching the GDR Team practice. I spoke to Heinz Grob, and he didn't say anything was off the record."

Grilho looked interested. "They have changed their system, perhaps?"

"Not as far as I could tell. Five forwards, two halfbacks who sometimes join the forwards on attack, though holding back somewhat, two fullbacks who act freely as sweepers, and a stopper in front of the penalty area."

"All moving as a unit, like an army on attack? The so-called blitzkrieg?"

"Then you know as much as I do."

"We all know what the others are doing. He knows my ideas, too; nothing is secret in this sport. One game and everything is clear. It is in the execution that . . . did Heinz say what he would do if the ball were suddenly to be stolen away and a long pass made into his underdefended territory?"

"No. Actually it was Professor Ziegler who explained his system, but when I asked that question, all he told me was that he had prepared for that, too. Big secret."

"Yes, that is a secret to me, too. So far, it has not happened in the World Cup Games. The German juggernaut is just too powerful. Or maybe the other teams were too frightened. We are fully prepared and we are not frightened. That makes a big difference. When people are overconfident, when they are sure they *must* win, and they meet with an unexpected obstacle, their whole world can fall apart."

"You wouldn't want to tell me what stumbling block you intend to place before their feet?"

Grilho recognized the allusion. "Are you a student of the Bible, Marc? I never knew that."

"I read it through, once, when I was a boy, and I occasionally refer to it for appropriate quotes."

Grilho now was tapping the ball back over his head with his left foot and tapping it back with the heel of the same foot, slowly rotating on his right foot as the ball arced over his head. "When I was a boy, we had no books in the house—books were a luxury, you understand—but we did have a Bible. Which my mother made us read, thank God. Until I left home—I was thirteen when I first went to the Rios team—other than my schoolbooks, the Bible was my only reading. I tell you this because even when Boni was a little boy, I read the Bible to him every night.

"One part I remember is this: 'Vengeance is mine; I will repay, saith the Lord.' That's from Romans.

"The *Lord*, not man, will repay, is the meaning of that statement. You may also remember, Marc, 'If thine enemy be hungry, give him bread to eat; and if he be thirsty, give him water to drink: For thou shalt heap coals of fire upon his head. . . .' Proverbs." Grilho trapped the ball under his left foot, lifted it slightly in the air, and with his right foot, gave it a hard, sweeping kick that drove the ball through the middle of the goal a good sixty yards away. He watched the ball go into the empty goal and turned back to Marc and Dahliah. "I mention this to show how my family—how Boni—could not have killed Gregor Ragusic. It is foolish of the lieutenant to think so, even for a moment. I do not say that Boni could not kill. In defense of the family, of a wife or child, of the mother or father, of the country, yes, that is permitted. In *defense*. But to murder a helpless person who is not attacking you? No, that is not within his character."

"Are you saying," Dahliah asked, "that Ragusic was helpless? Wasn't he once a star soccer player, World Cup level?"

"He did not keep in condition," Grilho said disapprovingly. "The body is a gift from God, lent, temporary, as is the mind and the soul. It must be kept—maintained—properly, clean and pure. 'Your body is the temple of the Holy Ghost. . . .' Corinthians. Gregor Ragusic defiled his body as he dishonored his mind. He was weak and fat. If he attacked, a child could have held him off or run away. Boni is big and strong; he would not have needed to kill Ragusic, even in self-defense. Therefore he did not kill him. You must make the lieutenant understand that."

"And yet," Dahliah persisted, "what about what you said? That, for family, in defense of the family . . . what if Ragusic were going to harm his father? You? Couldn't Boni have killed him under those conditions?"

Grilho's thin lips hardened and his jaw muscles stood out. His light coffee-colored skin grew darker. "I do not need protection. Boni knows that. I have overcome every barrier with honor and have lived within the Commandments all my life. As has Boni. Which includes, 'Thou shalt not kill.' "

"Except in defense of the family," Dahliah pointed out softly. "As you said before. With all due respect, Mr. Vargas—"

"Grilho," he said automatically. "Everybody calls me Grilho."

"Thank you. With all due respect, Grilho, and I do appreciate what you said about not needing anyone to fight your battles, are you sure Boni sees everything exactly that way? Might he not perceive you as needing his help in a bad situation? In a situation he felt you couldn't handle? One which would hurt you badly, and through you, his mother? And if the cause of that trouble was Gregor Ragusic, can you say, with certainty, that Boni would not have removed the source of that trouble out of love for you?"

"Is it possible, Miss Norman, that you are looking at everything backward? *I* am the head of the family and *I* am responsible for the protection of the family, my wife and my son in particular, and with respect for my father and for Mr. Hollingsworth, all the others, too. Most people look at me as only a soccer player. Some look at me as a head coach, too. Very few people know the responsibilities of a head coach. It is not like your baseball manager, I assure you. In effect, I am business head of the playing part of the Booters organization, answering only to Gregor Ragusic, or whoever the new owner will be. I am also head of the Booters family of players, many of whom are very young. Most people, in the United States at least, do not realize what this means. I have a good deal of responsibility of various kinds, and I handle these responsibilities very successfully most of the time. I am also head of several businesses which I take care of in my spare time. And of some charitable foundations, which is done in secret. Do you think a young man like Boni—he is very smart, but he is only twenty-two years old—must tell me what is happening in my own organization? Must help me take care of things it is my duty to take care of? Must *protect* me? Possibly it is the other way around, Miss Norman."

"I see what you mean," Dahliah was still speaking softly. "But that is not necessarily how Boni would see it, especially if he became angry at something Ragusic said or did. People do things in the heat of the moment that they would not think of doing upon reflection."

"Boni is training to be a diplomat, like his grandfather. He thinks, analyzes, before he acts. He would never do anything without thinking first."

"Was it you, Grilho, who told me that a good soccer player knows what to do and does it without thinking? Automatically?"

"I did not. I have always taught my players to think first, before the game, to analyze the pattern of play and find out all they could about the other team, so that their actions, no matter how fast, would be based on knowledge, not emotions. This I taught Boni when he was a little boy."

"Still, this was not a game. This was a loving son facing a man who was going to hurt his beloved father. Under those conditions—"

"If you are going to help the police, Miss Norman, to play detective, you should find out all you can about the other team first. Boni could not kill Ragusic; he was brought up half as a Hollingsworth. More than half. Hollingsworths command money, power, not violence. I came from the *favelas*. The *favela* is not a bad place—when I was a boy, a girl could walk there safely at midnight—but it is not for soft people. There, I learned to do what had to be done." His black eyes burned at Dahliah. "I have never forgotten."

"Are you confessing that you killed Ragusic?"

"Do not put words in my mouth, Miss Norman. I did not kill Ragusic and Boni did not kill Ragusic. You must tell the lieutenant that Boni will not be arrested."

"And if he is?" Dahliah pressed on. Marc wondered at

her insistence; he could tell Grilho was boiling mad. "Is it a father's duty to sacrifice himself for his son?"

"I have already made that clear, but do not read more into that than is there. Sacrifice is a last resort, when nothing else is possible, when there is no choice. It is better to plan the game far in advance, so that the sacrifice is unnecessary. I am a planner, Miss Norman. Boni will never be arrested, you may be sure of that." To Marc, Grilho looked very confident. "I will not allow it to happen. Never." Grilho trotted over to the touchline again and used the sole of his shoe to roll the end ball in front of him. He tapped the ball gently before him, took two steps, and kicked it with tremendous force toward the far goal, a good eighty yards away. The ball sailed over the crossbar of the goal. Marc had never seen so hard a kick in his life.

"I've never seen Grilho that angry before," Marc said. "In fact, I've never seen him angry at all."

"Anyone can be driven to that state," Dahliah said. "We all have areas of sensitivity that may seem relatively insignificant to an uninvolved observer, but to us, they have tremendous emotional impact."

"Yeah, well, you pressed the right buttons, all right. But don't do it again, especially around here. These are professional athletes we're dealing with, men accustomed to acting very fast, reacting physically, violently, almost instinctively. You could have been . . . could have been . . ." He couldn't voice the thought.

"Not with Grilho. People like him have inhibitors, instilled in early childhood, that prevent him from hurting a woman, a child, a helpless person, an animal."

"Until—how many times have you read about a guy

who suddenly goes crazy, kills his whole family, and all the neighbors say he was such a nice boy."

"Yes, but those are exceptions, reactions to great stress. Or a culmination of minor stresses. Perceived stress, that is, not necessarily something you would consider—"

"Exactly. These are a bunch of very keyed-up people, Dahliah. Very tense. They've been working toward this moment, the World Cup, for two years, and concentrating on it, practicing intensively, for six months. A player's whole career, the coach's, is riding on what happens in the final game. Pride, money, glory, honor, manliness, everything is at stake. And tomorrow is the big game against the best team in the world. And they're facing a referee who, they suspect, is not entirely neutral, in a sport where talking back to the ref can get you thrown out of the game. They've had their three best forwards injured. They know they're the underdogs. On top of that, Ragusic was murdered. Several of them are under suspicion. And you go needling Grilho in his most vulnerable spot? Attacking his family? I was ready to throw myself in front of you, to save your life. That last kick? It could have been your head."

"I knew what I was doing, Marc; I wanted to get his reaction."

"You got it. In spades. Lucky for you—and me—a ball was handy."

Just then, several of the players, in uniform, started coming out of the locker-room exit. "There's Boni," Dahliah changed the subject. "I have to ask him a few more questions." She trotted toward the big forward before Marc could stop her. He caught up with her, but not in time to keep her from greeting Boni and leading him toward the substitutes' bench. She indicated that Boni should sit on her right and patted the bench to her left. Marc had no choice but to sit on the side away from Boni.

"I've just spoken to your father," Dahliah said to Boni. "He indicated that you have a very close-knit family."

"On both sides," Boni agreed.

"I got the impression he would give his life for your mother."

"My mother is a goddess to him. In Brazil, grandmother Vargas ran—still runs—the family. We all would . . . the Hollingsworths, too. One for all and all for one. A long tradition; almost a religion."

"He also said he would give his life for you."

Boni looked at her unsurely. "What exactly are you getting at?"

"What if someone cheated him, hurt him badly?"

"You're crazy. My father would never . . . he never even got a red card in his life, and he's been fouled, attacked, hundreds of times."

"If he thought Gregor Ragusic would hurt your mother. . . ."

"My mother has nothing to do with Ragusic."

"Or if Ragusic were to hurt you?"

"Ragusic did not hurt me, could not hurt me. Even if he tried, I can take care of myself."

"I believe you're right; sorry I upset you." *Upset* wasn't the word for it, Marc realized, watching Boni's face carefully, measuring how to throw himself on Boni if he moved suddenly. This teasing of the animals could end disastrously if . . . and Dahliah had made a mistake seating Boni on her right, to keep his injured left leg next to her. One roundhouse sweep of his powerful, uninjured right leg could cut her in half. "I shouldn't have taken that approach," Dahliah said. "What is more likely is that you would give your life for your father. Isn't that so? Or should I say, *risk* your life? By killing Gregor Ragusic?"

Marc jumped up fast, before Boni completed drawing a deep breath, and stood directly in front of the tall forward, keeping an alert eye on Boni's massive right thigh muscles.

"I think it's a compliment," Marc said, trying to smile, "to be asked if you would risk your life for your father."

Boni let the breath out slowly. "Not quite the kind of compliment I value," he growled, "when it's linked to an accusation of murder." He drew another deep breath, seemed a bit more composed. "I would appreciate it if you and Miss Norman got the hell out of here. Now."

"Yes, sure, we have to go back to the office anyway, appointment with Mr. Witter." Marc grabbed Dahliah's arm, pulled her up, and started walking toward the locker-room exit with her. Ten steps and Marc felt a tremendous blow in his back, knocking him flat. The small of his back; the same spot all his other assailants seemed to favor. The pain radiated into his legs and belly. Dahliah helped him get up slowly, dusting him off. He turned his head painfully. Boni was standing there, scowling, leaning on the cane in his right hand, next to the row of soccer balls on the touchline, challenging Marc with his eyes, daring, encouraging him to come back and fight it out like a man. Marc was sure he would have hated being a goalie.

Dahliah held his arm tightly. "Don't be foolish, Marc; he's much taller than you." As she led him toward the exit, she leaned her head against his shoulder. "Would you really have thrown yourself in front of me if Grilho tried to kick me? I think that's sweet."

---

As soon as they left the stadium exit, Black Coat—the one who had pinned him to the wall after the press conference yesterday—approached them. Marc smoothly moved between the big man and Dahliah and kept walking toward the curb; the last thing he wanted was to have Dahliah involved. Black Coat politely tipped his hat, and to Marc's dismay, said, "Good afternoon, Miss Norman." Was everybody checking up on him, Marc wondered? "So nice to see you again, Marc." The voice was soft, low, and cultured; not quite the way Marc remembered it. Black Coat put his hat back on again.

"Yes, well, I'm in a hurry." No way was Black Coat going to attack him here, especially with Dahliah as a witness.

"Of course; you have so many important things to attend to. My director sends his compliments. He is so pleased that there was nothing in the press that would cause difficulties. It gives him great pleasure to work with such an understanding journalist. I take it there have been no new developments that might possibly change the status quo?" His eyes searched Marc's face urgently.

"No, no, nothing."

"And in the near future?"

"The police don't seem to have made much progress recently. That I know about. They have a tendency to work slowly."

"Yes, we are aware of that; they do have certain restrictions on their actions. Properly so, unlike civilians."

"The civilians are no nearer to any solution, either."

"I will convey those regrets to my director. Good day, Marc, Miss Norman." Black Coat tipped his hat and walked off briskly.

"What the hell was that about?" Dahliah asked.

"Remember I told you last night about the three guys who beat me up?" Dahliah turned around to look at Black Coat's retreating back. "Don't look," Marc said. "I don't want you to ever have to pick him out of a lineup. Forget what he looked like." Suddenly Dahliah looked frightened. "He's the UN guy. Don't worry. He just wants to make sure I don't make any waves until after the World Cup teams go home. Which," he added, "I'm not bloody likely to do, the way things are going." He held up his hand for a taxi.

"It'll be quicker if we take the subway," Dahliah said.

"You know I don't take subways anymore."

"Worried?" she joked. "I'll protect you."

"The taxi is for you; I'll meet you at home after I talk to Witter."

"You said *we* had an appointment with Mr. Witter. I have to talk to him, too." A taxi pulled up; Dahliah pushed Marc inside. Everyone seemed to be pushing him around these days.

"What do you have to talk to Julius about?" Marc asked.

"I have the handle on the story he wanted: the romance of Grilho and Kimberly Hollingsworth."

"You don't have anything. He didn't say anything."

"I'm a psychologist, remember? I got enough information so that I can put together practically the whole story. If I do a little research, I can get the facts I need to flesh it out fully."

"You can't. Shouldn't. Grilho doesn't want that story published. It's unethical."

"Ethics? In a newspaper? After all the outright lies I've read? The phony exposés?"

"Most of that is put out by the so-called victims themselves. As was once told to me by a wise old—it was Julius Witter himself, come to think of it—the best thing is good publicity, the next best thing is bad publicity, and the worst thing is no publicity."

"So, what's wrong with what I'm going to do?"

"With Grilho it's different. He really wants no publicity; he keeps his family life completely separate from his professional life. You heard him mention his charities? Foundations? I suspected, but I could never find a word anywhere about them. Grilho is—he's sincere. For real."

"And what if he's the murderer? Will you keep that quiet, too?"

Marc thought for a moment. "No, if he's the murderer, I'll write it up. Straight. But I don't believe it."

"Well, let me tell you something, Marcus Aurelius Burr. Grilho could easily be the murderer. A man that fanatical about everything could easily kill a man and honestly feel he was doing God's will, if that man did something evil that interfered with the way he thought the universe should be run."

"Yes, I'm sure of that, but I just don't believe it."

"And what about Boni? Not only is he Grilho's son, he's your friend. You *admire* him. Can you believe he's the killer? He tried to kill you, remember? Would you turn him in, too?"

"He didn't try to kill me. At that distance he could have hit me in the head easily; he's a striker and the league's leading scorer. He was just showing me how annoyed he was. At *your* questioning."

"Annoyed? He knocked you down. That ball was going a hundred miles an hour."

"Seventy, at the most."

"What's the difference? Don't pick on trivialities. The question is, would you turn him in if he was the killer?"

"Yes, and Jason Benjamin, too. And Cuffy and José. Even Frankie. All of them. Now you answer. Would you turn in Steve Vanderhook?"

She was shocked for a moment, then smiled. "You're jealous! I never would have believed it. Usually you're so passive when a man . . . don't be silly. I *live* with you."

"You haven't ever said you'd *marry* me."

"I said I'd consider it. Which is more than I've ever— why are you so insecure, Marc? Have I ever given you cause to—"

"Why? Because every time I see you with someone who's tall, blond, handsome, rich, and tall—"

"It's my professional manner, that's all."

"It's flirting, that's what it is. If I'm not tall enough for you, if you're not happy with me. . . ."

She took him in her arms. "Stop talking foolishness, Marc. If I ever want to leave you, I won't hint; you'll know. I don't want to leave, I'm not thinking of leaving, and I'm not interested in anyone else. I do like it when other men, good-looking, strong men, are attracted to me, but that doesn't mean I want anyone else but you. Now don't pick a fight; kiss and make up." She kissed him tenderly.

Mollified, sort of, he said, "You really mustn't write that story about Grilho and Mrs. Vargas. I'll drop you off at the house before I go to the office."

She hesitated, then said, "I'll talk it over with Nelda Shaver; see what she says."

"Oh, no, not her. She's a moron. She can't write, wouldn't know good writing if it bit her, and all she wants is gossip. I can tell you right now, if you ask her, she'll say yes. Guaranteed."

"Then I'll ask Mr. Witter. We could really use the thousand dollars."

"All he's interested in is increasing circulation." He sulked into the corner of the cab. Dahliah held his arm; it didn't help. It was going to be one of those days. *Another* one of those days. Like yesterday. Only with a different kind of beating up. A minor improvement, but gratefully accepted.

The taxi pulled up to the *Sentry* building. After Marc paid the driver he turned to join Dahliah. Blue Coat was already there. "How fortunate to meet you again," Blue Coat said politely. "And this must be Miss Dahliah Norman. How do you do?"

It was *definitely* going to be another one of those days, only worse. Much worse.

# 28

"For once in his life," Julius Witter said, "Marc is right. You mustn't write the story of the Grilho romance. If he had given you the interview, we could have gone ahead with a clear conscience. But for you to put together a set of conjectures based on his refusal to discuss the matter with you leaves us extremely vulnerable to a lawsuit. Grilho is not a person to be trifled with; he may look like a simple athlete and he speaks English with an accent, but he is a tough, competent businessman with a full legal staff."

"But you gave me the assignment yourself," Dahliah protested. "You asked me to get that story."

"I assumed that you would be able to charm it out of Grilho. Unfortunately, you took Burr with you. Not only is he singularly lacking in charm, but his presence has a dampening effect on everyone within a one-mile radius, which even your beauty and grace cannot overcome."

"I was counting on that money, Mr. Witter."

"But you didn't produce, Miss Norman. However," Witter softened, "I will do what I can to help you. Go speak with Nelda Shaver. Between the two of you, you may come up with an idea that will fit both "The Sporting Woman" and the Sunday Sports Section. I still have a thousand words open, and if you can complete it by five o'clock . . . it's the glassed-in office to your right, halfway down the floor. Go."

Dahliah went. "Why are you doing this, Julius?" Marc asked.

"Don't you think it would be interesting to our women readers to have a psychologist's viewpoint on sports matters? Might it not increase the readership of our Sports Section? And think of the good we'd be doing by bringing a husband and wife together so that they could discuss matters of mutual interest, such as sports. Would it not break down the feeling of isolation so many women have between Saturday afternoon and Monday night if they knew something about sports? I'm sure it would reduce the divorce rate significantly."

"When you start talking like that, Julius, about doing good for our readers, I count my fingers and check the gold fillings in my teeth. Know what I think? I think you're doing this, bringing Dahliah into your world, getting her used to a higher income, as another way to extend your control over me, another way to threaten to pull the rug out from under me."

"I truly like Dahliah," Witter said, "a lovely young woman who deserves better than you. This way, she can meet interesting people, men who are more worthy of her, better looking, stronger, richer, and it goes without saying, much taller. As for increasing my control over you," he sneered, "you may think I need more, but that is only because I have not yet found it necessary to use the full force of my intellect in my dealings with you. However, now that you bring it up," he said, as though the thought had not occurred to him before, "I shall keep it in mind, should the situation ever arise when I require more power over your insignificant destiny. Which I doubt." Witter took the black pipe out of his pocket. Marc moved his chair back automatically. "Now tell me what you've messed up lately."

"Messed up? Me? Not a thing. I've sent in my stories. On time. Everything you wanted, and more."

"Then why did Mr. Heisenberg call me this morning and warn me to keep an eye on you? He said he had gotten a complaint from a very high official in the UN, that you might be causing trouble, making wild accusations in the Ragusic murder case that would have serious repercussions in the international sector."

"Me? I never . . . you read what I sent in. You know that I—"

"What you sent in, yes. But what have you been saying? And to whom?"

"Nothing. Not a word, practically."

"No accusations against the German Democratic Republic?"

"Of course not. All I did was talk to the Americans."

"Very few of which are native Americans. Don't you realize how *international* soccer is? Why must I always have to explain the simplest. . . . Let me put it this way: It would be very gratifying if the murderer were not found."

"Not to Danzig. If I don't—"

"Yes, yes. I understand your cowardly attitude: Save me and the devil take the rest of the world. Very well. Since I must live with that, the murderer, should you be so fortunate as to stumble over some evidence, is not a member of a minority group. Or one whose apprehension would disturb one of our allies. Or, what is worse, disturb one of our enemies. Is that clear? Mr. Heisenberg was very firm on that."

"Everybody in America is a minority, or descended from a minority. There are no Indians on the team."

"Excuses in advance, Burr? These orders came directly from Mr. Heisenberg. There is a simple solution: Work it out yourself. Or, if your short-term memory is still malfunctioning, I've already suggested a way to solve the problem. *You* are as close to a nonminority as we have around here, and fortunately, your namesake was tried for treason in the post-Revolutionary days, so—"

"He was acquitted."

"No one remembers that, so all will be well if you confess to the murder."

"Me? Confess? You know I didn't kill Ragusic."

"Know? All I have is your whining denial. Which counts for very little; all criminals swear they're innocent."

"I'm not going to do it, Julius. Period."

"I can't force you, of course, nor would I, even if I could. But please remember that Danzig will arrest Dahliah if he doesn't have anyone else handy. I feel, in all honesty, I should inform her of this when she returns."

"Julius, you're a bastard."

"I take it that means you will, absent any other candidate acceptable to Mr. Heisenberg, sign a written confession to the murder for Lieutenant Danzig?" Marc nodded, wearily. "And that I will receive, in advance, a copy of that confession? With permission to publish the story? With my by-line, of course?" Marc nodded again, beaten to the ground. "Excellent. Now as to your regular work, why have I not received any stories about Lieutenant Danzig's progress? Gregor Ragusic was an important sports figure. Don't you think that rates five hundred words?"

"Danzig hasn't gotten anywhere. All I can say is that

he's interrogated some possible suspects and expects developments in the next few days."

"After the World Cup final game is over and the teams have left the country?" Marc nodded again. "And that he sees no international connections? Of any kind?" The nodding was getting to be a habit. "Excellent, my boy. The story is already half-written. You see how easy it is to be a journalist? Well, I won't keep you; you must be aching to get to your terminal. Five hundred words. Good-bye. I truly enjoyed having this little chat with you."

Dahliah came in, glowing. "Nelda and I," so now it was *Nelda*, Marc noticed, "have come up with a great story for the Sunday Sports Section. The men will love it, too. Sex. Why soccer players would be ideal lovers. Because they exercise so much, play such long, hard games at top speed without stopping. Perfect cardiovascular condition. Very flexible. Never get tired. And superstrong legs and hips. With huge muscles."

"Brilliant," Witter crowed. "Just what I was hoping for when I put you and Nelda together; perfect synergy. Don't forget to put in something about the psychology of the soccer player; how he must always be aware of the position and readiness of the people he is playing with. And some similar pyschological insights, with a few sexual innuendos thrown in. Go to any empty terminal, Dahliah, and write it right now. A thousand words. I'll get some file photos together that will emphasize the points you made. Marc has a short assignment to write, too, so he can edit your think piece when you've finished it. Then you can go home together. By five o'clock, Marc, if you please."

*Great,* Marc thought as he escorted Dahliah out of Witter's office. *Just what I needed to make my day complete.* There was only one thing missing from the whole rotten picture: Julius forgot to emphasize that gymnasts—using Marc as the perfect example—did not have big, strong thighs and hips. With huge muscles. And that these moronic women readers, regardless of the facts, would want their soccer player to be tall, too. Not to worry; Dahliah would put that in herself. Without prompting. And—minor matter—he had also committed himself to confess to the murder if he didn't find the murderer— the *proper* murderer—himself. At the right time. One with the specified national and racial characteristics. And mighty-muscled thighs.

# 29

When Dahliah and Marc got to the front door of their loft building, Brown Coat was waiting for them. The cherry—the *poisoned* cherry—that topped this day. How could Marc have forgotten that there was still one more Fate awaiting him? Didn't his luck—bad luck, naturally—come in threes? This afternoon alone, he already had gotten a hard time from Boni and Grilho. And Witter. One three. Then Black Coat, Blue Coat, and now Brown Coat. A second three. There had to be another three waiting in the wings. For symmetry. Three threes. But Marc couldn't think of anything else that could happen today. It didn't feel right, that he should be done with trouble this early in the evening, but there it was.

"How are you, Miss Norman?" Brown Coat asked, with a heavy German accent, his lumpy face breaking into what he probably thought was a smile, but would have frightened a pit bull. "I hope you are well. It gives me very pleased your acquaintance to make."

"Yes, well, this is, uh, Metzger," Marc introduced. "He works for—is associated with—and how is Mr. Jaeger?"

*"Der Oberst* to you his highest regards sends."

"You may thank Colonel Jaeger for his regards," Marc said. "If that is all?"

"I have come to protect you in this not-safe neighborhood against the criminal elements which in this dangerous city occupy."

"Then you should have met us at the bus stop."

"It was not possible from which direction you would arrive to predict. Here I was positive you to find."

"True. Thank Colonel Jaeger again for his thoughtfulness. Good-bye." Marc turned to unlock the door.

"Not necessary," Metzger said. "The lock for you already I open." To show how vulnerable Marc was? No need to rub it in; he *knew. "Der Oberst* would like to know if you have for the arrest of the criminal Benjamin arranged already."

"Unfortunately, I was not yet able to get sufficient evidence for the police. Yet."

"You are not correct way doing. Complete wrong. First the arrest, then the confession, *then* the evidence."

"I know, but the police don't . . . we have certain restrictions here that I am not allowed to . . . you understand. Bureaucracy. Very hampering."

"Stupid system. Incompetent. Please to remember that it must be complete done, finished, *before* the start of the game. *Der Oberst* is very firm on that. You understand?"

"Completely." Marc turned to go.

"Is Metzger your name," Dahliah asked, "or . . . what does it mean?"

"Translate?" Metzger smiled that smile again. "Butcher."

Marc wished she hadn't asked. The small of his back

was beginning to hurt him again. Thanks for the memory, Mr. Metzger.

---

"What the hell was that?" Dahliah asked, putting on her apron and moving toward the kitchen area. "All of that."

"Remember last night, when I told you I had been beaten up by three different guys? Those were the three guys. Black Coat, outside the stadium, was the UN; Blue Coat, the one at the *Sentry* office, was the State Department, and this one, Metzger, was the SSD, the East German secret police."

"He wants you to arrest Jason Benjamin?"

"Frame. Language difficulty. He means frame. They each want me to do something different. In every way. One wants me to sit on everything, forever, no one arrested for anything. One wants me to make sure they arrest Francisco Guzman, the kid who takes care of the equipment, but only after all the foreign teams leave. And this guy, Metzger, or rather his boss, wants me to make sure they arrest Jason Benjamin, but before the game starts." He sat down at the kitchen table and put his head in his hands. "And Witter, he wants me to confess that I killed Ragusic."

"You? But you didn't. You couldn't." Dahliah sat down opposite him. "Did you?"

Marc looked at her, amazed. "You, too?"

"I didn't mean it that way. What I meant is, if you did it, I'll stand by you. Help you."

"Bake a hacksaw in the cake?"

"Don't be silly. At the school, there are lots of big-wheel attorneys and people with connections to the police. Politicians. They all like me and if I needed. . . ." *Any of them tall?* Marc wanted to ask. Decided not to. "So if you did—I mean, if you *know* anything about—you know what I mean."

"Yeah, I know what you mean. Thanks." *What you don't know is that I did it all for you. And you'll never know.* "That was a good article you wrote about sex and the soccer player. 'Soccer Is Sexy.' Great title. Should arouse a lot of interest in soccer. And sex. Ragusic would have loved it. Vanderhook, too. Should boost attendance next year by fifty percent."

"Oh, do you think he will? Like it, I mean?" Was she blushing? Dahliah?

She was. Not much, but it was there. "Yeah, he'll love it." *Definitely* there.

"Do you really have to do a play-by-play tomorrow? We haven't had a Sunday off together for three weeks. Isn't the game on TV?"

"Not within a fifty-mile radius. Witter wants to have a special edition on the streets by the end of the ten-minute halftime interval; figures he'll sell at least fifty thousand copies, especially in the ethnic neighborhoods. Which, today, is practically all of New York. And another edition right after the game is over. Everything is arranged. They'll set type right off my modem. It's a big honor."

"But you've been working so hard, you're so tired lately, so worried, that . . . we haven't had a Sunday morning together for weeks. I love Sunday mornings. I look forward to them so—we're both rested, don't have to go to work, no responsibilities or anything. We can take our time and . . . it'll be so lovely. And then, I'll make a good, delicious breakfast, a special breakfast, and we can go back to bed again."

"We can still do it." He reached across the table and took both her hands in his, tenderly. "I can bone up on the statistics tonight—right after supper, in fact—and we'll go to bed early and wake up early and have lots of time together to do whatever we want. The game doesn't start till two, so if I'm there by one-thirty, that's all I need. We can even have lunch together."

Whatever he had to do to find the killer he could do after the game. Starting at two o'clock, with two forty-five-minute halves and a ten-minute interval, the game should be over by three-forty. Make that four, to play safe. So he had two hours to interrogate them all again. They would be very upset by the loss and maybe someone would let something slip. If not, Marc was no worse off than before, and at least Danzig would be happy to see him working. And if he had to go to jail, at least he would have had a wonderful morning with Dahliah.

The phone rang. It was Danzig. "Sorry to bother you on a Saturday night, kid, but I gotta know. What'd you find out?"

"Nothing definite yet, but I'm getting closer. Really. Much closer."

"What the hell do you mean, 'much closer'? It's been two whole days and I already gave you the two guys who done it. Just pick which one; I'll take care of the rest."

"But I don't have evidence. *Enough* evidence, I mean."

"Forget that TV crap; just get me a hole in the alibi. One lie, one lousy little lie, and I'll get the confession. I'm good at sweating perpetrators. First I get him alone, no lawyer, I explain what's gonna happen to him if he screws around with me. Usually that's when they talk, but if he's stubborn, then I take him down to the holding pen and show him the animals. He still don't cooperate, then I *begin* to put on the pressure, and I—"

"Yes, yes, I know." Marc had heard the story before, several times, in disgusting detail, and couldn't help feeling that Danzig was not only reliving his thrilling triumphs but was also envisioning Marc in the same helpless situation. Or Dahliah. "I've got a little more questioning to do tomorrow morning. Before the game, I mean."

"Not *questioning*, interrogation. How many times I gotta tell you? You're dealing with perpetrators, you gotta get tough. Put on the pressure. Tell them you know it's them, tell them you got witnesses, tell them the only way they get off easy is to make a deal. *Sweat* the bastards, you hear me?"

"Okay, okay, I know. I'll sweat them all."

"Not *all*. Don't you *never* listen to me? It's one of those two, the guys I told you. The black guy or the PR. Or maybe the other PR, but that's it. What's so damn hard about giving me a name?"

"I'm sure I'll have a name for you by six o'clock." *Sure, I'll have six names for him; a whole telephone book full.*

"And don't forget to sweat them. Give me all the dope you pick up; it'll save me time. I already wasted too much time on you already. Why don't you just do what I tell you so I don't have to make long phone calls?"

"You didn't have to bother calling me; I would've called you if I knew who did it by now."

"Yeah, well, that's what I'm calling you for. When you find out tomorrow, call the house; the desk sergeant'll know where I am every minute. Don't tell nobody *nothing*, not even your name. Some of those guys at the house got no respect; they'd do anything to steal my cases. So when you get—"

"Wait a minute, wait a minute. You're supposed to be watching over me, hanging around the stadium. You're telling me you won't be watching me? Aren't watching me? Protecting me? What if—"

"Hey, relax, kid; I work hard, you know, long hours. Got to have a little time to myself, know what I mean? It's Sunday, right?"

"But what if the killer—I mean, suppose he gets mad at me? You're setting me up, Danzig."

"Now why would I want to do that? Just use your head, will you? Ain't I better off with a witness than with a body? Just do what I tell you and we'll both be all right. I guarantee I won't be leaving Brooklyn tomorrow, okay?"

"Won't leave Brooklyn? That's supposed to make me feel safe? It could take you an hour to get to the stadium from some places in Brooklyn."

"So stall the guy, if it comes down to it. Or something. Just make sure to write the name down, just in case, and hide it where he can't find it after he—use your head, okay? Meanwhile, that ain't what I called you about. Something else came up. I just found out. The East German Team, they got threats against them by all kinds of kooks. Political and refugees and Polacks and Jews and regular Germans and anti-Commies and stuff like that. And soccer fans; they're the worst. Mobs all around their hotel, demonstrating and screaming, with bullhorns and honking their car horns and setting off firecrackers, big ones, to make sure the players don't get no sleep. And threats. The Germans even shut off the phones and asked for police protection. And on top of that, there's been rumors that the fix is in with the ref. People saying they're gonna kill the team and the coaches and the trainers and everybody."

"That's normal with soccer fans, especially for a World Cup final game. The police can handle that. You don't expect me to do anything about that, do you?"

"Hell, no; you'd be the last one I'd ask. You'd screw it up like you screw up every little thing I give you to do. Make things complicated. You sure you ain't holding anything out on me? That you think ain't important?"

"Hey, have a heart, Lieutenant. Ragusic was killed Friday morning. It's now Saturday night. I just finished talking once to each suspect; twice to a couple of them. What do you expect?"

"Yeah, well, that's what I called you about. The Germans are worried somebody's gonna bomb the hotel after the game if they win. And they're sure they're gonna win. So they're leaving direct from the stadium, right after they win the game. So just in case you was wrong about who done it, in case it was one of them, you don't have till six o'clock. You gotta give me the perpetrator by the end of the game." Danzig hung up.

Marc hung up, too. Bad things don't come only in threes; sometimes they come in ones. He turned slowly to Dahliah. "What's wrong?" she asked, the moment she saw his face.

"Nothing serious. Really. Only—I have to be at the stadium very early tomorrow morning, before practice starts." No way would Grilho let him even *see* anyone between the end of practice and the game. "We'll—uh— have next Sunday morning together, right?"

"Don't bother," Dahliah said icily. "I'm not in the mood. And I don't think I'll be in the mood next Sunday either. Or the Sunday after." She stopped preparing the salad and walked out of the kitchen area. "And you can make your own supper. Frozen nitrates or something. With *meat.*"

# 30

It barely registered on his bleary eyes that he was the first one to get into Koch Stadium; that the security guard had started the new page for Sunday with Marc's name at the top. Even though he had spent a full five minutes in the shower that morning, a really *hot* shower, he felt as grimy and as granular as the littered gray streets of the plaza surrounding the players' entrance. It wasn't just the fight with Dahliah the night before that had frustrated his angry, pillow-pounding attempts to sleep. It wasn't just the pain in his back, either, though that was the worst— the small of his back, to be specific—but the impossible, *unbelievable*, predicament he was in. From trying to *avoid* trouble. And to protect Dahliah, which she didn't understand, much less appreciate.

From the far end of the dark corridor, he could see Frankie Guzman, the next one to come in, unlocking the steel-mesh door of the equipment room. Two locks, one high and one low, requiring double turns each. So they had to be dead bolts. The lights in the room came on, and a minute later, Frankie came out, pushing the loaded clean-equipment cart that Marc had seen at the first interview. Frankie left the lights on in the room but carefully locked both locks before he pushed the cart into the locker room. There went another theory.

It was a full fifteen minutes later that Grilho came in. He walked quickly, purposefully into the locker room, just as Frankie came out pushing the now empty clean-equipment cart. It suddenly struck Marc—something from his last talk with Guzman. He walked over to the equipment room, getting there just as the boy was snapping the bottom lock closed. "Hi, Frankie," Marc said, leaning his elbows on the door's pass-through shelf in what he hoped was a friendly, casual manner, "one more thing. Didn't you tell me the other day that you distributed the equipment for the players the night before? So if the subway got stuck, you'd still be in the clear?"

"Yeah?" Frankie said suspiciously. "So what?"

"Well, I just happened to see you coming out of the locker room with your cart."

"You been watching me? What for?"

"I just came in. Happened to see you."

"Yeah? Who you kidding? But you wrong, man. I don't have to lie 'cause I'm clean. This is a *game* day. Grilho, he likes *all* the equipment in the lockers on game days, case somebody needs to change, or he don't like how something fits or something. Ask him."

"No, no, that's all right." Marc moved away slowly. "Got to run, now. See you." Another theory shot to . . . what theory? A vain hope that if he caught somebody in a lie, the murderer would immediately break down and pour out a full confession. Too much TV; that was the trouble. He had to cut down and read some good whodunits for a change. And he should have been tougher, the way Danzig wanted. No more Mr. Nice Guy.

Boni and Steve Vanderhook came in together. Marc waved and started over to meet them. Both tall, blond, and handsome. *See what you missed, Dahliah, by not being here with me?* Steve, a vicious smile on his face, raced his heavy wheelchair, fast, maximum speed, toward Marc, and just when Marc thought he'd have to dive to avoid being hit, Steve skillfully made a skidding racing turn and stopped dead in front of the elevator. He laughed as Marc peeled himself off the wall. "Very funny, Commissioner," Marc said sourly. "One of these days I'm going to write a column on how childish a grown executive can be."

"Hey, relax, Marc," Vanderhook said, still laughing, "why are you in such a bad mood? I had perfect control. And I have an excuse. All day long I have to be dignified, so if once in a while I have a chance to fool around a little . . . how's Miss Norman?"

*Is Dahliah what thinking about fooling around reminds you of?* "She sleeps late, just like other women. Lazy. Dull." *You wouldn't like her, Steve, really, Marc prayed.*

"I thought she was interesting and intelligent. I'd like to see her again; her views on the psychology of athletes are very stimulating. Is she coming to the game?"

"She's not really a sports reporter, so there's no place for her in the press box."

"That's no problem, Marc. I was invited by Gregor to watch the game from his special box, you know, the one that sticks way out from the roof over the top tier at midfield. The long, pointed thing that looks like the cockpit of a 747. It's really the best seat in the house by far:

tinted glass all around almost down to the floor, unob-
structed views of both goal lines. And very plush: carpeted, air conditioned, good sound system, closed-circuit
TV, a bar, refrigerator, a microwave for hot snacks,
comfortable sofas, everything. If Miss Norman would like
to . . . as my guest? Call her up; ask her. Or would you
rather I called? Give me her number and I'll invite her
myself."

"I don't think you understand, Mr. Vanderhook; Dahliah and I live together. We're sort of engaged. To be
married."

"Oh, I didn't mean. . . ." Yes he did, Marc decided.
Why else was he blushing? "When you introduced her on
Friday, you just told me she was working on a special
article. I didn't realize . . . sometimes I'm very obtuse. As
long as that's the relationship," Steve continued, "you're
invited, too, Marc, of course. There's plenty of room.
Under the circumstances, Mrs. Ragusic and the family
won't be there. No one will be there, and I didn't want to
watch alone. I prefer company."

"Thanks, Steve, but I can't. I'm doing play-by-play and
I'm all set up in the press box." Not quite true, but he
would be set up there shortly.

"Well, if you should change your mind . . . or Miss
Norman . . . just come on up; it's right off this elevator.
To avoid the crowds, I go up very early and come
down late, but you don't need me to escort you. Once I'm
up there I'll unlock the controls. You take this elevator.
Push the top button on the panel—it's unmarked—three
times quickly, wait one second and repeat two more
times. It'll take you to the top level, the door will open
automatically, and you walk right into the back end of the
private box."

"Okay, if I can. One more thing, Steve. When we spoke
on Friday, I was a little shook up. I forgot to ask you
something. You were one of the first people to come to the

stadium, right after Grilho, in fact. You said you went right upstairs to your office. When you did, did you see anyone in the corridor?"

"No, in my office. Grilho and I met for a few minutes to go over contingency plans. We agreed that I would send a telegram to FIFA for each serious violation the referee allows at the time of violation, not just after the game. I've already arranged with the TV network to provide us with a videotape from each of their cameras so that we can back up our claims."

"Will FIFA forfeit the game to us if we prove deliberate fouling?"

"Don't be silly. What we're hoping for is that word of what I'm doing will leak out and cut down the fouls to manageable proportions."

"Did you leave your office after that? See anyone else?"

"No."

"So Grilho could have killed Ragusic after he left you?"

"Or before, but he didn't. You know the man, and I know him better than you do. He's not the type. His character . . . it's impossible."

"Was he in uniform?" Grilho was the only other man on the team who wore six-stud soccer shoes.

"First thing he does. I think he feels uncomfortable out of uniform." Steve pressed the button for the elevator. The door opened immediately. He wheeled in easily and held his hand on the rubber safety bumper. "Going up?"

Marc shook his head. "Thanks, but I've got to get ready. Interview the—some of the players." The suspects, that is; who knew what might turn up.

"If Miss Norman decides she can't come today, tell her she can come around any other time for an interview. With you, of course," Vanderhook said, letting the door close. "Don't hold your breath," Marc said under his breath, and went off to talk to Boni. Damn, why wasn't he talking tough, making people sweat? He'd never get anywhere this way. He decided to act like Danzig from now on. Or as close as he could get. Which probably wouldn't fool anyone.

Boni was in full uniform, leaning on his cane, talking earnestly with José Velez in the corridor near the locker room. Not wanting to interrupt their conversation, Marc stopped a short distance behind them, but close enough to hear what was said. "Stop worrying," Boni said. "I've arranged to have a video camera crew, with telephoto lenses, follow whoever has control of the ball. Nothing but that. If they foul you, we'll have it on tape. Like instant replay."

"What good'll that do me or the team," José asked, "if I got a broken ankle? What the ref says, goes, even if they use machine guns. And you know they're gonna go after me, 'cause I'm skinny." He paused for a moment, then asked, "Does Grilho know?"

"Father is very old-fashioned. Gives everybody a chance to do what's right."

"Tell you what you should do, then. Pass the word around, what you're doing. Tell them you got three cameras going, full time, so they don't figure what angle is safe to take a cheap shot at me. Or the other forwards. Say any screwing around, you put the foul on TV. Those guys are very big on image. Maybe if you scare them I can walk out with my bones in good condition." He started to walk away, then turned back. "Hey, thanks for figuring out something. I'm gonna need all the help I can get." Velez went out to the field.

Boni, looking very unhappy, was still leaning against the wall when Marc walked over to him. "I couldn't help overhearing what you said," Marc told him, "and I want you to know I'll be watching, too. And if they pull anything too raw, I'll blast them in my Monday column."

"Yeah, thanks, Marc, but what good will that do? They'll be gone by Monday. And what can you see from the press box that the referee can't see? If he doesn't call it, it isn't a foul. You can't challenge him, either; you can get a red card for just looking cross-eyed at the ref."

"Whatever I can do, I'll do."

"Really?" Boni looked at him skeptically. "I didn't see anything in your column after the Bulgarian game. Where I got this." He pointed the cane at his left foot. "And two more of our starting forwards got killed."

"I wrote it, but it was cut."

"So what good can you do? You going to resign publicly if they censor your column again?"

Marc squirmed. "I can't afford to; I'm planning to get married. In the near future." Maybe the far future. "But I'll try."

"Yeah, sure." Boni smiled cynically. "Meanwhile, you're making sure we'll lose, upsetting everybody, being Danzig's stooge."

"You want the murderer to get away with it? Is that your idea of justice?"

"Ragusic was a mean, greedy bastard who hurt a lot of people and you know it. He deserved what he got. Justice? Yes, I think it was justice that he was killed. What he was doing to Father alone. . . ." Boni had that murderous look on his face again. "Why don't you just drop the whole thing, Burr? Danzig will never arrest anyone if you don't help him."

*That's what you think; he can always arrest me. And Dahliah. Maybe not for murder, but for something.* "Why are you so anxious for the killer to get away with it?"

"Because one of us has to have done it. This time it's a

good guy who kills the bad guy, and I want to see the good guys win, for once."

"Someone close to you?" Marc pressed harder.

Boni's throat swelled and the veins stood out on his forehead. He stood up straight, clutched his cane firmly in his right hand, and loomed menacingly over Marc. "You'd better not tell Danzig that," he growled. "If Danzig arrests my father, for anything, he'll have another murder to solve one day later. You. And you can quote me." He walked off stiffly. Marc noticed the big forward wasn't using his cane.

How to win friends and influence people. So what? With the number of enemies Marc had now, he didn't have time for friends. It was beginning to look as if the tougher approach brought results of a kind.

Jason Benjamin came out of the locker room. Marc caught his eye and hurried over. "Got a minute, Jason?"

"Yeah, I guess so," the tall goalie said. "Only not here. Let's go into the gym; it's not too popular to be seen talking to you these days."

They started walking down the main corridor. "What's wrong with talking to me? I quote accurately, I don't start trouble, and I really like sports, not like some of the other reporters."

"It's not sports," Jason explained. "It's that you're working for Lieutenant Danzig, trying to find the murderer."

"I'm not working for him," Marc said wearily. "And what's wrong with my trying to find the killer? Since when is it illegal, immoral, or fattening for a reporter to try to get a good exclusive? Don't you want the murderer found?"

"Sure, so I can give him a gold star. But actually, no. Why should I care? Whoever we get for a new owner has to be better than Ragusic. The way I look at it, the killer did me a favor."

They arrived at the gym, a brightly lit, clean, modern exercise center with carpeted floors and shiny chrome equipment, mirrors all around, and racks of light weights. Soccer players don't want to build up their arms and shoulders; ten pounds of upper-body muscle is just as hard to accelerate as ten pounds of fat. The far half of the room was covered by a large, thin mat for tumbling practice for the goalies, who spent a good deal of time airborne, diving through space to make their stops. It was also used by forwards who spent a good deal of their time on their butts after having been dumped in a hard tackle by a defenseman. Occasionally some of the forwards used the mat to practice the bicycle kick, a fancy maneuver in which the striker, his back to the goal, takes off from the passive foot like a high jumper, and in mid air with his body horizontal, swings the other foot vertically to kick the ball back over his head and into the goal. He hopes. Beautiful, when it works. Grilho used to do it about once a year, and he did it well, but damned few others did. He succeeded because he used the kick only when everything was perfect for it, not to show off.

A small area of bare floor was outlined for jumping rope. In one corner of the room was a bank of adjustable sit-up boards lined up in front of a row of stationary bicycles and treadmills. There were the various specialized Nautilus and hydraulic machines, a small complement of gymnastic apparatus, and three sets of vertical ladders fixed to the wall, complete with adjustable heel brackets and slant boards for stretching the calves and hamstrings. Near the single entrance was an open area for calisthenics.

Marc walked over to the quadriceps machine, the chrome-and-leather device used for strengthening the big muscles in the front of the thighs. "This where you rested on Friday?"

"It's the most comfortable," Jason said. "The head pad is like a pillow and there's a bend at the knees that really takes all the tension out of your legs."

"No one saw you in here?"

"My eyes were closed. If anyone peeked in here, he didn't make a sound. Anybody say anything to you?"

Interesting question. Marc tested. "Your eyes weren't closed when you walked here. Why didn't you say you saw somebody before?"

"Somebody said I saw him? To you? Who?" Marc kept his mouth shut, just smiled knowingly. Jason looked very uncomfortable, itchy, fidgety. After another minute of silence, he said, "It's possible that I—the light in the hall was dim. I think—keep in mind that it was in the other direction, so it wasn't like I was *near* him or anything. . . ." Marc still waited. "I think I might have seen Cuffy near the elevator. Sort of in front of the elevator. But I'm not sure it was him."

"Not *sure*?"

"Well, his back was toward me and he's dark-skinned and the light was dim and. . . ."

Dark-skinned? That told Marc something, too. "He was in uniform and you didn't know who it was?"

"Well, Grilho is sort of dark, too."

"Come on, Jason; Cuffy is twice as wide as Grilho."

"Not all over. They both have big thighs. We all have big thighs, even me."

"You could have saved us both a lot of trouble if you'd told me before. The first time." Marc stopped to think. "Were they wearing numbers?"

"Not for practice."

"What color was the uniform?"

"It looked blue, but it's hard . . . I told you, the light was dim in the hall."

"Hard to tell blue from red? Grilho was wearing the

260

opponent's colors for practice. It was Cuffy, wasn't it?"

"Look, anybody could be wearing any uniform; we all have extra sets in our lockers. I just wasn't sure, so why should I make trouble for a guy I like when I'm not sure?"

"A guy who is also one of the four remaining forwards? Your only chance to share the prize money and be on a World Cup winner?"

"I didn't even think of that at the time."

"But you did later, didn't you?" No response. "You have anything against Grilho?"

"Me? No, of course not. He's the greatest. Was."

"Then why try to throw the blame on him?"

"I didn't. It's just that . . . I really didn't. The light. . . ."

"I know. You said Grilho because he's the only dark-skinned guy around besides Cuffy. The way you're acting, you think Cuffy did it."

"I . . . Cuffy said he told the police he didn't go upstairs. I believe him. I didn't *see* him go upstairs; all I saw was him standing in the hall."

"Near the elevator."

"In the *vicinity* of the elevator. Don't make trouble for Cuffy, Marc. He's not the type to—"

"Who is the type, then? You? You told me you're the smartest guy on the team. You know what? I believe you. I think you're smart enough to drop hints, act like you're lying, just to make me think I'm pulling a story out of you, that you're trying to protect a buddy. When actually you're trying to throw suspicion on somebody else. And it makes me wonder why." Marc took a deep breath. "All you guys; I thought I knew you. And all of you are jerking me around. Nobody tells me the truth."

"Everything I told you was the truth."

"Yeah? Okay, I believe that, too, the way you put it. But the *whole* truth? Everybody's holding back something; every single one of you. And I'm wondering why. As far as I can see, one of you is the killer, and I'm not sure it isn't you, Benjamin." This time it was Marc who stalked off. It felt good to be the stalker, for a change.

# 31

As usual, Grilho was the only one outside this early, doing his bending and stretching and twisting exercises in midfield. Marc marched right up to him and said, "I have to talk to you, Grilho."

"Some other time, please." He did not stop his exercises.

"That will be too late. Practice starts in half an hour and you won't interrupt that. After practice, the players will be isolated, and I won't be able to talk to you."

"After the game I will talk to you. To all the reporters."

"This must be private and it can't wait till after the game." Grilho kept on bending and stretching. "Danzig is ready to make an arrest before the game."

Grilho stopped moving; stood very stiffly. "You know this for sure?"

"Not in so many words, but he's going to make an

arrest before the GDR Team leaves town. And I found out that they're planning to leave immediately after the game and go directly to the airport. The plane will take off as soon as they're on it. All the arrangements have been made."

Grilho's face grew hard, the flinty Indian look Marc had seen once before. "They expect trouble, which means they will give cause for trouble. My players are in good condition and we are ready for them. But there is more; I can tell from the way you look at me."

Marc squirmed. "It's only a rumor, but they say the fix is in. With the referee."

"To be expected. But I don't think they will try anything too rough. There will be too many cameras watching. But everyone is expecting that the referee will shade some close decisions against us. I have told my players to live with that, not to complain. We cannot afford a red card." He stared closely at Marc. "You did not come here to tell me only this. What is it? Time is short."

Marc braced himself. "When I last spoke to you, you didn't tell me you went up to the second floor shortly after you came in."

"You did not ask me. I went to see the Commissioner— it was only a few minutes—to confirm something we had previously discussed. It is easier for me to go to him than for him to come to me. It did not concern Ragusic."

"You took the elevator?"

"I do not need elevators for such a short distance. The stairs are quicker."

"Did you see anyone while you were up there?"

"The Commissioner's office is at the extreme far end of the offices, in the opposite direction. My back was turned when I went there."

"But coming back?"

"I saw no one in either direction."

"Would it surprise you to know that there were witnesses who saw several of your players on the second floor about the time of the murder?" Lying was getting easier and easier for Marc. Normal questioning, Danzig would have called it.

Grilho was remarkably calm. "No doubt they had business up there. That is where all the offices are."

"There are never any people in the offices that early, other than Ragusic. And none of them volunteered to the police that they were up there. Then, when they were identified by witnesses, they suddenly remembered. That includes you."

"It is natural. They were frightened of the police. As I was."

"Lieutenant Danzig intends to arrest one of them before the game starts."

"Boni will not be arrested."

Bingo! The Danzig technique had paid off. "You're sure of that? You fixed it? With the help of Grinell Hollingsworth? Even if Boni's the murderer? This is the morality you're so proud of?"

Grilho flushed. "He is not the murderer. If there is sufficient evidence, clear evidence, *proof,* then I will know what to do." Grilho looked ready to cry. Or to kill.

Might as well complete the slaughter. But first Marc stepped back, out of reach of any kick. "Danzig may not be allowed to arrest Boni, but he can surely arrest one of your starters. Before the game. A forward. Or your prize goalie."

"No!" The cry came suddenly, involuntarily, from deep inside Grilho. "No. It is not . . . they did not . . . the game!"

"How do you know none of them did it?" Marc pressed hard. "How could you know?"

Grilho regained control of himself. This was the man who never got excited, who helped back to his feet the opponent who had fouled him. He faced Marc calmly. "I

must complete my exercises, otherwise I will stiffen up."
He began bending and stretching again, ignoring Marc
completely. There was no way Marc could reach him, and
he was sure, no way he could startle Grilho again.

Marc jogged off toward the locker-room entrance. He
still had not spoken to Cuffy and José, and it was getting
close to the time he would be cut off from them, and them
from him, until the end of the game. For those few hours,
he would be safe.

José Velez was slouching in a chair in the locker room.
Marc motioned the slim forward to come out. Velez lazily
waved Marc to go away and stop bothering him. Marc
strode in angrily—he had had just about enough of these
guys' lack of cooperation, outright antagonism, when you
came down to it—and whispered into José's ear. "Do you
want me to say what I have to say in front of everybody
here? Or if that would embarrass you too much, I can
always call Danzig and tell him what I found out. Which?"

Velez got up fast and beat Marc to the door. He led Marc
past the gym entrance to the far end of the corridor and
turned to face him. "What the hell you trying to do,
threaten me? I been threaten by guys could eat you alive
and I'm still here."

"I'm busting my ass to help you and you're lying to me.
What the hell do you expect me to do, give you a medal?"

"Helping me? How you helping me?"

"You said you were going to tell Danzig what you did."

"I said *maybe*. Think about it."

"I figured you were telling the truth, so to cover for you,
to make it look like you did it voluntarily, I didn't tell
Danzig, either. Now I'm in trouble with Danzig. He's
going to want to know why I didn't tell him on Friday."

"That's okay; you cover for me, I cover for you. I'll tell
him right after the game; not mention your name."

"Nope, that'll be too late. And not enough. Why'd you
tell me you heard Ragusic's door close?"

" 'Cause I did. When I was coming up in the elevator."

"You couldn't have heard it from there. You heard it close when you closed it behind you, when you went into Ragusic's office."

"Who says?"

"The guy who saw you go in." Even in the dim light, Marc saw the tan face pale. Double bingo.

"He's the killer," Velez whispered. "If he saw that, he gotta be the killer. Who was it?"

"I don't know. Anonymous phone call to me." Marc didn't even blink when he said this; after the first lie, the rest come easy. *Harvey Danzig, you would be proud of me.*

"Listen," Velez grabbed the lapels of Marc's jacket desperately. "You got to put it out, around, that I never saw who did it."

"Why should I? You didn't level with me. You got me in trouble."

"Accident. You trying to get me killed."

"I'm trying to save you, José. You think the murderer will believe me if I say you didn't see him coming out of the office ahead of you? No way. He'll think you did see him and you're just holding out on the police to trade off if they ever get you on something—a missing green card for some member of your family, or running guns to the anti-Castro crowd. Whatever. Or maybe to blackmail him later. No, the only way you'll be safe is if we catch the murderer. And the only way that's going to happen is for you to start telling me the truth."

Velez looked badly shaken. "Look, I did tell you the truth. Just the time was off a little. I never saw the guy, I swear. When I got there, Ragusic was already dead."

"You were the first to find him, weren't you?"

"I guess. I seen plenty bodies when I was a kid; you don't forget them things. Ragusic—the blood was first starting to come up when I looked inside. I didn't have to go in; I knew. I also knew it was a soccer player."

"You knew more than that. You saw the shape of the head, the two heel cleats."

"Listen, you know who wears them on this team? Only two guys. Both of them rich and connected. I mean connected *good*. Even if I saw him *doing* it, you think it'd stand up? Hell, these guys are richer than the Kennedys. They could get a hundred guys who'd take care of me, my whole *family*, for a couple of bills each. And another hundred guys who'd take care of the first guys to make sure."

"What did you see? Talk."

"Nothing. I went to talk to Ragusic about money, figured this was the best time, now that I'm a starting forward. I knew the secretary wouldn't be there, so I went in fast and knocked on his door. No answer. I opened the door and there he was. I took one look, knew what the score was, and I took off fast. Not that fast. I took a quick look outside, through the crack, didn't see nobody, then I took off. Down the stairs. The whole thing took one minute, I swear, from when I ran up to when I ran down. I'm fast. And I didn't see nobody."

"Did you see anybody was missing, someone who came in later than he was supposed to?"

"I didn't see, and I didn't want to see. Things like that, the less you know, the better. Besides, how would I know who was supposed to be in the locker room at what time?"

"Then what did you do?"

"Got dressed fast and went out to the field. Figured whoever it was, let him think I was only interested in practice."

"You reported to Grilho? Did stretching?"

"Yeah, sure, when he came out."

"Came out? He wasn't there when you went out?"

"Not right away. Maybe a minute later. Why?"

"Was anyone on the field when you went out? Cuffy? Boni? Benjamin?"

"Nobody."

"Who was in the locker room when you came down-stairs?"

"Everybody."

"Cuffy? Boni? Benjamin? *Grilho*?"

"I don't remember." Very short. Velez suddenly shut his mouth firmly. When he spoke, his attitude seemed to have changed completely. He even smiled weakly. "Hey, we been out here too long; make people suspicious. I'm going back to the locker room. And don't worry, I'll tell Danzig what I did as soon as I see him."

Marc watched him walk away, certain that Velez had remembered. The only problem was, which one of the suspects was not in the locker room when Velez came in after finding the body? Assuming Velez had *found* the body and not—Velez had a habit of telling you only what he wanted you to know, and if caught in an inconsistency, giving out a little more, as little as possible.

Maybe Cuffy would know. If Cuffy was in the locker room at that time in the first place. Even if he was, it didn't mean that he didn't dash down the stairs one minute ahead of Velez. Well, only one way to find out.

Marc caught Cuffy just as he was about to leave the locker room. Cuffy groaned. "Make it fast, mon, I don't like to be late when Grilho calls practice."

"Okay," Marc said coldly. "Tell me why you lied to me about the last time you saw Ragusic."

"Me? Lie? I don't lie."

"I have a witness who saw you going upstairs first thing in the morning. That morning. In uniform." Why else would Cuffy be standing in front of the elevator at that time?

"Upstairs don't mean I saw Ragusic."

"I have another witness who saw you coming out of Ragusic's office. You lie to me once more and I'll tell Danzig everything I know." Marc meant it, too. Cuffy was a nice guy, maybe, but in a choice between Cuffy and Dahliah—between Cuffy and *Marc*—Cuffy lost every time.

"Couldn't nobody see me coming out of Ragusic's office. 'Less he was in the secretary's office. All he could see was me coming out of *her* office."

"Don't play games with me, Cuffy. My neck is on the line. Why did you lie?"

"Same reason everybody lie. 'Cause I didn't want nobody to think I killed him. They know I be up there and they look at my face, they know they got themselves a good murderer. All they need is for me to be black. You don't know what it's like, so don't you tell me how to be."

"What did you see?"

"Nothing. I knock on door, no answer, I go out right away."

"Dammit, Cuffy, tell the truth for once. If you don't level with me, you're going to have to talk to Danzig, and he'll get it out of you the hard way."

"And if I tell you something?"

"If you're not the killer . . . it'll help me find the real killer."

Cuffy took a long, hard look at Marc, then came to a decision. "I put my head inside, see he's on the floor, look fresh dead, and I get out of there fast."

"Did you see anyone up there? Or on the way up or down?"

"Nobody. Didn't want to see nobody, either."

"Where did you go when you got down?"

"Locker room. Try to look cool."

"Was anyone missing? Someone who should have been there?"

"Lots of people didn't come in yet. It was early."

"Boni, Grilho, Benjamin, Velez?"

"Didn't see none of them. José came in couple minutes later. That be all." He looked around; everyone else had gone outside. "Hey, got to go now; I be last again. Grilho, he be mad at me."

Marc let out his breath. At last, he had gotten the accurate picture. But what good did that do? Now he was sure of what he had suspected before. Everyone had lied, everyone had a motive, everyone had the means, everyone had the opportunity, and he didn't have the slightest idea who did it.

# 32

It didn't take Marc long to set up his play-by-play tools: the portable computer, with its modem connected to the telephone, ready to switch on; the stacks of cards for background on each player, coach, and official, color-coded blue for the U.S. Team, red for the GDR Team, and white—for purity—for the officials; the chart with the players' numbers propped up for quick reference; the diagram of the referee's twenty official signals; the electronic timer/stopwatch combination; the miniature TV hooked up to the closed-circuit transmitter; the large-print copy of the official rules; and most important, a thermos of hot herb tea, a container of vegetable soup, an apple, a container of certified-milk yogurt, and two bran muffins. And a pneumatic headrest for the waiting period. Which was now.

The game wouldn't start until two o'clock and it was

only a little after eight. Marc glanced out the slanted windows, looking down on the smooth green field where the blue team was bending, twisting, stretching; light, relaxing exercises before the game in perfect rhythm to the ever-present *"Tico Tico."* The players were moving in unison like a ballet company, smoothly, gracefully, in perfect harmony. It was not the calisthenic snaps and jerks athletes usually displayed, but more like the *Tai Chi Chuan* movements the Chinese favored, swaying, circling, bouncing in time with the fast rhythm of the samba. Only, Marc realized, there was no music. Not one sound in the locker room, in the halls, on the field. Nowhere. Yet down on the field, they were all moving in exact coordination. The music now beat in their heads, in their hearts, in their movements, like true Brazilians, like real *Cariocas,* residents of Rio. Grilho had succeeded in making the samba part of them when they moved, when they played soccer, when they *breathed,* so that now, no matter where each man was, he was moving in time with his fellow players, like ballroom dancers, able to gauge with a glance where each of his teammates would be two bars later.

There was more to Grilho than Marc had realized. He knew that this apparently simple, *natural,* perfect athlete was more than just a soccer player, but still Marc was surprised that he was surprised at how intelligent and deeply understanding Grilho was.

The question was, would this team of unnatural Americans, Americans who had to use their feet instead of their hands, this team of fancy dancing masters, this slender foil, be able to withstand the blows of the heavy saber, the invincible military march of the East German massed tanks moving to the march of *"Deutschland, Deutschland Über Alles?"* Germany, Germany, over everything. No, wrong, that was the old anthem, not the present one, which was—he didn't remember. No difference. Whatever it was, it had to be a somber march, military, not a fast, fun-loving dance tune, and as is all-too-often the case, the heavy tread of jackboots would soon crush the fluttering butterflies.

There was no point in watching the team exercise, nor later seeing the GDR Team work out. Neither team would show anything worthwhile for the opposing coach to take note of. Besides, he was tired. Last night, the way Dahliah had been acting, he had gotten very little sleep. Not that it was all Dahliah's fault—the fight was, yes, but not the *whole* night's sleeplessness—but as long as he was awake, his mind had gone to the *big* problem: Danzig. That took care of the rest of the night. And those bastardly suspects. If they had only told him the truth the first time around, he might now be closer to a solution of his troubles with Danzig. Now, all the time he had left was till the end of the game, plus whatever he could think of now.

Frankie? True he wasn't a suspect, a *real* suspect, but still, he had been the first one to come in after Ragusic. And he had access to any floor. No one noticed people like Frankie; they just took them for granted. And he had perfect access to Boni's shoes. No real good motive for killing Ragusic, unless Ragusic had caught him doing something criminal. Stealing, peddling drugs, whatever. Unlikely that Frankie would take such chances, or if he did, would let himself be caught. He did have a juvenile record, but nothing lately. Still . . . better leave him on the list.

Steve? Could Steve have seen something? It was very convenient for him that Ragusic had been killed; might not Steve have seen the killer and decided to keep his mouth shut? Particularly if the killer was someone he liked, such as Grilho or Boni? Both of them were needed for Steve's future plans for the league. A scandal would be bad for the image of the league; better an unsolved crime.

Grilho? He had motive, means, and opportunity; they all did. But was it in his character? Most certainly not.

Grilho would kill only in defense of his family. To protect Boni? But Boni was already protected. Between Grinell Hollingsworth and Grilho, Boni could probably assassinate the President and not even be arrested. But that was after the fact. Might Grilho have done it—wearing his own shoes—without considering that Boni would be suspected? Yes, if Boni was threatened by Ragusic and if you could believe that the cool, controlled Grilho could lose his temper that badly, that suddenly. Which was unbelievable. Would Grilho let his son hang for the crime? Never. If it came down to it, if there were no other way, Marc was sure Grilho would confess to the murder to save Boni, even if he didn't do it. But as of now, Boni was in no danger of being arrested; the fix was already in.

Boni? Possible. A sprained left ankle wouldn't stop him from kicking Ragusic's head in with his right foot, especially if he was carrying a cane or a crutch. Which he was. Boni could probably even climb the stairs, though the elevator was perfectly acceptable. He had no reason not to go see Ragusic, and if the murder was not planned, would not mind being seen going upstairs. He had been very careful not to tell Marc anything useful, not where he had been or what he had seen, and he had been very upset by Marc's questions. It seemed to Marc that Boni had been more concerned about the possibility that his father would be suspected than about protecting himself. But then, that was natural, assuming he thought his father may have committed the crime. Boni certainly knew more about his father's character than anyone else.

Jason Benjamin? By his own admission, the smartest man on the team. There were no witnesses that he had indeed slept in the gym. There was nothing to stop him from running upstairs, killing Ragusic, and then doing his sleeping in the gym. His feet were big enough to fit Boni's shoes—there had to be some way he could get hold of a pair—and the rest of the scenario would be just as Marc had first envisioned. Motive? Sure. At least as much as any of the others, maybe more. Forget that tack; they all had strong motives. With Ragusic, it seemed, the motive was a given. Means—hell, they were all soccer players. With mighty thighs. Opportunity? A three-minute disappearance was all that was needed.

Cuffy Royal? Lied about where he was at first, then admitted he was at the body within seconds after the murder. No more than a minute, for sure. If he was telling the truth. He could have described Ragusic's body just as well if he had been the murderer. And if he did come on the scene that soon after the murder, why didn't he see the killer running down the stairs or the stair door closing or *something*?

Which led to José Velez, the fastest man in soccer. Could José have been that fast? Sure. The stairs weren't far from Ragusic's office; neither was the elevator. He had lied, too, almost automatically changing his story as Marc learned more and more. He might have seen Cuffy coming out of Ragusic's office, or Benjamin, both easily recognizable, even from behind. Or he might have killed Ragusic himself and then seen Cuffy. His fear of the killer, the worry about the killer thinking José knew who the killer was, may have been real, or it may have been protective camouflage. No way to tell.

Which was another problem. Right now, Marc was alone in the press box, his back to the entrance, nothing but a pencil for a weapon. The killer could sneak in noiselessly—the carpet was heavy—and kick his head in. Marc swiveled around quickly. No one was there. But what could he do? Hang a sign around his neck saying he had no idea who the killer was? No, he'd just have to stay alert, back to the window, and be ready to run. No, not run; he couldn't outrun a soccer player. Be prepared to scream, bring the whole press corps running? If they came on time? Then another paper would get the story. His story. So unfair. After all he'd done. And almost lost Dahliah. Maybe already lost . . . and he'd had no sleep. So tired. The killer probably knew Marc didn't know who he was. Might be better to close—*almost* close—his eyes; *look* like he was sleeping—lean his head back against the pneumatic pillow and keep an eye on the entrance to the press room. Anyone who came in who didn't belong there had to be the killer. Trap him. That's what Danzig wanted, anyway. There was plenty of light shining on the entrance; easy to see the killer come in. The sun was getting higher, warmer. . . . Marc shifted slightly, head back a bit more, eyes watching the entrance through the slit. He stretched his legs out, relaxing, warmer, warmer . . . the pencil dropped out of his hand.

# 33

Marc opened his eyes in panic, but it was only Eli Rosen shaking him gently. "This is what I pay you for?" Eli kidded. "If I had a camera, you'd be buying me lunches for a month."

"I just. . . ." His heart was still pounding; it could have been. . . . Marc drew a deep breath and let it out slowly, relieved. "I was very . . . I've been under a lot of pressure," he explained. "Not getting much sleep." Thank God it was Eli, not the murderer. Asleep, he had been completely helpless, vulnerable. And the dream . . . what had he dreamed? Something about the murder, that he was sure of, but what?

"The game starts soon," Eli said, "and your computer light isn't on. Aren't you going to give them some background on the weather and the crowd and the mood?"

"Yeah, sure," Marc said, turning toward his terminal. "You want to copy mine or should I copy yours?"

"I have my own inimitable style," Rosen said. "It would raise suspicions if I started using good English for a change."

---

The U.S. Team won the coin toss and kicked off. John Geis rolled a short pass to his adjoining center forward, Teddy Pangos, who dribbled the ball a few yards before kicking a low pass to José Velez on his left, who was speeding toward the touchline. José took the pass on the run and dribbled toward the corner, trying to get near enough to pass to Geis, who had made his way deep into GDR territory. The five Red forwards fell back fast to consolidate with their three midfielders, trying to get two-on-one coverage of the Blue attackers. The two Blue halfbacks, Frank Santaro and Jan Lesko, had moved forward to follow the attack, but wouldn't go too far across the midfield line in case they had to pull back to defend against loss of control of the ball.

When José, already hard pressed, was ready to pass, he found no one free. Desperately he kicked a high cross toward the far corner of the goal, hoping to catch Cuffy Royal coming in fast from the other wing, but there were two Red jerseys dogging the Blue right winger and one of them, Johannes Waldman, headed the ball in an easy pass back to his own goalkeeper, Leopold Volker. Volker caught the ball, ran forward three steps, and threw the ball in front of Dieter Schotz, the GDR star forward. Schotz and Ludwig Bauer passed the ball rapidly between themselves, moving slowly toward midfield, until the full five-man forward line had caught up and was moving ahead like the vanguard of an army, funneling in toward the Blue goal. The four Blue forwards and their two halfbacks were already retreating into a defensive array, trying to drive the Red formation toward the touchlines, as the four Blue fullbacks pulled out to meet the challenge.

The defenders solidified in front of the penalty area and Jason Benjamin shifted back and forth to take the best cutoff position with each pass of the ball. The Reds suddenly converged in front of the penalty area, and as suddenly, broke for four different positions, spreading the defenders, who had been marking them closely, pulling them away from the penalty area, leaving Schotz with only two men between him and the goalkeeper. Schotz faked a pass to his left, dribbled around fullback Ian MacDougal, and made a run for the right side of the goal. Fullback Szalman Abbas made a diving tackle for the ball and missed, but forced Schotz to swerve to his right, reducing the angle of the shot.

Schotz faked a kick to the far side of the goal and booted a hard one for the upper near corner, but Benjamin wasn't fooled and caught the ball easily. The first attack by both sides was over. Neither side had scored, but Marc could see that, if this pattern continued, the German Team was going to have control of the ball far longer than the U.S. Team. Which meant more shots on the goal. Which meant, usually, more goals. And all this in the first five minutes of the first half.

Benjamin, with seven Reds near his goal, nodded to José Velez and booted a seventy-yard drive deep into the almost-empty Red half of the pitch. José, the speed demon, had taken off at Jason's nod and reached the ball before any of the Red defenders. He took the ball on the run and began dribbling toward the Red goal, waiting for the other Blue forwards to catch up. As soon as Teddy Pangos came up, José bounced a short pass into his path and made for the left touchline. Pangos took the ball a few yards toward the right corner as Cuffy Royal came tearing along the right touchline. Pangos slammed a low, hard pass to Cuffy, which Cuffy took on the fly and kicked right back toward the far goalpost, just as John Geis dashed in at full speed, faked a kick to right, and left-footed it toward the upper left corner of the goal. Volker had not been fooled, however, and reached the ball in time to punch it over the crossbar.

Since the defenders had last touched the ball before it went over their own end line, the Blues were awarded a corner kick. Jan Lesko, the powerful midfielder, ran up to take the kick, with the four Blue forwards spread out in front of the Red goal, each carefully marked by a Red defender. Lesko placed a low, fast kick toward the near goalpost as Cuffy ran forward to take the pass. Cuffy cradled the ball with his thigh as the ball arrived, turned and slammed the ball in toward the goal, but the angle was too sharp and the ball ricocheted off the goalpost. The ball was taken by Sepp Mies, the big Red fullback, and kicked diagonally down the field to Ludwig Bauer, one of the star Red forwards. Immediately both teams shifted roles, attackers became defenders and sprinted back to defensive positions in their half of the pitch, while the defenders formed their strong attacking line of five forwards and began advancing toward the Blue goal.

Halfback Frank Santaro came forward to slow down the Red advance and give Jan Lesko time to come back to work with him on defense, while the four Blue fullbacks, each marking a man, slowly moved out to break up the attack. The Reds moved forward slowly, inexorably, toward the Blue goal, dribbling and passing between each other across the field, but giving the Blue forwards time to catch up with the play. By this time all five Red forwards were within striking distance of the goal.

Suddenly Schotz, centered thirty yards from the goal, yelled. Bauer lobbed the ball to him as the other four Red forwards broke for the corners of the goal. Schotz carefully placed a high ball just outside the penalty area as Bruner, his tallest forward, ran to the spot, outjumped his marker, and headered the ball back to center as Schotz came darting in to hit a tremendous low drive directly ahead. Jason Benjamin dove for the ball and barely got his hands on it, deflecting it sideways, as Bauer came running in from the left and MacDougal from the right. They met with a tremendous crash but MacDougal, the fullback, was bigger and stronger and got his foot on the ball first. He forced it out to where Abbas could get a piece of it and punt it far out toward left midfield, where José Velez, like a mind reader, was already heading.

Marc checked his timer: Four kicks on goal in the first fourteen minutes of play. The pattern the game would take was becoming evident. This would be an all-out rough attacking game, with the ball control changing every few minutes, right after an attack was stopped. The Germans would form their powerful steamroller attack, their blitzkrieg formation, and march slowly and surely down the field into goal-attempt position. The Americans would rally, and with superhuman play, stop the goal, recover the ball, get it quickly into the underdefended enemy territory, make their play for goal, and be stopped dead. Control would go back to the East Germans, who would reform, march down the pitch again, and try for a goal. And sooner or later, they would succeed. This would be a war of attack, attack, attack, with the power of the GDR Team, the force of the five-forward line, wearing down the defense until one of their plays would get the ball past even Jason Benjamin. But Marc also noted how rhythmically the Americans were playing, how, when MacDougal kicked the ball out to left center, Velez was already on his way there. Like a team of mind readers, or more appropriate, the dancers of a chorus line, all knowing exactly where the other was at any moment, all hearing the same tune in their heads: "*Tico Tico*."

For the next ten minutes, play went as Marc expected, back and forth, a tennis match, except that the ball was in the U.S. half of the pitch longer than it was in the GDR half. Then, at twenty-eight minutes into the half, the Red team broke through. It started with their usual tactics, five forwards overwhelming the Blue defense, the four Blue forwards unable to mark every attacker until the ball was a good twenty yards into Blue territory, when the halfbacks could come into play. But by then the defense had been thinned out in front of the goal and there were too many attackers to mark closely or for a zone defense to be useful. This time, instead of spreading out the attack, leaving the defenders to guess which shell the pea would appear under, three Red forwards spread wide and Schotz and Bauer both broke parallelly for the goal at full speed, weaving short, fast passes between them, leaving Benjamin to guess which one would take the goal shot, and when. He was forced to stay in center position, shifting his weight as one or the other attacker had control. When Bauer shot, Benjamin was caught on the wrong foot and the ball went into the goal untouched.

Marc could see the crowd rise, and though all sound was turned off, the screams could be faintly heard through the glass of the press box. He could imagine the anger and the frustration of the Americans. Why, in half an hour of play, had not one offside been called? In soccer, offside is usually called every few minutes, giving the defenders an indirect free kick and completely disrupting the attack. With five forwards on the attack, it would have been very difficult not to have at least one attacker offside when they approached the goal, but Marc had noticed that the Reds had been very careful to maintain their rigid formation in a way that would avoid offsides completely. Besides, it was understandable that in the finals of the World Cup Games, referees and linemen would be reluctant to make any call in a debatable situation, would be a little more lenient than in an ordinary game. The crowd thought otherwise. As far as they were concerned, and to Marc this was obvious without hearing a single scream clearly, the referee was blind, a jerk, a crook, and the Commies all stuck together anyway. No matter. The Reds had scored the first goal with the game little more than a quarter over, and it was likely they would score several more goals before the game was over. Marc went back to his keyboard, and taking advantage of the pause after the goal, brought his play-by-play story up to date.

The ball was brought back to the center spot and the Blues kicked off. Moving smoothly and fast, they brought the ball along the right touchline well into the Red territory, but when Cuffy Royal put a high one within headering distance of the far goalpost, Teddy Pangos was outjumped by halfback Otto Seiler, who had been marking him very closely. And so the battle went, a war of attack, attack, attack, with control of the ball changing regularly as each side took its try—and often a shot—at the enemy goal; a battle remarkable for its lack of even minor fouls. Not once had the referee flashed his yellow card as a caution—though some of the tackles could have been called either way—and no red card seemed to be in the offing. Evidently Steve's meeting with the heads of the teams and the FIFA officials, and his threat of challenging, publicizing, every bad call, had had its intended effect.

The chess game proceeded with the players faking, running madly, trying to gain half a step on their markers so as to enable them to turn this slight advantage into a play leading to a goal shot, but both teams were too evenly matched to permit small gains to turn into scores. Then suddenly, as if at a signal, the entire Red team attacked as a unit, the forwards and the halfbacks crossing the mid-line, eight men on attack, leaving only two fullbacks to guard their goal. The Red forwards pressed ahead boldly, strongly, knowing that they could always find a man to pass to when attacked, and the ball drew nearer and nearer to the penalty area.

As the attack funneled toward the goal, the Red team spread out, spreading the overextended defenders with them, leaving Bauer and Schotz, left and right, in good position for a goal kick, with three other red shirts on each wing in position for a solo run. Schotz suddenly sped over toward Bauer and Bauer crossed back behind Schotz as the ball came arching over from the right wing toward the near goalpost. Bauer, who had a full-step lead on Mac-Dougal, trapped the ball on his chest and tapped it into the path of Ulrich Moser, who had come dashing in from the right touchline just in time to put the ball away into the far end of the goal. Jason Benjamin didn't have a chance; his fingertips were a full foot short of the ball. Score was now 2-0 in favor of the German Democratic Republic, at the end of thirty-nine minutes of play, with six minutes left in the first half.

The Blue team threw themselves into a series of individual attacks, all of which were frustrated by the conservative defensive play of the Red team, a chesslike pulling back, a consolidation, a waiting for the enemy to make a mistake. The Reds seemed content to use their front five forwards to break up plays and keep the ball in the Blue half of the pitch without making any serious tries at another goal. The remaining six minutes sped by in Blue frustration and futility and the half ended.

Marc typed the rest of the first-half story glumly, knowing that in ten minutes, the second half would start, that it would continue for forty-five minutes of play exactly like the first half, and that the U.S. Team would lose ignominiously, be shut out 4-0. As he would. And there was nothing he could do about it, either the game or his own skin. No way would the cavalry come charging up at the last second to save the good guys; no way would the murderer come up to the press room, and with tears in his eyes, confess and beg for understanding and forgiveness. Which Marc would gladly give him, if he had the chance. Which he didn't.

# 34

The East German Team opened the second half with a short kick forward, Bauer to Schotz, who immediately passed it backward to his halfback, Otto Seyler. Marc was shocked to see that the Germans had changed their formation completely, from their all-out-attack blitzkrieg formation, with five forwards and a weak defense, to the impenetrable *catenaccio* defensive formation made famous by the Italians. The "big chain," with its *libero*, the sweeper, operating behind four fullbacks and three halfbacks, all on defense, had led to countless 0-0 games and was, for all practical purposes, a highly static formation. True, there were one or two strikers left near midfield, ready should a counterattack develop, but these would come from sudden, unexpected opportunities rather than planned total-team attacks.

The Red strategy was clear; rather than try to run up a

huge, lopsided score, and take the chance that the Americans would get an opportunity for a shot on goal, they would play it supersafe and be content to win the World Cup 2-0. This, then, was the technique that Professor Ziegler had alluded to when Marc had watched the GDR Team practicing in the Meadowlands. It would work, too. It might make for a dull game, a boring game in which the U.S. Team dashed itself futilely against the unyielding stones of the *catenaccio* as attack after attack would be broken up by the tight sealing of the penalty area in front of the goal, but it would ensure that the GDR Team became the new World Champions and would hold the World Cup for the next four years.

Marc could actually see the angry booing from where he sat, the fans standing up, the cupped hands in front of their mouths focused on the red-shirted players who were, after all, only following the orders of Heinz Grob, their Head Coach, who had to follow the orders of whatever commissar had decreed that Ziegler's strategy was the way to win.

For twenty minutes the Blue team attacked and for twenty minutes it lost the ball before penetrating the Red half of the pitch more than thirty yards. It was easy to get past the two forwards, whose only function, it seemed, was to move the attackers aside toward the touchlines, whereupon these forwards, too, fell back and joined the other eight defenders. But once there were ten defenders protecting the goalkeeper—and the attackers had to leave at least three men to protect their own goal in case one of the Red shirts broke loose—it was impossible to get closer than thirty-five yards from the Red goal line, and the deeper the Americans penetrated, the denser and more effective was the defense. The Reds could play man-to-man and still have three loose men in front of the penalty area to take care of any Blue who managed to get that far.

Marc could see the excitable Teddy Pangos, the wild man of the league, getting angrier and angrier, frustrated at every attempt to get a play going that would allow for a try on goal, dashing here and there, trying to gain a half step, a quarter step, anything that would let him get past the barrier of Red uniforms. Finally, desperately, he pulled loose, slammed a short through pass to John Geis between two Red halfbacks, and sped left as Geis tapped the ball back to him. Teddy took the ball down the left touchline, using José Velez in a series of wall passes where José worked as the wall that Teddy was passing the ball to, and getting it back from, as he went past defender after defender. As José and Teddy approached the goal line, Teddy passed fast to José and broke for the near goalpost. José volleyed the ball to Teddy, and just as Teddy was about to kick the ball, he was crashed into from the right side by Sepp Mies, the big Red fullback. Pangos fell to the ground, knocked out, as Mies passed the ball gently to Volker, the goalkeeper. When it was clear that Pangos would not rise, the referee blew his whistle to stop play.

The crowd stood up, screaming. Even through the glass Marc could hear them screaming, and he didn't have to be a lip-reader to know they were screaming, "Foul!" To Marc, it was obviously a foul, charging the opponent rather than the ball, which called for a direct goal kick—an almost sure score—but the referee did not signal any foul. It was a judgment call, to be sure, but how could Mies be trying for the ball when the ball was on the far side of Pangos? But what could be done? Dissenting from the referee's decision was itself a violation and called for a penalty. The medics finally got Pangos to sit up, but it was clear he had been injured and could not continue to play. Grilho had no forwards left. With only twenty-five minutes left to play and down by two goals, he was forced to substitute a halfback, Peter Franczak. The game was lost. Sepp Mies was smiling smugly. Cuffy Royal was staring threateningly at Mies, as though ready to take on the big German right then and there, but John Geis took the burly black forward by the arm, spoke into his ear, and led him away.

The game restarted, but with even less momentum than before. Grilho had assigned Franczak to be right winger and sent Royal to center to team up with John Geis, but the Blue attacks were weak and ineffective. The fresh Franczak was trying hard, but he was not quite able to fit into his unaccustomed role as a striker. The Reds calmly gave up any semblance of an attack, being content to continue their impenetrable defense for the rest of the game, pulling back even their two forwards to ten yards behind the midfield line. Whenever they took control of the ball back from the Americans, they would punt the ball deep into the Blue territory and sit back, waiting for the tiring Blues to bring the ball back to them to be outmanned and overwhelmed again. Cuffy and John kept pushing the center, using the speedy Velez to bring the ball along the left touchline toward the corner, but once José kicked a cross near the goal, there would be two fullbacks marking Geis and two more marking Royal, with a sweeper waiting behind to protect against any breakthroughs.

After ten more minutes of frustration, John Geis came up with a brilliant move. After José took the ball down the touchline, John ran back toward midfield as Cuffy dashed from his usual position near the far goalpost, sprinting parallel to and just outside of the penalty area, toward the near post. Instead of a high pass, Velez kicked a low boomer right into Cuffy's path. Volker moved to cut off Cuffy's kick, but on the run, Cuffy volleyed the ball back low to John Geis, who was now speeding diagonally across the field toward the far post, a full step ahead of his startled marker. John caught the ball on his chest and had just dropped the ball to the ground for a clear shot at the goal when Sepp Mies hit him in the ankle with a low, sliding tackle. The ball drifted toward Volker, who picked it up easily. John Geis was on the ground, writhing in pain, clutching his ankle. The whistle blew, but the referee was not holding up a card, not even a yellow card.

The crowd was on its feet again, screaming even more loudly than before, so loud that this time it could be clearly heard in the press room. Even the blasé, hardened reporters were muttering. Now Marc understood why Ziegler was not concerned about leaving only three men behind on defense. If it looked as though the Americans were going to score, big Sepp Mies, the GDR secret weapon, would just foul—put out of the game, if necessary—the striker who was going to get the goal. And from the look on Mies' face, the big fullback was enjoying it. Worse, the referee would not show a red card, would not permanently remove from the game, any GDR player who committed a major foul, even if the bastard used a gun.

It took a full ten minutes for the crowd to settle down. Marc could see the police who were guarding the field holding their nightsticks firmly, ready to protect the Red team and the referee, even though, Marc was sure, they would have loved to turn the crowd loose, and even—first taking their shields off—join the boiling mob in doing unto the Red team what any red-blooded American should have done.

There were only fifteen minutes left to play. Not only were there no forwards on the American team to substitute for the injured John Geis, but putting in a second halfback would mean having two halfbacks on the team, playing forward, in positions they were not used to. And both of these would be second-string halfbacks, at that. Ridiculous, Marc thought. Might as well pack up his terminal and spend the remaining fifteen minutes thinking about the Ragusic murder.

Then Grilho walked out on the field. Grilho? Yes, *Grilho*. It was him. Walking out on the field to play. TO PLAY! Forty-two-year-old Grilho, who had not played a professional game in four years, was going in to play forward for the U.S. Team. With the score 2-0. With fifteen minutes left to play. Against the greatest team in the world. With a referee who wouldn't call a foul. The crowd stood up, shocked into silence, then cheering, cheering, as though a god had come down from Olympus to right the wrongs of mere humans.

Grilho reported to the referee, said a few words to his teammates, and the game started again. Volker punted the ball deep. Franczak took it and passed it easily forward to Grilho. The well-rested Grilho dribbled it at top speed down the middle of the pitch, easily evading the defense, twisting and turning around them, faking them off balance, until he was within thirty yards of the goal, with Franczak twenty yards behind him. Volker was alert but not worried; between him and Grilho were three fullbacks, waiting, ready to stop anything the little brown man could do.

As Grilho broke the tackle of the last halfback, with the three fullbacks practically forming a wall between him and the goal, with each of the other forwards double-teamed, he began running at full speed toward the fearsome Sepp Mies, who was braced firmly for the impact. Suddenly, as Grilho was almost on top of Mies, he heeled the ball backward hard to Franczak, who immediately volleyed the ball back toward Grilho. Grilho stopped a foot short of the hunched Mies, reversed, took one step back, and threw his body horizontally through the air in the bicycle kick, catching the ball on the instep of his free foot just as it came to him and kicking it backwards, over his head and over the heads of the defenders, into the far corner of the goal. A GOAL! The U.S. Team had scored a *goal*. *Grilho* had scored a goal. In one minute of play. The miracle had come about. The stands went crazy, erupted, exploded. "Grilho—*Grilho*—GRILHO!" the crowd screamed. You could see it with your eyes closed, hear it with your ears shut. GRIL-YO—GRIL-YO—GRIL-YO—and his teammates were screaming, too, jumping, punching the air, dancing—dancing—*"Tico Tico"*—to the beat of the triumphant, joyous samba.

When order was finally restored and the clock was started again, there was a new atmosphere on the field. The Blue team was ready to fight, to win, to blast through the Red chain defense. When Dieter Schotz kicked off forward, easily, to Ludwig Bauer, so that the ball could be passed back to the middle of the GDR crowd, to be stalled for the remaining fourteen minutes, Cuffy Royal ran to challenge the giveaway, causing Bauer to hurry his pass back to Moser, who had to run to his right to get to the ball. But meanwhile José Velez was speeding toward Moser, just in case, and attacked the Red forward in a beautiful sliding tackle.

Moser did not lose control of the ball completely, but he had to get rid of the ball in a hurry and his pass was lateral and slow, giving Franczak, who was still relatively fresh, a chance to get his foot on it and deflect the ball toward Grilho. Grilho dribbled the ball forward a few yards, faked left, right, then left again, and put a short pass right in front of the charging Cuffy Royal, who was cutting diagonally across the pitch toward his far goalpost. Cuffy picked up the ball in a half-volley and booted it low and hard just ahead of José Velez, who was darting down the left touchline, a full stride ahead of his marker. Cuffy reversed and ran toward his near goalpost as three defenders closed in on him to block the intended high header for goal.

Meanwhile Grilho ran a curving path, starting toward the middle of the goal in case José's pass was short, and two more defenders pulled in ahead of him, bracketing him to prevent the projected header. Just as José came in line with the penalty box, Grilho broke left for José's near goalpost, gaining a full step on the defenders who were braced to outjump him. José slammed a low pass with his left foot right at Grilho, chest high, as his markers tried to catch up with him, both ready to tackle him as soon as he dropped the ball to the ground for his kick.

Amazingly, instead of absorbing the force of the ball on his chest and letting it fall to kick level, Grilho jumped and caught the ball in his groin, bent in half to cradle the ball, half twisted in the air, and with a bump that would have done credit to any stripper, jerked the ball with his hips into the lower corner of the goal, just ahead of Volker's outstretched hands. Goal! *Another goal. Two goals in two minutes.* Using a maneuver that had never been seen on a soccer pitch before. Marc immediately tapped the name into his terminal—the Grilho Bump—gaining secondary fame for himself.

The stadium was roaring, exploding, everyone standing, explaining to each other, to whomever would listen, what a wonderful, marvelous, *miraculous* play this was, the greatest of all time, the greatest that could *ever* happen, that after this, anything else, any other game, would be *nothing* compared to this once-in-a-lifetime unbelievable, magical, *supernatural* sign from heaven. And the chant started again: GRIL-YO—GRIL-YO—GRIL-YO—over and over and over and the crowd wouldn't stop. Then Grilho disengaged himself from his surrounding, adoring, *inspired* teammates and stepped forward, in midfield, calmly, calmly holding his hands up for a moment, palms out, turning around slowly so that he faced, acknowledged, the cheers of all the people, then put his hands down, signaling that the game was not yet over, that the game must still go on. There was immediate silence. Grilho signaled them all to sit down, and they sat. The referee placed the ball in the center circle, on the center spot, and blew his whistle. The last thirteen minutes of the final game for the World Cup had started.

The Red team had changed to a 4-2-4 formation, mirroring the Americans. With the score tied at 2-2, they could not afford to play pure defense and hold the Americans to a tie; they had to shoot for a win, a clear win. Who knew what would happen in overtime, with the Americans in their present winning mood, with momentum on their side? And if it went into a shoot-out? With Grilho, who had never failed to score on a one-to-one with any goalkeeper, and with Jason Benjamin in the cage, the odds were that the Blue team would win a tie-breaking shoot-out. No, the GDR Team had to score a goal, had to win within the next thirteen minutes, or else. They could no longer afford to take the risks of a five-man forward line; Grilho could slip too easily behind that line to face a depleted defense.

This was to be skill against skill, force against force, with the odds favoring the Reds. The Blues did not have a single first-team forward, while the Reds still had their best men in the game. The Blues had Grilho, true, but how much longer could a forty-two-year-old man continue? How long could his freshness stay fresh, his magic work? Now that they knew what he could do, they could defend against it; there could be no more bicycle kicks, no more Grilho Bumps, no more tricks up his sleeve. And if all else failed, there was always Sepp Mies. If Grilho came *near* the goal again, Sepp Mies would take care of him, but good. Even if the attack were so blatant a foul that the referee *had* to give Mies a red card, had to take him out of the game permanently, without Grilho the Americans were, for all practical purposes, a bunch of undisciplined, disorganized amateurs. Once the big, burly Sepp Mies smashed the slim little Grilho, that would be that. After one hit, there would be no need to worry about overtime, or even about a shoot-out.

Bauer kicked forward to Schotz, who immediately began to dribble toward the center. As Franczak attacked, Schotz drove a long pass to Moser, his left flanker. Moser took the ball forward twenty yards before being stopped with a hard tackle by Jan Lesko. Lesko passed the ball to José Velez and the attack and counterattack was on. For a full ten minutes, control of the ball changed ten times, with the play so intense that it seemed the men were fresh out of the locker room. Neither side could get within thirty yards of a goal line as the battle—the chess game, really—raged, each side trying to get the small advantage that would permit it to convert an inch to a yard, and a yard to a shot on goal.

Finally, a combination of short passes, a run down the touchline, and a fast cross to the near goalpost gave Schotz an opportunity to take a shot at the Blue goal, with Bauer coming across to pick up a deflected save, if any, by Benjamin. Abbas dove in front of Schotz's kick and got the tip of his shoe on the side of the ball, just enough to deflect it to where Benjamin could get both hands on the ball as he fell and immediately curled into a protective fetal position around the ball. Bauer, charging up, almost kicked—and looked as though he would have enjoyed the feeling—Benjamin in the head, but pulled back at the last second.

Benjamin got up fast, looked around as he took his allowed four steps, and punted a tremendous seventy-five-yarder down the middle of the pitch, into open space, directly ahead of where Grilho, slipping away unseen, was sprinting as fast as he could. Desperately Otto Seyler ran forward to the ball, but Grilho beat him by two steps, turned him around with a fake hip swivel, and proceeded down the center, angling toward the right goalpost. Fullback August Roebling came out to meet him—or even to slow Grilho down until Sepp Mies came over from his position—and Grilho, still speeding, let him come close and then, as soon as Roebling had committed himself to the tackle, lobbed the ball inches over Roebling's head and continued his sprinting dribble toward the right goalpost, leaving the fullback sprawled on the ground.

Sepp Mies came running, desperately, parallel to the goal line, to where it was clear Grilho would take his goal kick as Volker, unwilling to commit himself too far in advance, moved more slowly toward his left goalpost and slightly in front of the goal line, afraid to come out to meet Grilho, who was capable of whizzing around him like a ghost or even kicking a swerve around him. At the last second Mies dove feetfirst to meet Grilho, spikes aimed directly at where Grilho's knees would be. Grilho, with his amazing control, stopped dead, put out his right foot, placed the sole on the ball, and pulled it back toward him, leaving it stationary on the ground. Mies, already sliding, went past Grilho with a yard to spare, unable even to hook his foot into Grilho's ankle. Grilho had his right foot pulled back, ready to kick as Volker dove for his left corner. Grilho slammed his right foot into the ball as though he were trying for a long pass, and with perfect timing, rammed the ball off his right instep directly into Mies' face, caroming the ball off his face straight into the far corner of the goal, five yards away from the off-balance Volker. Sepp Mies' face dissolved into a red smear as the seventy-mile-an-hour ball ripped across his nose, mouth, and cheeks, taking with it bloody white skin and showing new red emblems on the white hide.

Goal again! The *winning* goal! Three goals by Grilho in

fifteen minutes. Thirteen minutes. Less than two minutes left to play and the momentum, the spirit, was with the Americans. On the field, Grilho was surrounded by his teammates. Cuffy Royal lifted Grilho all by himself, hoisted the slim, brown hero to his shoulders, and marched him triumphantly to midfield, followed by the rest of the team, as the crowd went crazy. The East Germans were standing around in a ragged circle, shoulders drooping, their backs to the seats, waiting. The medics were working over Sepp Mies, carefully wrapping his broken face in gauze, lifting him to his feet, helping him walk off the field.

Again, Grilho lifted his hands for quiet. There were still almost two minutes left in the game and the game, the beautiful game, must go on. The crowd was silenced swiftly and the substitute fullback, Helmut Voss, checked in. Marc typed his name into his terminal for the record, but it didn't matter. The game was over and everyone knew it. Everyone but the East Germans, who bravely kicked off directly ahead and mounted their fiercest attack of the day. Every pass was challenged, every ball that came near a Red jersey was fought over bitterly. Kicking and elbowing was the order of the day, and charging from any angle did not bring any whistle from the referee. The Americans entered the fray joyously, taking advantage of the referee's fear of calling a foul at this time and under these conditions. Truly, his life was at stake and he knew it; no way would the police be able to protect him from the mob should he make a call against the Blue team after the leniency he had shown the Red.

Tackles were fierce and fast, with cleats aimed at shins as often as they were aimed at the ball. Then the crowd started counting, backwards, "Ten, nine, eight, seven"— louder and louder—"six, five, four, three, two! One! OVER!" The referee looked around, blew his whistle, and ran for the GDR locker-room entrance, followed by the Red team. The crowd spilled out onto the pitch, mobbing the Blue team, hugging and kissing them, and the police stood by, not even trying to stem the overwhelming wave. Grilho was hoisted up and marched around the field, a full procession, then Jason Benjamin, Cuffy Royal, José Velez, Abbas, MacDougal, Franczak, Lesko, Santaro, the whole team, even those who hadn't played. And Teddy Pangos, John Geis, Boni, and the rest. Around and around, until Grilho held his hands up.

Again, as if by magic, everyone was quiet. Marc turned on the sound. Grilho's words came out clearly. "I am very proud that I have finally played in a World Cup Game, although I regret the circumstances that made it possible. As we must all do, I took the opportunity that was given to me by God and used it as well as I could. I am fortunate to have been able to play with such a great team, with such good men. Soccer is a game in which every player must do his part, where a goal is the result of each player's work. Thank you for your support. Now we must rest. Please let us down and we will all meet you outside later." Quietly, under the spell of these simple words, the bearers of the winning team slowly let the players down and moved aside to let the Blue team, the team that had just won the World Cup for America, go to its locker room.

Marc quickly typed the last few sentences of his story into his terminal, using the simple words as Grilho had, letting the power of the event speak for itself. He folded his terminal, put everything away in his briefcase, and prepared to leave. Then he remembered. Danzig. How could he have forgotten? Danzig would be here any minute and Marc had nothing to tell him. Not a thing. Except, of course, the name of the murderer. The name of the. . . . Well, of course. It was so obvious. That last play . . . actually, he could have known from the first. The trouble was, there was no proof. Not even a shred of evidence. Danzig would never believe him. He would be taken off to jail and charged. And Dahliah would also be arrested.

Maybe if he spoke to the murderer, appealed to his better nature . . . hah, that was a joke. But what else could he do? Whatever he did, he was lost. The only thing left was to do what Julius Witter had told him to do: confess himself. Whatever you said about Julius, you had to admit he was smart. Shrewd. Farseeing. Mean. Well, give it one try. Then, when it failed, get a lawyer and confess—to someone other than Harvey Danzig. He trudged off to meet the murderer.

# 35

The elevator doors parted and Marc walked forward, down the long aisle between the closets and the service counters of Gregor Ragusic's private personal box, the command post that reminded Marc of the interior of a 747 with the pilot's bulkhead removed. Steve Vanderhook was sitting in his big new wheelchair at the very front, the glass-enclosed observation post from which you could see every inch of the field, facing the arena where there were still a few die-hard fans waiting to get another glimpse of their heroes.

When he heard the elevator doors open, Steve turned his chair slowly in place to watch Marc approach. His face was still flushed with happiness and pride. "Wasn't that the greatest game of all time?" he asked. "Isn't Grilho the wonder of the ages? I haven't been so happy in—for as long as I can remember."

"Well, yes," Marc said hesitantly. "It was a great exhibition of skill and talent. And brains. And psychology. Grilho read the GDR Team like an open book. But I—"

"I hope you're going to make a big play of this in your column," Steve interrupted. "Not just for Grilho, though he deserves everything you can say about him, and more, but for the good of soccer. If you write it strongly enough, if you tell the whole story, you may inspire a whole generation of American boys—and girls, too—to take up soccer as seriously as they play baseball and football. It's important, Marc. Very important. We don't need any more—" he waved at his useless legs—"any more injuries like this." He smiled ruefully, then with joy. "And how do you like the way Grilho took care of that bastard Sepp Mies. You know, people think Grilho's soft. He isn't. Grilho is polite and a gentleman, but he doesn't allow anyone to get away with anything for very long."

"Yes, well . . . you don't think that last play was deliberate, do you? Come on, Steve; there's no way Grilho could have set it up that perfectly. Too many indeterminable factors. How could he know that—"

"No, no, I don't mean he set up the whole play with the intention of getting Mies in exactly that position, just that he instinctively—when the situation showed itself—without really thinking . . . he just knew what to do when he had the chance to do it."

"Yes, exactly. He did what he had to do when the opportunity arose. Almost the way you did," it was time to say it, "when you killed Gregor Ragusic." Marc's back still hurt, badly, and that reminded him of the terminal and attaché case he was carrying. He put down the terminal and the case as far from Steve as he could. Even though Steve was chair-bound, he had powerful arms.

Marc wasn't sure how Steve would react to what he was going to hear and there was very little room to move in the pointed prow of the observation post.

"You're saying that I—Ragusic? That's ridiculous, Marc, and you know it. Impossible."

"No, not really. I mean, yes, it's impossible that you kicked his head in, of course, but. . . ." How should he say it? The whole purpose of this was to persuade Steve to confess. Try to act understanding, sympathetic. "Look, Steve—Commissioner—I know Ragusic was a bastard, trying to expand the league too fast so he could push through his ideas, his rule changes."

"Which would have ruined soccer in the United States and ensured that we would never have a chance at the World Cup again. And which also would have made soccer as dangerous as football. But what has that to do with—"

"Yes, exactly. You didn't know—he didn't tell you—about expanding the league in one big jump until the day before he was killed. You thought the expansion would be slow, that you would have a chance to persuade each new owner of the wisdom of keeping soccer as it is. Then he told you . . . see, Ragusic was smart, but not as smart as he thought he was. And he liked to brag. He told me about his plans, tried to enlist my support, the day before he was killed. You couldn't have learned about them *after* he was killed, so he had to have told you the same day."

"Isn't that circular reasoning? He could just as well have told me that a week ago."

"No, he couldn't. He told me he was going to tell the other owners—*explain*, was the way he put it—right after the final game, to get their support. So he wouldn't have told you that beforehand so you could do your arm-twisting in time to scuttle his plans. But he couldn't resist gloating, showing how smart he was, how help-less you were, so he must have told you the same day he told me. Probably that very morning. Thursday morning."

"Are you taping this conversation, Marc? Without my knowledge or approval?"

"No, no, I would never do that. Look." He knelt down and opened his attaché case on the floor. "See? Nothing's running." He stood up again. "What I want is . . . look, you go to the police. Not Lieutenant Danzig. Someone higher up, someone you have influence with. Take your lawyer with you. Explain the situation, that Ragusic was destroying everything you've been fighting for these past twenty years. That you tried to dissuade him but he wouldn't listen. That he laughed at you, that this was the only way. For the good of the sport, for the help of the handicapped, to avoid having more paraplegics from sports-related injuries, everything. You're very popular, you'll have a good press. I'll write a column in your support."

Steve Vanderhook thought for a moment, then said, "Marc, you're wrong. Nothing of what you've said makes any sense. I'm a paraplegic; how could I kick Ragusic's head in?"

"You didn't. From your exercises, from the use of your crutches to move when you have to, your arms are very strong. You put a soccer shoe on your right hand and smashed Ragusic's head in. That's how."

"Marc," Steve sighed, "you know I can't stand without the use of both crutches, that it takes me a full minute just to get my crutches out, lock my leg braces, and lift myself up. And when Ragusic sees me drop one crutch and grab a soccer shoe to hit him with, do you think he's just going to stand there and let me hit him as I'm falling?"

"No, of course it didn't happen that way. At first, I

thought it was a spur-of-the-moment kick, but then I realized it had to be planned. You decided to kill him right after he told you what he was going to do, on Thursday morning. So you came in early on Friday morning. Not the first one in, that would have been too suspicious, but early. You knew there would be no one on the second floor but you and Ragusic. Actually there were several people up there, and one of them almost saw you, but there was no way you could have figured that. Had you seen anyone, you would merely have postponed the murder until the next day. Anyway, you got the shoe—the pair of shoes—which was another clue. Why a pair? Well, one reason was to make it appear that a soccer player had done the deed, to emphasize that Ragusic was killed by a kick. The other reason was that you had no choice; you had to take a pair of shoes."

"And how was I supposed to get a pair of shoes? I really don't know how to pick a lock."

"You didn't have to. When Frankie Guzman left the equipment room to distribute some equipment, you wheeled up to the mesh door and stuck your hand crutch in through the slot in the mesh door—backwards. You held the crutch by the tip, the curved handle inside, and hooked a pair of shoes from the pile on the floor near the front of the room. They're tied together in pairs by the laces, so you took the pair. You stuck them into the quiver that you keep your crutches in and took the elevator upstairs. Once in your office, you took them out, untied them, put one shoe—the left—into the bottom of the quiver and the other behind you on the chair seat. On the right side. No one would notice that your crutches were sticking up a little more than usual."

"And I went to Ragusic's office and stood up with one crutch," Steve said sarcastically, "with the shoe on my other hand and chased him around the office till I caught him?"

"No, what happened was . . . see, Ragusic had a tendency to stick his face into mine—yours, anybody's—when he was making a point, showing how smart he was, how he could dominate you. You grabbed his tie, held him in place for the second it took to get the shoe from behind you, and smashed his head in. The angle of the cleats was exactly that which would appear if some soccer player had kicked him sideways, with a karate kick. When Ragusic fell, you smoothed out his tie, put the shoe into your quiver, and took off, peeking out into the hall before you left his secretary's office. The next day, you disposed of the shoes in a place no one would ever find them. Or destroyed them."

"You have a vivid imagination, Marc; you should be writing whodunits. Wherever did you get this idea?"

"At the end of the game, when Grilho made that powerful kick that evened the score with Sepp Mies. When a soccer player wants to use his maximum power, get the greatest speed or the greatest distance, he kicks the ball with a swing, with his instep. That's why, today, almost all the place-kickers in football are ex-soccer players. Grilho's kick—I'm sure that making the goal was his prime intent, but I'm also sure that he also wanted to teach that bastard a lesson—was with his instep. No soccer player would use a karate kick; it's unfamiliar to him, feels wrong. Instinctively, he would sweep his leg, use his instep. I wondered, knowing you, why you would want to implicate a soccer player, frame a soccer player. Especially Boni. It's not like you, Steve." Marc was truly troubled.

"I would never frame anybody, Marc. Never."

"I know; I realized that just now. You picked the nearest pair of shoes you could reach from the opening in the equipment-room door; didn't realize whose shoes they were until after Danzig spoke to you. So what are you going to do now, Steve? What I suggested before . . . it would work. Everyone would understand."

"No one would understand, Marc; you can't understand anything unless you've walked a mile in another man's shoes." He grinned wryly at that. "Joke. Unintended. I'm not trying to make you feel bad, Marc, and I'm not looking for your sympathy, but it's clear to me from what you've said that you haven't discussed this wild theory of yours with anyone, much less Lieutenant Danzig. If you had, he'd laugh you out of town. Or send you for a psychiatric examination. I'm not going to take your advice, which is based on a completely erroneous set of assumptions. There is no evidence to back up anything you've said, much less anything that could be used in court. Even if everything you said was true—and it isn't—there is no way I'm going to turn over the control of the U.S. Soccer League to anyone else. This is my baby and I'm going to see that it's done right for the rest of my days.

"I'm going to leave now; the crowd has thinned sufficiently so that I won't have any problems in the elevators or the corridors. I'm going to carry out my duties, to protect the league and its players and its fans, to the best of my abilities. If you want to go to Lieutenant Danzig with your wild story, go ahead. I hope you won't—it will cause me some inconvenience, and if there is any resultant scandal in the papers, any breath of scandal attached to my name that would hurt the league, I will resign rather than see the game disgraced. Is that what you want, Marc? If it is, do it. But if you do, realize the implications. Do you think whoever takes my place as Commissioner will love soccer as much as I do? Do you think he will keep the game as pure and as beautiful as I will? Do you think he will fight to keep the game *safe*? Do you want to see more paraplegics in sport?"

Steve's normally calm, beautiful face was red, strained,

almost tortured. "I have a suggestion for you, Marc. Look outside. See how beautiful the pitch is, how perfect. Think what a great day this has been, what you've seen today, the miraculous play of Grilho. Then decide." Steve turned his wheelchair and moved down the narrow corridor slowly. When he reached the elevator, he pressed the button. He did not look back.

Marc slowly turned around and looked down at the field through the huge windows. He could see every inch of the pitch, and some of the area outside the touchlines, too. The afternoon sun was shining brightly and there was peace on the land. And maybe Steve was right. The problem was, what would he tell Danzig? And what would Danzig do if he did?

He turned to ask Steve if maybe—and there was Steve, bearing down on him in his wheelchair at full speed, with his crutches extended like the horns of a raging bull. Time seemed to stand still, everything slow and clear. There was no place to move where the horns would not catch him, pierce him, thrust him out of the big windows on to the seats a hundred feet below, the punctures, the wounds, undetectable in the smashed body, his smashed body.

Without thinking, Marc fell to the floor, flat, his head turned away from those stabbing horns. Then he felt the wheels of the massive chair, with Steve's weight added, hit him hard, fast, passing over his back, the small of his back—right where it hurt the most—and the curve of his neck, jumping up and over, taking off, from the springboard of Marc's body. And Marc opened his eyes to see Steve floating through the big center window, his long, beautiful, gold hair streaming out behind him, a Viking on his funeral pyre slowly blowing out to sea, surrounded by a halo of shattered glass, fragments gleaming, catching the afternoon sun, rainbow flashes haloing the handsome head, still erect and proud, as the slow, graceful curve took him down, down, down, out of sight. Then something else hit Marc hard in the small of his back, and he heard the shot and felt the blow on the back of his neck and the remnants of the crystal mist, the tiny splinters of glowing glass, were still falling, falling, slowly falling, and he saw no more.

# 36

He opened his eyes; Dahliah was caressing his forehead with a cool hand. She looked worried. Good; that showed she still cared for him, even if he wasn't a big, blond, handsome murderer. Enough of that. Poor Steve, who wanted only to help, to save lives, to keep people from being paralyzed. He had been put into the position where he had to kill Gregor Ragusic for the good of the game. Marc was sure of this; he remembered, now, the tortured look on Steve's face as he was racing toward Marc—he was ready to sacrifice Marc, to sacrifice his honor, and to kill again to keep the league and the game pure and beautiful.

Marc could move his hand, his forearm, but all else—it was his back. And his neck. He was paralyzed. A paraplegic. Worse. A quadriplegic who could move only one hand. That wheelchair had to have weighed well over a hundred pounds. And Steve? At over two hundred pounds? Three hundred pounds hitting his back and his neck at twenty miles an hour. And that second blow. And the shot. Hit him in the neck. Clean through the spine. Left only one nerve, his right-hand nerve. It wasn't love; Dahliah was *pitying* him. He would never walk again. He closed his eyes so she wouldn't see the tears.

"Is it too bright?" Dahliah asked. "I can turn down the lights."

"No," he murmured. "Not the light. It's . . . oh, God, I can't move."

"You're not supposed to move, darling; you're in traction. All the way up. It's only for two weeks or so, if you lie quietly. The doctor said that after you've recovered, a few weeks of physiotherapy, massage, light exercise, stretching—hanging would be very good for you—you should be as good as new in three months."

"I'm not paralyzed?"

"No, of course not. Just some ligament damage and some temporary displacement of the vertebrae. Rest, muscle relaxers, anti-inflammatories, and maybe some tranquilizers if you get too restless. I'll come to see you every day."

"Steve?"

A shadow passed over her face. "He landed on some seats. Died instantly. The doctor said he didn't feel a thing."

Sure. After he landed. But what about on the way down? Or did Steve want it that way? Would it really have been possible to stop short after he hit Marc and sent him through the window? Could he have decided to go with Marc, all the way down, to preserve the legend of the Vanderhooks?

"That's enough," Danzig growled. "I told Witter I'd leave you be for a while, but enough's enough. Let's get it over with; I got other cases to take care of. You're under arrest for the murder of Commissioner Steven Vander-hook; I'll read you your rights right now."

"Wait a minute!" Marc yelled. "Wait a minute. Arrest me? For the murder of—You're crazy. He tried to kill me."

"Really?" Julius Witter said, sounding very pleased. "You have the story?"

"Don't give me that crap," Danzig yelled. "I was there and I saw the whole thing. You purposely fell down like I seen in karate movies and threw him over your head outta the window. I forget what they call it, but I seen enough of them to know."

"You were there?" Marc tried to turn his head, but it was hopeless. "Where were you when he was trying to. . . . When were you there? How did you get there? What's going on?"

"Yes, excellent questions, Marc," Witter's voice was stronger now. "You seem to be learning the basics of reporting. Yes, Danzig, where, when, what, how, and why? That will determine the who. Especially the why."

"Whatta you mean, why? I came there to protect him. Like I told him I would."

"A little late, weren't you, Lieutenant? What were you doing, and where were you doing it, while my star investigative reporter was risking his life?"

"It was Sunday, that's what I was doing. And the traffic was extra heavy; everybody in Brooklyn was out in the streets. Damn soccer game, that's what the trouble was. Otherwise I would have been in time to save the Commissioner's life from your investigative reporter's karate attack. Which he learned from Miss Dahliah Norman; I had her checked out, too, just in case."

"How did you know where Mr. Burr was?"

"How? I arranged with him before that I would meet him right after the game, make the arrest, and give him the story. That's how. Only—"

"You didn't have the slightest idea where I was!" Marc

shouted, making his head hurt more. "You got into the elevator to go up to the press-room floor but Vanderhook had pressed the call button and the elevator took you up to Ragusic's private crow's nest."

"Yeah? And that's where I saw you throw him outta the window. With my own eyes. And I'm putting you under—"

"Wait a minute," Marc said. Now his neck hurt as much as his head. "In order for you to see him go out the window, to see him hit me, you had to have been up there the moment he turned around and started for me. That wheelchair moves fast."

"Well, of course. As soon as the elevator doors opened, I saw—"

"And you chased him. The chair. You're the one who—"

"Now take it easy, take it easy. I was trying to save your life."

"Save my life? You're the guy who shot me in the neck!"

"Shot you? Me? You ain't shot. All that happened was . . . I was trying to save your life. Like you asked me to, remember? You're always asking me to save your life. So I did."

"He was trying to kill me. You had your gun out; why didn't you shoot him?"

"What the hell for? All I saw was a poor cripple in a wheelchair that was rolling towards you and there you was, getting down in a karate position, ready to throw him outta the window. You're the one I shoulda shot. And didn't you once tell me—that other time when I saved your life—that I shouldn't shoot in your direction?"

"That was different. Now I know what happened. You wanted to get me on an assault against a poor cripple in addition to the other charges; to shoot me in the middle of an attack on the Commissioner, that's what you wanted.

You were going to shoot me, kill me, and then you could blame me for Ragusic's murder, too.''

"Yeah, then why was I chasing the wheelchair, trying to stop it?''

"With your gun out? Now I know what happened. You tripped, didn't you? And landed on my back. The small of my back. With your knees. You're the one who crippled me. And the gun went off, didn't it? Right against my neck. The recoil. You're the one who almost broke my neck.''

"Hey, take it easy. The carpet was very loose or something, that's how it happened. Perfectly natural. In the line of duty. Besides, I didn't shoot you; ask the doctor.''

"No." Marc had a sudden revelation. "You didn't shoot me. You shot Steve Vanderhook. In the back. That's why you were so anxious to arrest me, blame me for his death.''

"Who, me? The medical examiner says he died from the fall. A hundred feet onto the backs of some seats.''

"The medical examiner didn't even examine him, did he? Julius, I want—''

"Now wait a minute," Danzig interjected. "What's the sense of making a big fuss about this? I mean, the Ragusic case is closed, right? Otherwise, why was *you* up there?''

"Yes, Burr," Julius said. "You did solve the case, didn't you?''

Marc tried to nod; it didn't work. Now his back hurt.

"With evidence?" Julius persisted.

"Enough to fry him. Vanderhook, I mean.''

"You don't really want to make trouble for Lieutenant Danzig, do you?''

"The hell I don't. I want him to hang.''

Julius hastily addressed Danzig. "I take it you are willing to forget about the petty details of my minor involvement in this matter, as well as the *Sentry*'s and Miss Norman's? Even Mr. Burr's?''

"Hell, yes. You know me, Witter; I don't hold grudges. That is, if . . . assuming. . . ."

"Yes, of course. Assuming." Julius spoke to Marc again. "Need I remind you that you did withhold evidence and that by so doing, you caused me, the *Sentry,* and yourself, not to mention Miss Norman, a good deal of potential, very expensive difficulty?"

"What do you want, Julius?" Marc asked wearily.

"I suggest that you give Lieutenant Danzig whatever evidence you have, that you tell me the whole story, and that I write it up myself in such a way to ensure that Lieutenant Danzig gets the credit for breaking the case."

"That's all? And what do I get out of it?"

"Of course, Lieutenant Danzig will completely forget about any involvement I, we, all of us, have had in this case."

"It's not enough." Marc clenched his teeth stubbornly. "Let everything come out."

"I might be able to arrange a big raise for you. Say twenty-five per week?"

"Say fifty?"

"Out of the question; you are embarrassing me with Mr. Heisenberg. Due to your past raises, my budget is already several percentage points above the minimum I swore to uphold."

"I'm sure Mr. Heisenberg will be very interested to learn how his Sports Editor in Chief and Lieutenant Danzig conspired to hush up the murder—Steve might already have been dead before he hit the ground—of the last of the Vanderhooks and about Danzig's attempt to frame a Hollingsworth for the murder of Gregor Ragusic."

"You are a grasping little miser, Burr, with the instincts of a pit viper who has no respect for the profession of reporting, but very well, I will make the sacrifice and see if I can explain it to Mr. Heinsenberg."

"And Dahliah gets paid for the pictures she took of Ragusic's body."

"Of course. Standard rates."

"She's not an employee. A thousand dollars toward our air-conditioning system."

"She was on assignment, Burr."

"Not that assignment, Julius."

Witter sighed. "Very well, but that is the maximum I can do."

"One more thing. Don't faint, Julius; not money. Are there any heavyset guys outside, waiting? In overcoats?"

"Three. Unsavory-looking characters. All heavyset. All in overcoats, despite the weather. They seem not to be talking to one another."

"Okay. Give them these messages. Brown Coat: There is no evidence of any involvement by any citizen of the Warsaw Pact countries. Blue Coat: There is no evidence that any member organization of the UN is involved. Black Coat: There is no evidence that will interfere with any existing or potential arrangement with any other country. The unfortunate accidental death of Commissioner Vanderhook was the result of actions by an American citizen for purely domestic reasons. Got that?"

"Clearly. Would you like to write up the story behind those messages one of these days? In the near future? I can have a stenographer at your bedside in half an hour."

"Never. Or yes, if you wish, but under your by-line, Julius."

"On second thought, I think not. Is that all? Then give Lieutenant Danzig the evidence."

Marc told the story quickly and precisely, in reporter's terms. He could hear Witter's cassette recorder going. Witter would write the story himself, under his by-line, giving Marc no credit, other than as victim. Let it be.

"There ain't one solid bit of evidence," Danzig complained. "The Chief ain't gonna buy this."

"There is one bit, but it's enough. The shoes, the murder shoes, are probably gone forever. But for Vander-hook to get them out of Ragusic's office, especially while he was wiping out the carpet marks of his wheelchair, he had to put them into his quiver, the leather thing he carries his hand crutches in. There was no way he would call attention to that by having it changed in a store, so there has to be blood and other tissue, identifiable as coming from Ragusic, in that quiver. And that's still there."

"Okay," Danzig said, relieved. "That's it. Gotta go now; lots of other cases to solve." He left quickly.

"Not bad, Burr," Julius said, "but I'll have to hurry to get this in tomorrow's edition before Danzig tips off the whole world."

"One more thing. Dahliah's column. It makes sense for it to go on Nelda Shaver's page, but it's to be sent in by modem from my portable terminal. I don't want Dahliah picking up any bad habits from Nelda. You understand? Especially with me here flat on my back."

"Acceptable," Julius said. "Now I've got to go. There are such things as deadlines, you may recall."

"One more thing," Marc said.

"We have already agreed on the money," Witter said firmly.

"Not money; just want to tie up a few loose ends. Get on the phone and tell your secretary to take down my column."

"What are you going to say?" Witter asked warily.

"The new Commissioner of the U.S. Soccer League has to be Grilho."

"With his son as star forward of the Boosters? No good."

"Boni is going back to school to become a diplomat, which is what he really wants to do. This way, he can claim he can't play anymore because his father is the

Commissioner. That will please the Hollingsworths and ensure their full support, which will guarantee that Grilho is voted in unanimously. Grilho will be happy, and for the next four years he'll have a free hand, and the league can expand slowly. And there will be no changes in the rules."

*So Steve will have won anyway*, Marc thought. *Some good will have come from his sacrifice and from Ragusic's death.*

"You know, Burr," Witter said thoughtfully, "there is still hope for you." He hurried out.

"Alone at last," Dahliah said. "You were masterful, darling." She bent over and kissed him. Marc was relieved to find that his sensory nerves were still working well.

A nurse came into the room. "I'm sorry," she said, "but visiting hours are over."

"Buy something for me, Dahliah," Marc said. "When I get home, I want to find a set of heavy adjustable barbells."

"But I thought that as a gymnast you didn't want to— won't that build up your thighs?"

"Exactly," Marc said.